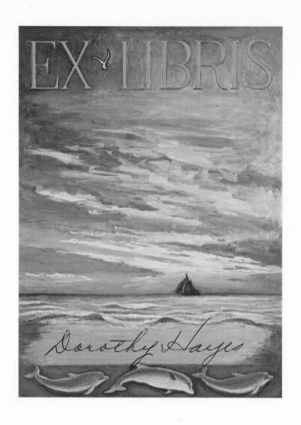

EX LIBRIS

Dorothy Hayes

BEYOND THE SOUND OF GUNS

BOOKS BY
EMILIE LORING

THE TRAIL OF CONFLICT
HERE COMES THE SUN!
A CERTAIN CROSSROAD
THE SOLITARY HORSEMAN
GAY COURAGE
SWIFT WATER
LIGHTED WINDOWS
FAIR TOMORROW
UNCHARTED SEAS
HILLTOPS CLEAR
WE RIDE THE GALE!
WITH BANNERS
IT'S A GREAT WORLD
GIVE ME ONE SUMMER
AS LONG AS I LIVE
TODAY IS YOURS
HIGH OF HEART
ACROSS THE YEARS
THERE IS ALWAYS LOVE
WHERE BEAUTY DWELLS
STARS IN YOUR EYES
RAINBOW AT DUSK
WHEN HEARTS ARE LIGHT AGAIN
KEEPERS OF THE FAITH
BEYOND THE SOUND OF GUNS
BRIGHT SKIES
BECKONING TRAILS
I HEAR ADVENTURE CALLING
LOVE CAME LAUGHING BY
TO LOVE AND TO HONOR
FOR ALL YOUR LIFE
MY DEAREST LOVE
I TAKE THIS MAN
THE SHADOW OF SUSPICION
WHAT THEN IS LOVE

BEYOND THE SOUND OF GUNS

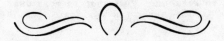

EMILIE LORING

GROSSET & DUNLAP

PUBLISHERS, NEW YORK

BY ARRANGEMENT WITH LITTLE, BROWN AND COMPANY
PRINTED IN THE UNITED STATES OF AMERICA

BEYOND THE SOUND OF GUNS

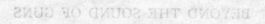

I

MID-SEPTEMBER. A morning warm as summer. Clouds, puffy, white and cottony, with gun-metal centers and raveled gold edges, slowly moved across the translucent blue sky patterning the earth with fantastic shadows. Peak above peak rose mountains, in pairs, alone, mysterious, majestic, their tops snow-capped, their defiles deep purple, their sides and bases splashed by the red and yellow of wild currant. Rabbit brush and sunflowers fringed the road. Silence save for the hum of locust and cricket.

Kit Marlowe stopped her horse on the brow of a hill deeply scarred with wavy trenches made by soil-erosion experts. She sniffed the fragrance of wild sage. Was there also a smell of rain? Did the dark centers in the clouds mean a storm? She glanced at the distant snow-capped mountains which seemed within finger reach in the clear air. Their outlines weren't so sharp as when she had started out.

She was at least three miles from home. Should she go on? In New England she had been weather-wise, but she hadn't had time in the two weeks she had been at the Double H to become familiar with storm portents. She patted the glossy neck of the bay with her gloved hand. The tinkle of half a dozen Indian silver bangles set with turquoise turned one enormous, white-rimmed brown eye in her direction.

"Come across with advice, Rusty. Shall I go on? Did the

shake of your silky mane mean 'No' or was it to dislodge that outsize fly on your nose?"

She looked back at her brother's ranch. It was as if she were seeing it through the small end of a field glass, distance shrank it to miniature proportions. Barbed-wire fences stretched on and on in a valley dotted with grazing cattle. A creek looped and curved and glittered like a silver ribbon. The large, rambling, two-story white house with a shelter belt of cottonwoods behind it, in a flower-bordered lawn, shone like a pearl in an emerald setting. Near it snuggled a smaller, much smaller duplication, the guest house — the Dude's Rest, a one-time cowhand had named it.

The still immensity of the country gave her the shivers. Robinson Crusoe landing on his desert island must have felt like an atom in a boundless wilderness as she felt now. The grazing cattle appeared restless. The angry bellow of a steer had an ominous note. BARK. Bark. B-a-r-k, a coyote was sounding off in the distance. That last added a macabre touch which didn't help her adjustment to her present life.

She had learned the functions of the various whitewashed buildings that squatted within hail of the homestead. Bunkhouse, flanked by a towering woodpile, barn, with a great corral, foreman's cottage, blacksmith shop, granary and icehouse. The real-estate broker who had sold Dick the property three months ago had assured him that it was a complete outfit for cattle raising, well stocked with the best breed of Herefords, that the fall roundup would show him thousands of dollars of sirloins on the hoof, that there was a competent working force ready to carry on under the direction of a new owner. Was Dick, a veteran of World War II at twenty-eight, the man to do it?

The high-power salesman had neglected to impress on his victim's mind the fact that the property was fifteen miles from a highway, thirty from a neighbor, fifty from the nearest city, that a stage brought the mail from there to a post office ten miles from the ranch.

Had the man seen that his prospective customer was in a don't-give-a-damn mood? Dick had been an easy mark, bitter, scarred, his left arm useless. He had been horribly hurt just before the mission in the Pacific Theater after which he had been reported missing, by a letter from Lois Langley, his fiancée, telling him that as she was terribly in love with an officer she had met while serving with the Red Cross in England, she was breaking their engagement and considered herself free to marry the other man.

"Not that I would have stopped her, crippled as I am, but she might have waited till after my return to break the glad tidings," he had protested savagely. After which in a to-hell-with-everything depression he had bought the ranch.

"Why didn't you talk with me first, why, Dick?" she had asked from a frightened certainty that he had made a tragic mistake.

"*Why?* Didn't the Grands train you and me in the conviction that it is better to make a wrong decision than to get the habit of leaning on another person for advice? I decided. From the time I was a small boy I've had a ranch complex. I have the ranch. I put two thirds of the money I inherited from Grandfather into it and signed a mortgage for the balance. I've got to fly. If I ditch I'm cleaned out. If I've guessed wrong, as I did about a girl, it's just too bad." In a sudden shift from defiance to wistfulness which had wrung her heart, he asked: —

"Can you take it for a while, Kit, until I get adjusted? Except for Grandmother, we're all that's left of the family. We ought to hang together."

"Can I take it! Try to get rid of me, Captain. Watch me make the headlines as Kathryn, the world's ace cowgirl." She had tucked her arm under his and laughed, a shaky attempt with her eyes full of tears, but it passed. "Perhaps that isn't what the female of the species is called but you get what I mean."

It had taken weeks to find substitutes for her many war jobs, but here she was and remote as the ranch seemed from civilization here she would stay while Dick needed her. In time he would forget the Langley girl. She had never seen even a picture of her; Dick had met her while at an officers' training camp.

Why worry about her? Keep everlastingly busy was the answer and to date she had found plenty to do. She thought of the formal afternoon and evening clothes she had brought and laughed. There's humor in almost every situation. You can take it so long as you keep laughter in your life, Kathryn Marlowe, she told herself.

A soft whinny brought her back to the present, a big drop of rain on her cheek shocked her to the realization that while she had been absorbed in the past, the clouds had ganged up to obscure the sun, that rain was spattering into the dust of the road.

She wheeled the horse and started down the hill. Could she reach the house before her gabardine jodhpurs had changed from soft beige to a drenched brown? No hat to worry about. The feel of the rain on her dark hair was grand. Lucky it was short, lucky that dampness tightened the wave to curls.

Great drops pelted like machine-gun bullets. The wind had

risen and slapped at the sleeves of her green crepe blouse. Thunder rumbled behind the hills. Reaching home was out, but she could make the small building at the foot of this hill for shelter from the storm. A line rider's camp, Dick had told her one day when they passed it and had explained its use. It snuggled at the bend of a creek outlined by willows already turned reddish brown.

"Get a move on, Rusty," she encouraged the bay, but the horse had been trained to descend a hill with care and cautiously picked his way down, sliding occasionally in what appeared to be a roaring river of mud. Thunder crashed, wind whistled. Tree branches reached and writhed against the sky like the arms of an enraged octopus grabbing for its prey. Rain soaked through her thin blouse till it fitted snug as the skin of a green avocado.

In front of the one-story brown building she slid to the ground before she noticed the gray horse hitched under a connecting shed. A Winchester rifle in a leather scabbard was strapped to the well-worn saddle which was adorned with silver filigree, a coiled rope was tied beside the saddle fork. Was a cowhand already in possession? Rusty pricked his ears and whinnied. The gray answered. As she tied the bay to the rail the door was flung open.

"See who's here," a rough voice exclaimed. She didn't like the two little flames that flared in the man's near-set greenish eyes as they swept over her skin-tight blouse. She didn't like his heavily lined, leathery face with its high cheekbones and she hated his thin mouth when it stretched in an ingratiating smile and revealed the glitter of a gold right upper molar. He could be cast for a Wild West outlaw and would look the part.

Behind him, tin plates, cups and pans on a rack shone like polished silver; a bedstead of poles held a rough tick; from the ridgepole hung a large oil lamp, and when the man moved she caught a glimpse of a potbellied stove, a table made of old boards and wall shelves filled with tin cans, their colorful jackets proclaiming that mammoth tomatoes, peaches, apricots and plums lurked within.

Through her mind flashed a write-up of this state she had read when she knew she was coming to the ranch. "Time marches on, but time has not changed the peace and security of these wide open spaces."

Maybe not, but how would the writer of that blurb react to the man smirking at her, a man in the early thirties, perhaps. His red and blue plaid shirt, his brown corduroy cowboy pants, his tan leather boots with their high heels were dry; evidently he had sufficient weather sense to get under cover before it rained. Was he one of the hands on Dick's ranch? There were ten in the bunkhouse. They looked alike to her.

"Step inside out of the rain, ma'am." With a flourish he swept off his big, shabby, broad-brimmed blue Stetson with its silver filigree hatband, and flashed the gold molar in an encouraging grin. "You won't be intrudin'."

Thunder crashed behind the hill. The heavens poured forth a deluge. Kit crossed the threshold and backed against the door to hold it open.

"Certainly I'm not intruding. This line rider's camp is on my brother Richard Marlowe's ranch. Why shouldn't I step in?"

What had Dick done to the cowboy that would wipe the grin from his face and set flames in his eyes again?

"So — o you belong to the Marlowe outfit? You tell that smarty-pants brother of yours that a city slicker like him can't turn Skip Cane down without givin' him a reason. Get that?"

He had moved quite close to her. She didn't like his glare.

She didn't like his nearness. She didn't like the smell of liquor on his breath. The completeness of the living quarters terrified her.

"Yes, I *get* it. Now get this. I'm not deaf, don't stand so near." As with a cocky grin he moved a step closer, she laid a protesting hand on his arm. "Keep away."

"Say, who do you think you are, pushin' me round?" His angry voice was loud and echoed in the cabin, so loud that it drowned the sound of rain on the roof.

"Who is pushing whom?" inquired a deep voice.

Help, or another of the same kind, Kit wondered as a figure in a drenched gabardine trench coat materialized from the white sheet of rain. A military cap was pulled down to meet clear gray eyes which darkened to black as they moved from her face to that of the man crowding her against the door.

"Skip Cane in person." The voice had an edge in it. "What gives?"

"It's you again, is it, *Colonel?* I'm plumb fed up with you nosing into my personal affairs. I ain't in the Army. I ain't no longer on your pay roll. What business is it of yours who's pushing who?" The cowhand set his thin mouth in an ugly line.

The officer wiped the moisture from his face with a wet sleeve and slapped his cap against the doorjamb to remove the rain.

"You may be surprised to know it, Skip, but I'm making it my business." He looked at Kit. "Were you pushing him?"

"He stood too near. I put my hand on his arm to keep him away."

"Standing too near has become a habit of yours, Skip. You've been deferred because you're a good cowhand and the country needs cattle. But if you keep up this sort of thing the town fathers will draft you. Not that we particularly want your type in the Army, but you make good fighters."

"Says you."

Kit's throat tightened, her heart thumped as Cane doubled his fists and stepped forward with a murderous glint in his eyes. The officer regarded him above the light he was applying to a cigarette.

"No dice, Skip. Quit throwing your weight around. I don't brawl in this uniform or in the presence of a lady."

"You're telling me." The cowhand clapped on his broad hat. His eyes glittered with hate. "Gone all out for this dame, ain't you? You won't get far when she knows you're Rex Danton who gypped her man into buying run-down Double H Ranch. Double H for Health and Happiness, your uncle, the Old Boss, named it. Laugh that off. Fat chance the new owner has for them."

"Beat it and beat it quick, Cane."

The low, authoritative voice had instantaneous effect. The cowhand stamped across the room. Rain ran off the broad brim of his Stetson in tiny rivers when he stopped outside the threshold.

"Next time, *Colonel,* I'll catch you when you're not in uniform or with a lady. So long."

II

KIT LISTENED till the splash of a horse's hoofs was lost in the beat of rain against the roof. Her eyes were on the bronzed face of the officer at the door.

This was the man who had sold Dick the ranch, "gypped" was the word slimy Skip Cane had used. He didn't look like a cheat. His fine mouth encircled by a white line of anger was grimly set. Lines, deep as if inked, radiated from the corners of his gray eyes, grave, as if they had seen things which had left their tragic impress. His nose was large and clean-cut. His dark hair was lightly touched with platinum at the temples.

"Gypped." The word echoed through her mind. "Gypped." Was it as bad as that? Had Dick put his small personal fortune into a hopeless flop?

"You're wet and cold." Through his angry absorption in the departing cowhand, had the officer sensed her shiver? His smiled warmed her as he pulled off his trench coat and laid it across her shoulders.

"This is dry inside. Better keep it on till heat from the stove gets in its work on your clothes. We'll have a fire in a minute. Close the door till I get it started, will you?"

"I prefer it open."

"We may get smoked out, but, you're the doctor."

His amused smile and shrug made her feel like a schoolgirl at the awkward age. Backed against the door she clutched the sides of the trench coat together across her breast to cover her wet, clinging blouse, watched him as he opened the door of the potbellied stove.

"Somebody's been burning stuff here." He pulled out a piece of blue denim, scorched around the edges, the size of a man's large handkerchief. A strip of newspaper came with it.

"The guy who left the stove in this condition violated the social ethics of the range rider." He was looking intently at the cloth he held. "The hospitality of the cow country is boundless. A visitor is welcome, but he is supposed to leave a camp in as good condition as he finds it, not burn his old clothes in the stove and leave it clogged."

He dropped the scorched scrap to the floor and kicked it out of sight, poked inside the firebox with a stick before he stuffed in paper and kindling and touched it with the flame of his cigarette lighter. When the fire was well started he pushed in a chunk of wood from a pile.

"You'd better come nearer and dry those wet clothes," he advised without turning. "You don't have to hold back that door. It will remain open."

"You seem familiar with the place."

"Why not? I spent my vacations on this ranch for years." He drew forward a wooden chair. "Sit here. I judge by your voice that you've accepted Skip Cane's profile of me. Even so, let's not fight. You may be surprised to know that I'm fed up with conflict, temporarily off the beam, as it were."

She glanced at the array of ribbons on his tunic, at the silver eagle on his shoulder, at the castle on his collar. Evidence to the fact that as an officer in the Combat Engineers, he was justified in his aversion to more fighting. I'll bet girls go all out for you and you don't give a button on your tunic for them, she thought. She abandoned the protection of the door and perched on the edge of the chair.

"That's better. You needn't be afraid of me. Just between us I wouldn't care if I didn't meet another woman, young or old, for the duration. To quote Skip Cane, I'm plumb fed up with them. That statement ought to help you relax."

He tucked another chunk of wood into the stove and opened the draft in the door. Had he, like Dick, been turned down by the girl he loved?

"That will do the trick." He raised his voice to make it heard above the roar of flames up the chimney. The air became cloudy with smoke. She coughed.

"As I remarked before, this should be shut, unless we want to choke to death. I don't." He closed the door.

"Masterful type," Kit observed in a stifled voice and wiped her smarting eyes.

"We get that way in the Army. How long had Skip Cane been here annoying you?"

"He was here when I arrived. When he discovered that I came from the Double H he blasted my — Dick because he had refused to hire him."

"Which refusal showed that the new owner is a judge of men. Skip is an A 1 cowhand but a troublemaker in the bunkhouse. He's a menace on a ranch. As you may have observed, I'm his special hate. It was my painful duty to order, by long distance, his discharge from the Double H." From his trousers pocket he drew a package of cigarettes and offered it. She shook her head.

"No thanks."

"Won't accept one from me because you've been alerted against me? There are two sides to every story, remember."

"I don't smoke." The warmth of the fire was driving the chill of the storm from her body and spirit, the air had cleared. "I can but I don't care for it. Lucky, isn't it, when cigarettes are becoming scarcer every day." The sudden remembrance that she was being friendly to the man who had gypped Dick stiffened her voice. "Did you own this ranch before you sold it to Richard Marlowe?"

"Are you his wife?"

"I asked a question first."

When he smiled, even white teeth accentuated the deep bronze of his face and the brilliancy of his gray eyes.

"The chair recognizes the lady from the East. I inherited Double H Ranch a year ago while I was overseas. It had been running under the foreman, Joe Carr's, oversight for months before it was sold to — your husband?"

"Was that Wild West outlaw right when he said Dick had been 'gypped'? Ooch, the fire is hot." She threw back the raincoat. Already her blouse had returned to its normal lines.

"The new owner has not been gypped. That 'run-down' crack of Skip Cane's was a spite bomb. The stock and buildings have been kept up to the high standard my uncle, the Old Boss, required, Joe Carr saw to that." He drew the other chair in the room forward. "Mind if I sit down? Dampness sets my right leg aching as if my four wisdom teeth and one or two of their collaterals had gone on a jumping rampage. What do you think about it?"

"Your aching leg?"

"Quick on the come-back, aren't you? I want to know if you take my say-so or Cane's for the justice of the word 'gypped.' "

'My reaction changes with the time of day. At one A.M. War Mountain Time — I've learned that since I came — when the wind rips and roars at my window, coyotes yip outside and the ranch dogs bark their heads off in response, I could cheerfully strangle the owner who unloaded on us. When I arise and greet the smiling morn, all blue and gold and snowy white, and hear the roar of planes above the clouds on their way back from night-bombing practice to the field at the Fort beyond the city, I'm not quite so low in my mind." Oh, dear, she was being friendly again when she should be scathingly contemptuous or indifferent.

"It's a great country. After we have finished cleaning up the savages I shall come back to live and work. I owe that to the boys from here who won't return." He closed the draft in the stove door. The roar in the chimney ceased. "I'm an engineer by profession."

"Richard Marlowe is a lawyer. He knows no more of ranching than a baby. He was heartsick and discouraged because of crippling injuries and was an easy mark for a conscienceless real-estate agent. Not that it will lick him," she defended passionately. "Dick has what boxers call the fighting heart, the will to come bouncing back every time one is knocked down."

"Fond of him, aren't you?"

"That's too tame a word. I adore him."

"Lucky guy, no wonder he has the will to bounce back with you to cheer from the side lines. He's finding it rough going here now, but he'll work into it. The job is so darned worth while. Ranching is a productive industry of enormous significance in the history and life of the nation. You'll like it better when you know and really see this country. Towering canyon walls, spectacular falls, petroglyphs on rocks, antelope herds, elk, buffalo and its quota of mountain lions and grizzlies. I'm selling you my home state. How'm I doin'?"

"Fine. Go on. I'm almost sold."

"You ain't heard nothin' yet. Grand people, with a wide, wide world outlook. The majority of the important ranchers have a house or a *pied-à-terre* in the city. Plenty of amusement.

Hiking, fishing, mountain climbing and camping in spring and summer. In November pheasant shooting. In the winter, big game hunting. If you're socially-minded, Mountain Lodge, twenty miles from here, part resort hotel and part dude ranch, is filled with guests from East and West. Some come for health, some card addicts come to meet other card addicts, many for sports."

"I'm not looking for amusement. I want to help win this war. I didn't join one of the auxiliaries because I was all the family Grandmother had left at home. Sometimes it seems that I just can't bear it to live here doing housework and chores, when the Government is begging for girls and women to serve in the hospitals. I feel like a parasite. I'm a Nurses' Aide, Red Cross ambulance driver, I've been hostess at a USO."

"You are helping by getting an ex-soldier back to normal thinking and living, aren't you? Rehabilitation, the experts call it, is a war job of tremendous importance. Besides that, you'll find plenty of ways here to put your shoulder to the wheel, help is so infernally scarce. You may even find a use for your hospital training. A ranch can produce casualties of which you've never dreamed. So can mountain sports."

"You talk as if I wanted people to be hurt so I can help. I don't. What kind of sports?"

"Skiing, tobogganing, bobsledding, skating, dog-sled racing. Want to place a little bet that the new owners of the Double H will be rooting for the ranch in a couple of months?"

His smiling assurance was match to tinder. She rose in a sudden surge of anger.

"I don't bet and I hope you get what you deserve for unloading a property you didn't want on Dick." To her horror she felt the sting of tears behind her eyes. Rex Danton might think she was putting on the sob-sister act in an attempt to have him take back his ranch. "I'm going. Thanks for the coat and for the fire."

"Don't thank me. It isn't my fire." Standing, he was no longer smiling, his face had set in grim, fighting lines. "Better wait. It's still rain — " The door was flung open.

"What goes on? In God's name what are you doing in this camp, Kit?" an angry voice demanded.

"Dick!" Kit took a quick step toward the man glowering at her from the threshold. Rivulets of rain dripped from the brim of his sombrero, cascaded down his poncho. His dark, tormented eyes snapped. The red edges of a large, circular scar on his left cheek stood out like a fiery ring on his thin, pale face. Had anxiety for her drained away his color?

"Did you rain down?" A cliché if ever there were one, but the only words that came to her mind. From the corners of her eyes she could see the officer standing with one hand thrust in his trousers pocket, the other holding a cigarette as if waiting. Waiting for what? She had an uncanny sense that she was at a crossroads.

"Saw smoke rising like a signal fire from this chimney. The camp hasn't been used by a range rider for a month," her brother explained. "Been at the corrals all morning, when I returned to the house found Ma Snell with a bad attack of jitters. You had been gone so long she was afraid you were lost in the storm. Her Ouija board was on the kitchen table. She'd been working that for all it was worth hoping she'd get a communication as to your whereabouts."

"She might have at that." The officer tossed his cigarette into the stove, shut the door with its isinglass windows. "Curious about the renascence of the Ouija board in wartime, isn't it? Ma Snell has an uncanny skill at getting mystic messages.

In case you are wondering how I know, Captain Marlowe, I'm Rex Danton, nephew of the original owner of the Double H."

At least he wasn't afraid to acknowledge who he was. How would Dick react to that name, Kit wondered. She had never voiced to him her fury at the agent who had sold him the ranch. If he was bitter toward the man he had never given a hint of his resentment.

"Rex Danton? One-time Major Rex Danton, the owner from whom I bought, aren't you? Damned glad to unload, weren't you?"

"Yes and no." Dick's angry flare had sent a surge of red to the officer's hair, surprise had darkened his gray eyes, but his voice was under control as he explained pleasantly: —

"Yes, because when I get out of the Army my profession will leave no time for ranching. No, because I love the ranch which was my happy hunting ground from the time I was a small kid till I enlisted. Does that answer your question?"

"And how. Come on, Kit. You don't mind a little rain." Richard Marlowe pulled off his poncho and flung it across her shoulders. "Wear this. I've been wet before."

He pushed her ahead of him through the doorway without giving her a chance to speak. She fought an urge to glance over her shoulder at the man standing in the middle of the cabin. After all, he was the former owner of the property and it would have been decent to be courteous to him. Possibly he had not known to whom his agent was selling. Experience warned her that this was not the psychical moment to suggest it. The desirability of a swift change of subject was indicated by Dick's mood. As her bay and his black slushed side by side past an open roadster she ventured: —

"Perhaps I wasn't glad to see the former owner of the

Double H. When I stepped into the line rider's camp I found it occupied by a cowhand, by name Skip Cane. He reminded me of the old-time buckaroo who shot up everyone in sight in the Wild West movies to which you dragged me when we were youngsters. I couldn't have been more frightened if I had seen a rattlesnake in a corner coiled to strike. You'll have to admit I'm not a coward, but something about the man — in that setting — gave me the heebie-jeebies."

Her expedient had worked. Dick's resentment at the former owner of the Double H receded into the background.

"Did the guy touch you?"

"No. When he discovered who I was his fury at you for not hiring him boiled over. He called you a city slicker in a voice drenched with threat. Why didn't you hire him, Dick?"

"Joe Carr, the foreman, had warned me he would appear, that while he is an efficient cowhand, none better, he keeps the bunkhouse in a ferment, that where he is there will be fifty-seven varieties of hell popping. He is blackballed at the ranches in this part of the state. Did he threaten you?"

"No, but he came too near. When I put my hand on his sleeve to keep him at a distance, he demanded, 'Who do you think you are, pushing me around?' At that precise moment the Army established a beachhead."

After that they rode for a mile without speaking. Kit had learned that it was wiser not to force conversation. The air was spiced with the strong smell of wet sagebrush. The leaves of the cottonwoods were lacquered by rain, each pine needle sported a diamond pendant. As they neared the ranch house the deep mellow notes of a bell drifted through the storm.

"There's the wash-up bell. We should have invited Colonel Danton to have noon dinner with us, Dick. I have been informed recently that the hospitality of the cow country is boundless. We didn't measure up to specifications. I assume that the soaked car we passed near the camp was his. He's thirty miles from the nearest neighbor and fifteen from the highway. We feed even our enemies in the prison camps."

"Maybe we do, but we don't feed that guy. Don't you know who he is?"

"Only that he's a much beribboned Colonel in the Combat Engineers and once owned the Double H."

"He's the man who stole my girl. The officer for whom Lois Langley threw me over."

"*Dick!* Did you know that the ranch was *his* when you bought it?"

"Sure, I knew. Even if I was a darn fool to buy, you don't think I signed the mortgage with my eyes shut, do you?"

III

AT THE WINDOW of the camp Rex Danton watched
the two riders until they were mere dark shadows in the rain.
When the splash of hoofs on a muddy road had died away he
put out the fire in the potbellied stove and picked up the piece
of scorched blue denim he had kicked out of the girl's line of
vision. He hadn't been mistaken, there was half of a stenciled
letter on it. Once it had been red. He frowned at the strip of
newspaper which still clung to the cloth. The date of publica-
tion was intact. He whistled.

"What goes? What goes?" he said under his breath before
he tucked cloth and paper carefully into the pocket of his trench
coat. Had Skip Cane burned the stuff? Could be.

The sun was shining again, the sky was a clear, cloudless
blue, a soft pine-scented breeze was billowing the Stars and
Stripes on the flagpole, when he drove his roadster into the
garage at Mountain Lodge, the rambling caravansary built
of enormous logs, surrounded by cabins, which his uncle, Peter
Danton, had had built in company with four neighboring
ranchers. Spread on a fertile plateau three hundred feet above
the surrounding country it was set against a backdrop of
majestic mountains with towering white peaks. The project
had been a grand conception and a financial success.

On the broad porch Rex looked out over the purple-gray
and green stretches of sagebrush, wooded knolls and lush

green valley glinting with shining creeks with game trails, like dark threads, following their curves. The scattered buildings of a distant ranch brought the girl in the line rider's camp to the forefront of his mind again. Confound it, she and her aversion had been pricking like a splinter in his memory even while he had been considering the significance of the piece of blue denim he had rescued from oblivion and deciding on the best use to make of it. "Kit." The name suited her.

He had been on the way to the Double H, to welcome the new owner and offer any information he had gleaned from experience that might help, when the rain had sent him beating it to the line rider's camp for shelter. If one could trust the storm signals displayed in the eyes of the girl and Marlowe it was darn lucky he hadn't reached the ranch. Could she really believe he would gyp — that was the word Skip Cane had used — anyone into buying the property? Why not? What did she know about Rex Danton?

Unseeing gaze on the panorama of earth and sky, he visualized her oval face tanned to a golden brown; her beautiful large eyes — were they blue or black? — set in spectacularly long lashes; her dark hair, clinging close to her proudly held head, the beautiful line of chin and throat. Her drenched clothes had revealed that she was slight without being thin. Her finely shaped hands were tipped with nails not too long, not too red. Expressive hands. A huge turquoise ring on the right third finger matched the stones in the silver bangles from wrist to elbow. If she were Marlowe's wife —

Why the dickens stand here mooning over the conclusions of an emotional girl — or was she a woman? He had plenty of problems to work out, besides the one he had picked up today, and was that something, he asked himself before he entered the spacious lounge. In its center loomed a stone chimney with a fire burning on each of its four sides. He crossed to the office in the corner.

"Reckon you got caught in the shower, Colonel," observed Collens, the thin-faced, prematurely bald, old-young clerk. "Tst! Tst! Your cap is kind of out of shape. I obeyed orders and didn't let on to the other guests that you arrived late last night, though the news got around you were expected. Here's your mail."

"That wasn't a shower, it was a deluge, Colly. I've been away so long I'm rusty on weather signs. The inside of my car was a small-size swimming pool before I reached the Double H line rider's camp at the foot of the hill. Sure these letters are for me? What a bunch, and I came here on leave to get away from it all."

"I reckon the ranchers around are pretty glad you're back. We're all awful proud of your overseas record, Colonel. I'll bet a lot of the envelopes are invitations. The letters aren't the whole of it. Phone's been ringing for you most of the morning."

"Good Lord, was it the Fort?" Was he being recalled so soon? After three years in the service he had been given two months' leave to recuperate from a serious machine-gunning and only a week of it had passed.

"No 'twasn't the Fort — gosh, I'd hope not an' you just out of hospital. It was a lady phoning from the city. Said she'd give you a buzz tonight about seven. She wouldn't tell her name."

"Tonight about seven." The words set up a rhythmic chant in Rex's mind as he showered and changed to a fresh uniform. It couldn't be — Coatless, he was brushing his hair furiously before the mirror when the name flashed in neon letters on the screen of his mind. Arms upraised, brush in each hand, he stood like a mechanical toy which had run down for want of winding and glared at his reflection. It couldn't be she. The last time he had seen her she had declared she would stay on her overseas job till V Day.

"You sure had me scared," he told the looking-glass man. "For a minute I thought we had to fight that battle over again — and boy, oh, boy, was it a battle? I meant it when I told the girl in the cabin that I was off women, young or old, for the duration."

"And they call this a leave," he exclaimed aloud as at seven o'clock he sealed, stamped and added the last letter to a sizable pile. There had been the resignation of the manager of his uncle's oil field to answer. Oil. More oil, the Government was demanding, and the man had regretfully admitted he was not equal to the job. He wasn't, but with so many men in the service where could one be found to take his place? There had been regrets to send to invitations from friends to spend a week or as long as he liked on their ranches. He would make no visits this time. Freedom, absolute freedom. A leave with no obligations to be entertaining was his dish.

He regarded thoughtfully the letter he had written to the real-estate agent asking for details of the sale of the Double H ranch. On second thought he wouldn't send it. An interview would be more satisfactory. Much as he hated it, he would go to the city tomorrow and have a talk with Cal Smiley. He could judge from his manner whether he had deliberately put over one on Captain Marlowe. Also, he would land the piece of blue denim with the strip of paper and its betraying date line in the right place.

In the lounge, Seth Carter, a tall, stout man in dinner clothes with iron-gray hair and slightly bulging eyes, which reminded Rex of a pair of blue and white glassies he had treasured as a boy, met him with outstretched hand.

"It's grand to have you back, Rex. Zowie, man, wouldn't your Uncle Pete have been bursting with pride if he were here to greet you." A short, wheezy cough put a period to his enthusiasm, but only for a second. "We're lining up to give you a great reception in town, lad."

This was what he had feared, to avoid which he had come to the Lodge.

"That's mighty kind of you all, sir, but hold it off, like a good fella, will you? Wait till the others return. Each of our townsmen who slugged across a beachhead inferno, who bayoneted his way over Normandy hedgerows, who went through hell in the Pacific, should be counted in. I — I — I've been ordered to keep quiet, avoid all excitement for a while. When the machine gun got me in the leg, the fever mussed up the works here" — he tapped his left breast. His conscience pricked. That excuse was bunk. His heart was beating out its job, twenty-four hours a day without a hitch.

"That's bad. Sure, I'll give the high sign to the boys to head it off for the present, Rex. We hadn't planned a horntootin' hullabaloo, you understand, but a celebration that would be a worthy tribute to you and our other boys, living, k — killed," he cleared his voice, "or missing, who have given their best that this horrible slaughter shall not happen again. Think you'll be fit later?"

"Sure, I'll be sound as a nut, after a few weeks of this life. I'll be around for some time. I've been ordered to report to Washington when my leave is up. I may get a call before."

"I hope you won't be sent back to the front. You're terribly needed here, Rex. Your Uncle Pete's wells supply oil for war use. The man who's handling them isn't equal to his job. He knows it, all right. Here's the wife. We're staying at the Lodge for a few weeks to see if I can lick this wheeze. It isn't contagious, thank God. I hate like thunder being away from home but I promised the Doc I'd give it a try. Sally, our daughter, came with us, but went back to the Circle Q to check up on a carload shipment of cattle we sold. She comes pretty near knowing as much about the business of the ranch as I do. She'll be back tomorrow."

A tall, fresh-skinned woman in a gray frock as silvery as her hair joined them.

"Serena, you remember Rex Danton?"

"Remember him? As if I could forget him." Her smile set her blue eyes sparkling. "Wasn't he the wild man in my Sunday School class? Wasn't he a magnet that drew the attention of all the little pigtailed girls — our Sally among them — in the next class until they were removed by a distraught teacher to a remote locality?" Her eyes shone like sapphires behind tears, the gay raillery of her voice changed to gravity. "I've followed you with my prayers, Rex."

He cleared his throat of a troublesome huskiness.

"They must have been what pulled me through many a time when I was in a spot, Mrs. Carter."

" 'Mrs.' You used to call me Aunt S'rena, Rex."

"Aunt S'rena it will be from now on. There go the dinner chimes. May I sit with you tonight?"

"Try to escape, just try, that's all." She slipped her hand under his arm. "You're my boy, now. You know — " A quick catch of her breath. "You've heard — "

"*Not* Seth, Jr. Not young Seth?" Rex's words were a shocked protest. He was their only son. So that accounted for the break in Seth Carter's voice when he had said "killed."

She held her under lip tight in her teeth to steady it and nodded.

"D — don't let his father hear you," she whispered. "He

was with a plane carrier in the Pacific. Pilot. Seth senior has been wonderful."

Wonderful was an understatement, Rex thought, as during dinner Seth Carter reported the gossip of the community without once referring to his own grief and loss. At his first opportunity he steered the conversation in the direction he had wanted it to take since the moment they had been seated at the table.

"Have you met the new owner of the Double H?" he inquired.

"No. I drove over to welcome Captain Marlowe to our part of the country soon after he arrived. Didn't see him, he was out with a couple of hands running lines. Joe Carr, he's still there as foreman, scratched his grizzled head and suggested that the neighbors hold back from coming for a while; that the nerves of the new boss seemed kind of raw, he didn't want to see folks. Marlowe was ditched in the Pacific. The enemy strafed the rubber boat and he, the pilot, was the only survivor of the crew. He was reported missing. Three months later he was discovered on a small island, in a native hut, weak and almost dead from wounds."

" 'Missing' is a tragic word but there's always a glint of hope in it."

"Right, Rex. Captain Marlowe is bitter about his injuries. There's a story going the rounds that a girl had given him his time while he was in the Pacific Theater, which, if true, doesn't help in his readjustment to life."

"Poor, bewildered boy. You should have gone again, Seth." Rex caught the glint of tears in Serena Carter's blue eyes. "Joe Carr's an A 1 foreman, proud of his job, intensely loyal to his late boss and the Double H brand, but not sympathetically understanding of the problems of youth. If young

Marlowe is bitter he needs friendliness and help all the more."

"He has it now, Serena. Joe told me he was expecting his sister Kathryn. She must have arrived by this time."

Sister. His relief to know that the girl he had met was not Marlowe's wife was absurd, Rex assured himself.

"Has the new boss had experience ranching in the wide-open spaces?" he inquired. "Quote, 'where the deer and the antelope play'?"

"No, and from what I hear this country seems appallingly wide and open to him. There's a feeling in the community that silver-tongued real-estate agent, Cal Smiley, landed him for a sucker. They don't blame you, Rex. You put the property in his hands to sell and he sold. Sorry you felt you had to dispose of it."

"Hated like the dickens to do it, sir. In normal times I would have held on to the ranch for my children and grandchildren when or if I had 'em, but when you're living in the inferno of battle, your own future, to say nothing of the future of a next generation, seems a mere glittering mirage. The transfer papers came while we were under furious bombardment. I signed and shot them along p.d.q. knowing that my number might come up at any minute, that if they weren't signed, disposing of the ranch would be one more load on my sister Barbie's shoulders. I got mine the very next day. I'm darned sorry if the new owner thinks he's been — gypped, but I don't feel in any way responsible."

"You're not, no one thinks you are," Seth Carter assured earnestly. "If Marlowe had the guts to win a D.F.C. — I understand the decoration was pinned on by one of the highest ranking Marine officers — he has the right stuff in him to see his investment through."

"Maybe, but to start ranching from scratch is a mighty big

order and takes a different kind of courage. I'll have a talk fest with Smiley tomorrow and get to the bottom of the deal. I kept Rushing Creek for myself for vacations, I couldn't let it all go. If you remember, it is four miles northeast of the home ranch, has about a hundred acres, with a stone house built into the sloping hillside and the other necessary buildings, log cabin, a storehouse, bunkhouse, barn and corral. Uncle Pete bought the land years ago from Old-Timer Pratt, tore down his log cabin, built the house and kept it up to the minute as a fishing and hunting lodge."

"Sure, I remember it, it's the envy of every woman in the county. Built in different units on the various levels. I've had some bang-up whoopees at Rushing Creek — and boy, how that creek can rush in the spring when the mountains feed it melting snow. There's a swimming pool in the basement that opens off the second terrace. The outfit was so luxurious your uncle's friends side-stepped its real name and called it 'Pete's Folly.' We — "

"Phone call for you, Colonel Danton," a teen-age boy in scarlet livery glistening with gold braid and buttons announced at his elbow.

"Who is it? Did you get the name?" Rex settled more firmly in his chair as Collens's words flashed through his mind — "Said she'd give you a buzz tonight about seven."

"No, sir. Mr. Collens didn't tell me who was calling. They're holding the line, Colonel," the boy reminded.

"All right. All right, I'm coming. I'll be seeing you later, Aunt S'rena." As he turned away from the table he heard Mrs. Carter say : —

"Rex was afraid of that call, Seth. Why?"

"You're darned tootin' I'm afraid of it, if it is from the person whom I suspect is on the other end of the wire," Rex agreed to himself as he crossed the foyer. "Here I go straight up to the firing line and boy, how I'd like to run."

In the booth he picked up the receiver.

"Rex Danton speaking."

"Rex, *darling*." He flinched at the ardent voice. Never had he given her reason to use that word or tone to him. "I'm here."

"Where's here?"

"In the biggest hotel in the city which is twenty miles from Mountain Lodge where you are staying, I understand. Mother is with me."

"So what? Thought you intended to stay on the overseas job till the last enemy gun had been silenced."

"Don't be such a kill-joy, Rex. I did intend to, but I broke down in Italy — nerves shot to pieces, by the blood and horror to say nothing of the mud. I was ordered home and told to get into the mountains. I remembered how you raved about your family's ranch and decided that that country was the place for me."

"How did you locate me?"

"*I* read the papers. You had a great write-up. The article copied from a local paper stated that you would spend your leave in your home town. After that, it was easy. Here I am. All thrills at the prospect of seeing — "

"Make your message short, please. Servicemen want to telephone." The metallic transcription interrupted.

"How maddening. As if my call wasn't important." Rex visualized the pout of the red lips at the other end of the line. "Just in case you care, you're not my only reason for coming to the Wild and Woolly West. I must see you, darling. To-morrow?"

"All right. All right. I'll take you and your mother to lunch.

For Pete's sake ring off. Give the servicemen a break. Good night." He snapped the receiver on the hook.

"Hope 'twasn't bad news, Colonel." Collens's sympathetic query stopped him as he crossed the lounge. "Folks don't turn a muddy white like you are 'less someone's dead or they're fightin' mad."

"You've said it. Fightin' mad fills the bill — and how." An idea flashed into his mind, "Colly, I'm checking out tomorrow."

"Tst! Tst! Aren't you comfortable here in your uncle's suite? Yours now, though, isn't it? Where you going?"

"That, Mister Collens, is something I'm not telling. If anyone asks you, you don't know. Get that? *You don't know.*"

IV

A STEEPLE clock in the city was striking twelve. Rex Danton rose from a chair in the office of Smiley, Inc., Real Estate, and looked down at the gray-haired, coatless, white-shirt-sleeved man opposite, whose feet in glistening tan shoes were propped on the desk, from whose mouth a long black cigar protruded at a belligerent angle. Cal had grown old in the last few years, he thought, must be about forty-eight now and looked every day of it.

"I'm not satisfied with your explanation of the sale of the ranch, Cal," he declared gravely. "Captain Marlowe has come out of the war partially disabled, you should have made sure he knew what he was taking on before you passed the final papers."

Smiley tipped back his swivel chair at an alarming slant. His thumbs were thrust into the pockets of his black and white checked waistcoat, a squad of fountain pens deployed in the upper left pocket, a tan leather belt adorned with silver filigree girdled his too, too solid waistline.

"What's all the shootin' about, Rex? The guy got the ranch he wanted at a bargain and you got your price. So what?"

"I feel responsible because I believe Marlowe was talked into buying a property entirely unsuited to his experience and needs. You're a super-smooth salesman, Cal, when you want to put across a deal."

"Sure, I'm a smooth salesman. That's why you gave me the job, wasn't it?" Smiley's suavity went out like a candle flame in a puff of wind. He dragged his feet from the desk and rose. His small eyes, set like a pig's in folds of plump, red cheek, contracted to points of green light.

"I don't like your insinuation that I put across a raw deal, Rex. You put the property in my hands to sell. I sold at your price. Now, you're beefing about it."

"I'm not beefing, I'm just darned sorry to see a man who had enough handed him in the war get another tough deal."

"Why so sure it will prove tough? Ranching may put the guy on his feet physically and pep him up mentally. Marlowe said he'd always wanted a ranch in this state. He's got it. So what? I hear he's come home carrying Old Man Depression on his shoulders. It's a bad break for that sister he's imported. She's something out of this world when it comes to looks, I hear."

"Who told you about her?"

"Now, now, keep your shirt on, Colonel. Skip Cane got an eyeful of her. He dropped in this morning, early, sore as the devil because Marlowe wouldn't take him on at the ranch. He thought I might have some influence with the new owner of the Double H."

"Don't try it. You know as well as I do that Skip's a trouble-maker."

"Woman trouble and how. Sure I know. You don't think I'd recommend him, especially where there's a pretty girl, do you? There are still a few details of the sale to be cleaned up which will necessitate several calls. I'll do my best to perk up the lady's spirits. I've got quite a lot on the ball when I start."

He rubbed his left cushiony hand with its spectacular diamond set in a broad gold band over the other. His fatuous grin roused Rex to fury. Did the smooth guy think Kit Marlowe would welcome his calls? He had another think coming to him. The gleam of satisfaction in Smiley's watchful green eyes warned him that he was reacting according to plan. He hurriedly dropped the anchor of self-control. It held. He laughed.

"You and Sinatra, the Voice. I haven't forgotten your reputation as the most sought-for bachelor in town. Hand over one set of Rushing Creek Ranch keys, will you? Keep the other. I'll take a look-see at the place while I'm in the neighborhood."

Smiley reached into a drawer at the side of the desk.

"Here they are. Thought perhaps you'd open up your apartment in the city. Not thinkin' of baching it at the ranch, are you?"

"In these days of scarcity of help? Be yourself, Cal. When does Marlowe make the last payment on the Double H?"

"Next month. Say, you aren't planning to buy it back, are you?" Anxiety had wiped away his smile.

"Buy it back! I'm in the Army, man, remember; besides, I'm not the only heir to Uncle Pete's property. With cattle, oil interests and city houses, Barbie and I have headaches enough."

"Gosh, Rex, I'll be glad to dispose of a lot of the stuff. I've got a market." Smiley was all eagerness, resentment forgotten.

"I'm sure you have. My sister and I will get together soon to plan what we'll hold."

Smiley followed him to the door, opened it with a flourish and administered an approving slap on his shoulder with the other hand.

"Atta boy. Give me a ring if you decide to sell. I'll do my darnedest. Say, why don't you stop and lunch with me?"

"Thanks, I have a date. I'll be seeing you."

Returning the salute of men in uniform Rex strode along the wide street bordered with sentinel rows of cottonwoods, lined with up-to-date business buildings, noisy with traffic, crowded with lunch-bound clerks, businessmen and shoppers. He thought of his sudden hunch to put in his leave at Rushing Creek, side-step Mountain Lodge and its social whirl and the girl he was on the way to meet. Was it a cockeyed or divinely inspired plan? Time would tell. He thought of Smiley's question, "Say, you aren't thinking of buying it back, are you?" He had been thinking that very thing and it was what he would do through a third party, Seth Carter perhaps, if he were convinced that the Double H was proving a burden to the new owner.

He arrived at that conclusion and the hotel at the same time. As he slowly mounted the steps he was aware that his stomach was putting on the sinking act it had staged when he had jumped into the water from an LST ramp on D Day and with his men behind him had slogged through the surf to the beach under a sky swept with enemy shellbursts.

"Here I go," he muttered and swung the revolving door.

She was waiting for him in the foyer, a hatless, blond-haired girl in a tweed suit which matched her light blue eyes in color. She was whiter and thinner than when last he had seen her, perhaps she had had a nervous breakdown, though he wouldn't put it past her to make up the yarn. Hadn't he learned there was no truth in her?

"Darling!" Her impassioned greeting brought the eyes of every person within hearing distance to his face, which he realized had gone darkly red. He ignored her eagerly extended hands. Not discouraged, she tucked crimson-tipped fingers under his arm and clasped her other hand over them.

"Isn't it wonderful to be together, both of us safe and sound after the horrors we have seen, Rex?"

"Where's your mother? Isn't she lunching with us?"

"She is hunting for a dwelling place for herself and che-ild. Seriously, we're crazy about the climate, she hasn't had a touch of hay fever since we arrived and usually the poor dear suffers the tortures of the damned at this season. We'd like to find a small house outside the city. Know of one?"

"I haven't been back long, but long enough to know there isn't so much as a one-room apartment vacant in the county. Table for two, Wilson?"

The gray-haired, hawk-nosed maître d'hôtel beamed a near-tearful welcome.

"It's grand to see you back, Mr. — Colonel Rex. Luckily your favorite place is unoccupied." He drew out a chair at a table near a sunny window in a *Salon Moderne* if ever there was one. "Madam will sit here?" He opened menus. "I hope you've come to stay, sir?"

"Not for long, Wilson. Marching orders due any day." He ignored the girl's shocked "*Rex*" and gave his entire attention to ordering the luncheon. The vigorous rhythms, the whispers of strings, of a full-throated orchestra playing the "Victory Polka" came over the air.

"Remember when we danced to that at the Red Cross Canteen, Rex? Wasn't it divine?"

The waiter deposited first-quarter moons of Persian melon before them and departed.

"Listen, lady." Rex was aware that his voice lacked the light touch he intended. Why not when his pulses were beating a tattoo of anger? "You take an awful lot of punishment, don't you? We danced together on and off for a week, went to a few movies, then I heard you were engaged to a Captain in the Marines who was staring down death in the Pacific Theater. I wouldn't cut in on another man's girl, no matter how much I wanted to, and to be quite honest in your case, I wasn't tempted."

"But, Rex, I told you the engagement was just war hysteria. Darling —"

"For Pete's sake, quit that Hedy Lamarr 'darling.' It's a hammy piece of acting you're putting on and you know it. I told you then, I tell you again now, that I never have felt the slightest interest in you except as a fairly amusing companion." Exasperation roughened his voice. "Believe it or not, you're getting to be a nightmare. Do you go after every man you meet as you've been after me?"

She'd never forgive that insult. What else could he do? He had told her in London that he wasn't in love with her, never would be; he had answered her one impassioned letter to that effect, and still she persisted. If her eyes had been flames they would have scorched him.

"You flatter yourself that I followed you here, don't you? If you'll think back to our phone conversation last night, you may remember I told you I read the papers, that I had a second reason for coming to this state. Your technique for getting rid of a guest is simple — and successful. I don't care for luncheon. Just a word more. I hate as intensely as I love. Good-by."

She left the table before he could rise. The gray-haired waiter who had arrived with ample orders of broiled guinea hen inquired anxiously: —

"The young lady is not ill, I hope, sir?"

"She had a phone call. She won't be back. Cut out the dessert I ordered."

After luncheon, which he enjoyed in spite of the smarting consciousness that he had been infernally rough to a girl, brief case in hand, he entered an office in the Federal Building. A man with a World War I button in the lapel of his brown tweed coat, who was sitting at a desk, sprang to his feet, seized his hand and shook it vigorously.

"Gosh, it's great to see you, Rex." His keen black eyes twinkled with laughter. "Don't tell me you've come to report that cattle have been stolen from the Double H."

There was a rumor that FBI Tim Blaney was half Indian; he looked it with his high cheekbones.

"No. I used to get the thrill of my life when I was sent here by Uncle Pete to make that report. I have a hunch, Blaney, that I've come about something even more important." He threw the piece of blue denim with the strip of newspaper to the desk. "Take a look at that."

Tim Blaney picked it up. "Where'd you get this?" He ran long, bony fingers through his short, crisp black hair.

Rex told him. "Marlowe said it was a month since a line rider had used the camp. Is the red stencil part of a letter?"

"It is. P. Could be that the other letter was W. Get it?"

"Sure. I had a hunch it might be that. If it is, I've brought it to the right place."

"You said that Miss Marlowe and Skip Cane were in the line rider's camp when you found this?"

"Only Miss Marlowe. Cane had gone."

"That cowhand was at the Double H at the time the last bunch of cattle was stolen. Never could tie anything on him but I don't trust him. He may be mixed up in this."

"But the portion of the newspaper used for kindling is dated a month ago."

"What does that prove? It might have been left there by a line rider. Forget this till you hear from me. Don't let anyone know you found it. Information has an unbelievable way of getting round, and doubtless more than one person knows that a POW's blue fatigue was burned in the line rider's camp."

"Okay. I'm planning to spend a few weeks at Rushing Creek. Get in touch with Chang Loo, Uncle Pete's late houseman, will you, Tim, and send him there, pronto?"

"He'll be glad enough to go. He wanders in here once a month for the pension money the Old Boss left him, looking like a lost soul."

An hour later with a sigh of relief Rex headed his roadster toward his ranch, glad to get away from the ceaseless movement of human beings in the city streets. From the car radio came a man's voice.

"Hidden guns pound at Allied Lines."

The announcement flashed a picture with sound on the screen of his mind. A picture of screeching, groaning cats and trucks and jeeps rushing and slowing along a road, of the glaring eyes of bulldozers as they shoved and twisted and pulled regardless of the menace of buried shells, of falling bombs as they performed titanic construction feats. Would the time come when the memory of resulting tragedy would dim?

He hastily tuned in on another station. Over the air came the soaring, singing rhapsodies of Tschaikovsky. The music was like a soothing touch on his smarting heart. He looked off at the distant mountains that raised white peaks against masses of rolling clouds. Somewhere in the canyon of violet haze at their base spread the Double H.

He had been back in this country one week and already he had acquired two enemies, Cane, and a girl. "I hate as intensely as I love," had been her corny exit line. Sounded like a threat. Two! He was optimistic. Make it four. Hadn't Kit Marlowe been definitely unfriendly and hadn't her brother's voice and eyes burned with hate when he exclaimed, "Rex Danton? One-time Major Rex Danton?"

He swerved the roadster to avoid hitting a sage chicken. As it scuttled into the rabbit brush beside the road his thoughts returned to Marlowe. Why should he be sore at him? Double H with its acres and acres of rich grazing land was a good buy at the price he had paid for it. The black Herefords were the finest bred. Uncle Pete had repeatedly turned down better offers. The buildings were in excellent shape. The new owner had been living at the ranch long enough to realize its value.

Yesterday he had started for the Double H with the intention of offering his help to solve many of the problems which were bound to crop up for a man strange to the life. His friendly intention had been sidetracked by the storm. Why not go now? Rushing Creek Ranch was four miles beyond on the same road. Why let the animosity of the brother and sister switch him from his desire to be of service? They might show him the door. So what? Better that than to wish later he hadn't been a quitter.

"Dick has what boxers call the fighting heart," Kit Marlowe had declared. He grinned at his reflection in the mirror above the windshield.

"To continue her quote, there's nothing the matter with your will to bounce back every time you're knocked down," he informed the man returning his gaze with intent gray eyes.

When he reached the brow of a low hill he stopped the roadster. Ahead spread a magnificent valley glinting with blue lakes and winding creeks, that retained the sagebrush flavor and a hint of the splendor of the old West. The rambling white house with its great fireplaces and wide porches had meant home and adventure to him. Now, looking at it after three years' absence he could realize that even in its frame of colorful flower beds it might seem frighteningly lonely to a man and girl from an Eastern city.

When he stopped on the drive before the house, laughter and a snatch of song drifted from the long bunkhouse. "Bury me not on the Lone Prairie," an untrained, but musical baritone voice pleaded with operatic fervor to the accompaniment of a guitar. No sign of life about the house. If the two persons he had come to see were not at home he would call on Ma Snell, who had been cook and housekeeper at the Double H for years.

As the gate in the white picket fence clicked behind him a slender figure rose from the middle of a mass of yellow marigolds, towering white boltonia and cherry-red phlox, a girl in navy-blue slacks and tangerine pullover. A dirt-caked trowel was clutched in a white cotton-gloved hand, blue-black hair waved over a proudly held head, startled dark eyes regarded him, red lips were parted in surprise in a slightly dirt-smudged face.

"As I'm alive, see who's here," the apparition gasped. Then with a troubled glance toward the house — "Why did you come?"

"Why shouldn't I come? You didn't think I'd let you get away with hating me, did you?" Rex replaced his cap at a jaunty angle. "You can't keep a good man down, gal." As she continued to regard him more in sorrow than in anger, he parleyed : —

"Why should you treat me like the dirt under your feet because your brother bought a ranch I owned?"

With another glance at the house, she moved a step nearer, said in a voice so low he had to bend his head to hear : —

"It isn't only the ranch."

"For Pete's sake, then what is it? Let's have the awful truth. Quick. What have I done?"

"You stole my brother's fiancée."

Was she quite out of her mind? He hadn't seen a girl for months, except —

"I told you I had a second reason for coming to this state."

The words echoed through his memory. It couldn't be? Things didn't happen that way, and yet, she had said she had broken her engagement to a Captain in the Marines. Dick Marlowe had been with the Marines in the Pacific Theater.

"What's the name of this girl I stole?" he demanded grimly.

"As if you didn't know — Lois Langley."

His heart and brain and pulses came to a clanging stop. Lois Langley. The girl who had threatened, "I hate as intensely as I love." As if he were looking on from another world, he saw himself pull a handkerchief from his pocket, heard his voice saying : —

"Don't be foolish, Kit. Come here and let me wipe the smudges from your lovely face."

V

KIT pushed away his hand. She resented the throb that his tender, "your lovely face," had sent pulsing along her veins. He hadn't denied it. Ever since Dick had told her yesterday that Rex Danton was the man for whom Lois had thrown him over she had hoped it would prove a mistake. His stunned expression when he had heard the name convicted him.

"Now that you know why you are unwelcome here I wish you'd go." She glanced nervously toward the house. Dick was changing his clothes after hours of riding. He was tired and bitter. He had insisted on mounting a bucking, bawling horse and handicapped by his stiff arm had been thrown.

"Could be I didn't come to call on you." The cold voice gave her the shivers. "I'll shoot round to the back door and say howdy to Ma Snell. She's baked cookies for me since I was teen-age. I'll keep out of your brother's way, that's what you're jittery about, isn't it?"

"I'm not jittery. I'm — good grief, here comes a car. Do people drop in to *call* in this country? I've been planting tulip bulbs. I thought I was safe till supper. It is too late to dash to the house. I'm a sight."

"You are. It's a pity you didn't let me remove those smudges. The one round your right eye is a beaut. Perhaps it is Lois Langley coming to see your brother. She's in the city with her mother. She lunched with me today. An episode entirely coincidental, as they state on the screen. Good-by."

Kit stared unbelievingly at his straight back till he disappeared round a corner of the house. Evidently his wounded leg didn't handicap him. He moved with the lithe ease born of the perfect play of muscles in superb condition. Lois Langley here? Incredible. She had lunched with him. He needn't have been so cocky about it.

The sound of a car stopping derailed her train of thought. A silver-haired woman in black and a hatless girl in forest green were at the gate. Could this be Lois, this pretty girl, with short auburn hair, smiling, lovely mouth and brown eyes — eyes that had known tears, she realized as she walked forward to greet them. She flung down the trowel she was clutching and slowly drew off her stained gloves.

"Miss Marlowe?" The woman's voice was as charming as her smooth, fresh-skinned face. She had the manner and assurance of one who had been accustomed to the best in life for generations. "I'm Mrs. Seth Carter, your nearest neighbor when we are at home on our ranch, the Circle Q. At present we are staying at Mountain Lodge. This is my daughter, Sally. We've come to tell you how glad we are that your brother has taken over the Double H."

Not Lois Langley. Kit drew a long, ragged breath of relief and offered her hand.

"Thank you both. Won't you come in?"

As they walked toward the house Mrs. Carter commented on the magnificence of the view, on the flamboyant color in the flower border so late in the season, on the scent of phlox, while Kit wondered if Ma Snell would give notice if she were asked to boil fresh water for tea. Sally stopped when they reached the door.

"I've left my roadster spang in front of the gate," she explained. "I'll park it behind Rex Danton's car further along the drive. Other neighbors may drop in."

Kit's cheeks burned. If the girl knew that Rex was here what would she think when he didn't appear? Of course he wouldn't. Hadn't she told him to go home or words to that effect?

"I always loved this room with its great beams across the ceiling." Mrs. Carter stopped on the threshold of the library that stretched from the front to the back of the house. "Always have a feeling of warmth and comfort when I step into it. The books that cover the walls on each side of that enormous fireplace look as if they had been read and reread, the deep, dark green chairs as if designed to rest a man tired from a long day in the saddle. I can almost see Peter Danton seated at the grand piano running his fingers over the keys. He loved music. He had several homes but this was his favorite."

"It's a pity his nephew felt he must sell it," Kit said and instantly regretted the edge in her voice which had brought Mrs. Carter's questioning eyes to her face. "Won't you take off your coat? My brother, Dick, insists upon having this roaring fire, he brought home a touch of malaria from the Pacific. The heat reduces me to a comatose state."

"You'll get used to it. I like big fires, too." Serena Carter slipped off her black broadtail jacket. "This house is heated with a coal-burning furnace. The fireplace alone for this room wouldn't provide enough heat in our winters. Peter Danton was the first to substitute a furnace for stoves and I remember how the old-timers shook their heads and muttered, 'Plumb crazy.' When he installed electricity, the ranchers' wives went on a sit-down strike till they had it."

"I haven't yet recovered from my surprise at finding a telephone here, an up-to-the-minute white kitchen, which might have been lifted from a home-magazine ad, an electric range, two refrigerators ditto, and a freezing unit."

"Oh, we do ourselves very well in this country in material comforts. The fire and your flowers put heart and soul into this room, bring it alive. The pink button chrysanthemums in the crystal bowl are perfect, the two roses in the slender silver vase under the portrait of that lovely white-haired woman with the spectacular sapphires between the windows are Pink Perfection, aren't they?"

"Yes. The lovely woman is our grandmother who brought up my brother and me. Our parents died when we were quite small and the Grands, as we called them, took over. She is a very young grandmother, and an active one. Up to the minute in fads and fancies — collecting perfumes being one of them — but a rock-bound Puritan when it comes to principles and morals. She heads the Red Cross ambulance corps in our city, but, I judge from her letters, has as little idea of what ranch life means as a babe in arms. The garden was another luxury that surprised me. I've been planting tulip bulbs, on the 'If Winter comes, can Spring be far behind' theory. Will you excuse me for a few moments? A cup of tea or a glass of sherry is in order."

"Tea for Sally and me, thank you. She'll be here in a moment, then she'll open up the gate-legged table against the wall for the tray. When Rex and his sister were here on their vacations, though our daughter was ten years younger than Barbie Danton, she practically lived at the Double H."

When it came to the ladies, Colonel Rex Danton apparently had what it takes, Kit thought as she left the room. Had he meant it when he said he wouldn't care if he didn't meet another woman, young or old, for the duration? Phooey. It was definitely a line. He —

Her train of thought ran off the track as she stopped on the threshold of the large kitchen. With a red poppy-splashed apron over his uniform, Colonel Rex Danton, D.S.C., was spreading slices of bread at a white table. Tall, curvaceous Ma Snell, with an enveloping white apron over a pink and green plaid gingham, her gilt-blond transformation in a swept-up hair-do, with an artificial gardenia tucked into its glistening coil, the coloring of her round, smooth-skinned face a triumph of make-up art, was cutting chocolate cake into pie-shaped pieces, chattering as she cut. On a center table were the Sheffield tray and the silver teapots and kettle, Marlowe heirlooms which had descended to Kit.

"What *are* you doing, Colonel Danton?"

"Preparing the cup that cheers, for neighbors, Miss Marlowe. Ma Snell exhumed your citified tea equipment from the small pantry. Can't let them go away hungry, 'tain't done in this country. Don't tell me you're so inhospitable that you've told the Carters, also, to go home."

"I *haven't*. I'm *not* inhospitable. I adore having guests. I came to ask about tea." Kit picked up a crumb of the chocolate frosting. "Mm, how delicious. Lucky you had that ready, Ma Snell."

"I knew we'd have company today, so I baked it." The woman glanced at a table with a green and white checked cloth on which were an overflowing workbasket and a Ouija board. She drew a lugubrious sigh before she added, "Company and trouble was the message I got. But today's ain't so awful as the mess of trouble that is coming here later," she added in a portentous voice that set Kit's nerves pricking.

"You hit the jackpot with company, the Carters qualify for that, Ma Snell. I'm here too, you don't mean that I spell the trouble in your prophecy, do you?" Rex Danton inquired. The woman gazed at him adoringly as he teased her.

"You know I don't. But you're not here to stay," she sniffed and regarded him with tear-filled eyes. "You've went and sold the Double —"

"Sure, I'm not here to stay. Haven't you heard I'm a first-class fighting man?"

"You bet I've heard." She chuckled, a large woman's chuckle. "You don't s'pose I need to be told you're a fighter, do you? It's my guess you've fought in this war the way you fought cowhands twice your size an' rode buckin' bronchos an' bulldogged steer when you was a boy."

"Hey, soft-pedal my guilty past, Ma Snell. Wipe the tears from your eyes and take the tea tray to the living room for Miss Kit and I will —"

What appeared to be a forest-green whirlwind blew in the back door.

"Rex! Rex! I saw your road — ster." Sally Carter's voice broke on the last word. She looked up at him with drenched eyes. "When news came you were in a hospital terribly hurt — you're the same as my brother — and Seth, Jr. gone — I thought I would *die*. I just couldn't take any more. I honestly thought I would *die*." She hid her face against his shoulder. He smoothed her shining auburn hair tenderly.

"Here I am, Sal, sound as a nut. Ma Snell has carried in the tea tray. Be a good gal and take this load of sandwiches and cake to the library, will you? Miss Marlowe wants to tell her brother you're here." He offered a tiered mahogany stand with a plate on each shelf.

"We call it a curate's comfort at home." Kit smiled at the girl. "Your mother will think a lot of savages have moved into Double H ranch if we leave her alone much longer."

Holding the laden stand Sally Carter looked at her, then at the man standing by the window.

"Jeepers," she said, "something tells me this is it, stout fella."

"For Pete's sake, Sal, don't you begin to see into the future. Ma Snell already has given Miss Marlowe a bad attack of heebie-jeebies by her doleful prognostication of trouble."

"Boy, oh boy, has old Snelly been at the Ouija board again? Trying for advice on a fourth husband? Don't you mind her, Miss — "

"Kathryn, but Kit to you, I hope."

"Sure, it will be Kit to me. I was Sally to you the minute I saw you. You're a knockout. This way to the dining car." She kicked open the swinging door to the hall and disappeared.

"She's a great kid and good medicine for you," Rex declared gravely. "Seth, Jr., to whom she referred, her only brother, won't come home."

"How tragic. How do these mothers and fathers *bear* it? Their smiling courage is magnificent." Kit brushed her fingers across wet lashes before she demanded belligerently, "Why do you think I need 'good medicine'?"

"You're set to resent everything I say, aren't you? A few moments ago when you spoke to Sally was the first time I have seen you smile. A girl with a dimple in each cheek should cut out the grim act. I'm glad the Carters came. They own the most sensational ranch home in the state. Mexican hacienda type with servants in character. Hollywoodish sort of outfit that's right up your alley, I'll bet. When Mrs. Carter was a kid her mother married a *hacendado*, rich as Croesus, high-class family. Seth Carter had the house, which had been her home till she married, reproduced to hold the choice Mexicana his wife had inherited and collected."

"They sound like story-book people."

"They are the best type of *real* people. Sally's a grand sport. She's a trick rider, a whole lot better than some of the professionals who tour the rodeos. You can have fun with her. Better get a move on. Your slacks and pullover are okay, but your face needs washing — definitely. Your guests are waiting."

"Mister Emily Post to the rescue. You've missed your vocation, Maestro. You should edit a Your Manners and Morals column, you'd be a smash hit." On the threshold she looked back over her shoulder. "Been nice meeting you. Good-*by*."

That ought to discourage him from coming to the ranch. With Dick in his present aggressive mood, likely to go off like a hidden mine at any minute, even a Colonel of Combat Engineers isn't safe, she thought, as she ran up the back stairs. The faint sound of voices drifted up from the library.

Richard Marlowe in gray slacks and a matching coat over a powder-blue pullover was standing at the window of his room staring out at the mountains, their white caps tinged with pink from the slanting sun. Kit thought as she had thought many times before, "He is one of the handsomest men I've ever seen."

"Dick." He turned at her breathless whisper. "Dick, we have callers, neighbors from the Circle Q. Mrs. and Miss Carter. Go down, quick. I had to leave them to arrange for tea, I feel as if I'd been gone years. Hurry, will you? I'll freshen up and — "

"Why did they come? I don't want to see anyone. They'll ask me how I — "

"Phooey! Don't think so much about yourself." His startled glance reminded her that for the first time since his return she had shown impatience with his depression. Perhaps she had been feeding his bruised ego with tenderness. "I want to meet the neighbors if you don't. Please go down. I feel as if I were in a nightmare trying to push things and people along. That incessant sound below like the tide lapping the beach is, doubtless, the voice of Ma Snell telling the story of her life — or ours. Why don't you *move?* Okay, if you won't, I will."

She dashed into her dressing room, hastily bathed her face and hands, wielded a powder puff and lipstick and started down the stairs. Was the sound of wheels in the distance another car coming or was Rex Danton departing? When she reached the threshold of the living room Sally was arranging cups and saucers. Ma Snell broke off in the midst of a sentence and lighted the alcohol lamp under the silver kettle. She threw the match into the fire.

"As I was sayin', Mrs. Carter, I'm sixty-five and I've had three husbands. Ain't I done well?" She smoothed her blond hair, placed roughened red hands with blood-red nails on her ample hips and preened with satisfaction.

"That depends on the point of view, Ma Snell. I'm sixty and I've kept the same husband for thirty-five years. I think *I've* done well."

"Thirty-five years with one man. Hearin' the same complaints over and over, seein' the same face day after day. Christmas. That may suit you, but I like change. Kettle's boiling, folks," she informed before she left the room.

"My brother will be here in a moment, Mrs. Carter," Kit announced as she entered the library. "I hoped you were having your tea." She crossed the room and drew a chair behind the table which held the silver tray and its shining equipment.

"We are in no hurry, my dear. Ma Snell has been confiding her doubts of your 'fittin'-in' before you came, quote, 'I'm used to men, I didn't want a woman nosing round my kitchen,' and her intense admiration of you now that you are here. She said, 'It's sure a treat to have another female to talk to.' "

"We have grand woman-to-woman talk fests. Subject, largely MAN. His virtues and his faults. Her confidences are sometimes embarrassing."

"I imagine they would be. She reported that Rex Danton is here. Would you mind very much if he had tea with us?"

"Mind?" Kit's light response was a triumph of will over apprehension. What would happen if Dick found the accepted lover of his one-time fiancée in the library? "Of course not. Sally, sound the mess call in the kitchen for the Colonel, will you?"

"Sure, I'll get him. I don't know why he's skulking out there. Can't be that he's fascinated with Ma Snell's elderly curves."

Mrs. Carter laughed as her daughter disappeared into the hall.

"Skulking isn't the word I would apply to Rex Danton. Even as a mischievous small boy he was ready to own up and take punishment for his pranks — and they were many. His father was Peter Danton's brother. He and his wife were killed in a motor accident when Rex and his sister were in college. I hope I haven't butted in on a strained situation, by suggesting that he have tea with us. I knew by your voice when you spoke of the sale of the Double H that you are misjudging him. He is much troubled that Smiley sold your brother the ranch —"

"Why should he be?" Dick Marlowe interrupted curtly from the threshold. "I'm of age and in my right mind. I wasn't drugged before signing the transfer papers."

Good grief, Kit groaned mentally, was he determined to be bitter and unfriendly? Exit these charming Carters from her life after this angry outburst.

"Richard, I want you to meet our thirty-mile near neighbor from the Circle Q," she said and wondered what would happen next.

"Mighty friendly of you to come." He grasped the hand Mrs. Carter extended. "This is a grand country." A smile fused his thin face with life and color. "Now I know there are grand people in it."

Kit had the sensation of having been dropped in an elevator. What had happened to change his mood? Voices in the hall. Sally and Rex Danton. Now what? She sprang to her feet tense with anxiety, as the girl stopped in the doorway with the man in uniform looming behind her. For an instant his steady eyes met and held hers.

"Hold everything," they warned as plainly as if he had spoken. She forced hers away to look at her brother. Before he could speak Sally stepped forward with outstretched hand.

"Thrilled to meet you, Captain. Jeepers, those beastly Japs nicked you, didn't they? I hope you gave them *hell* in return."

"*Sally!*" her mother exclaimed.

For a startled second Dick stared at the girl, then gripped her hand and laughed.

"You've said it, Infant," he agreed and laughed again. "Their plane did a comet into the sea — and did that comet have a long fiery tail." His eyes hardened. His jaw tightened as he looked at the man standing in the doorway but his voice was courteous as he greeted: —

"How are you, Colonel Danton?"

Relief relaxed Kit's nerves and left her limp. No scene. Dick's good manners held. Cheers.

"It seems like old times to see you in this room, Rex," Mrs. Carter sidetracked Rex Danton's reply. "When Ma Snell brought in the tea tray she reported that the Ouija board had foretold company at Double H and — " She stopped. Listened. "Voices outside. Another delegation of neighbors to welcome you and your brother, Miss Kit?"

Before she finished speaking Dick Marlowe had left the room to answer a knock at the front door.

"*Lois!*"

His shocked exclamation echoed through the library. It stopped Kit's heart. With Lois Langley and Colonel Danton in the same room anything was likely to happen.

"Ma Snell prophesied more trouble and here it is." Rex Danton's low voice beside her sent it plunging on again.

VI

"MY SISTER KIT, Mrs. and Miss Langley." Though colorless from shock, Richard Marlowe easily performed the introductions to the others in the room.

The woman and girl dressed in identical light blue tweeds, with identical black pillboxes, tilted at an identical angle on their blond heads, had swept into the room on a wave of scent.

"Suivez Moi," if she knew perfumes and she did, Kit assured herself. They looked enough alike and of an age to be sisters. To judge by Dick's expression — or lack of it — they might be the most casual acquaintances instead of his one-time fiancée and her mother.

"Won't you take off your coats, the room is so hot," Kit suggested and realized they were the words she had spoken to Mrs. Carter. Had surprise and consternation shrunk her mind to one-idea dimensions?

"We will, won't we, Mother?" Lois Langley suited the action to the word. Dick Marlowe responded to the caressing glance she cast over her shoulder and helped her remove her coat while Rex Danton performed the same service for her mother. For all the world like a Broadway comedy, George Kaufman directing, Kit thought. She hurriedly swallowed a nervous chuckle and became busy with the tea things.

"You can't realize what this homelike room means to me after the horror of war-smashed Europe." The pathos of Lois Langley's voice matched the hint of tears in her eyes.

Kit caught the tightening of Mrs. Carter's lips. Was she thinking, as she herself was, that the two men present, one standing at each end of the broad stone mantel, might have even a keener realization of the contrast than had the girl curled up in the wing chair?

"It is a heart-warming room," Kit agreed because she felt tenseness in the silence.

"And do our hearts need warming." Lois uncurled, sat forward and set her teacup and saucer on the small table beside the chair.

"I might as well confess the horrible truth and get it over." She looked up at Richard Marlowe. "We've come to throw ourselves on your hospitality, Dick, darling. When I inquired at the hotel how to find your ranch, the clerk, who knew we had been hunting for a cottage, said you had a guest house you might rent. Do let us have it. We can't find a place to stay in the city or outside it and — "

"Don't let that get you down," Sally Carter interrupted blithely. "There are plenty of rooms and half a dozen cabins, if you are the exclusive type, at Mountain Lodge, only twenty miles from the city, with a smooth all-weather, non-skid, dustless oil-surface highway connecting it with the marts of trade, as they say in the prospectus."

"Really?" Lois Langley's eyes narrowed in antagonism as they met the girl's. "Advertising must be your business, you do it so well, Miss Carter. Perhaps you're the agent for Mountain Lodge?"

"Advertising is not my business and I'm *not* an agent." An angry surge of red colored Sally's fair skin, her eyes sought Rex Danton's across the room. Kit caught the warning shake of his head in response.

"You wouldn't turn me over to a country hotel, would you, Dick, darling?"

Kit waited tensely for her brother's reply to Lois's pleading eyes and voice. Would he be fooled by the act she was putting on? Had he forgotten that she had thrown him over for the man standing at the other end of the mantel who appeared absorbed in the cigarette he was lighting? This was his home, she was the girl he had loved, still loved perhaps, the guest house was his.

"Why, of all places in the world, did you pick this state, Lois?" he evaded.

"I was ordered to the mountains. The shock of hearing, while I was overseas, that you were missing was too much on top of the strain of work and horror. Then, I read in a paper that you had been found, had been hospitalized. The account told of your decoration, of your medical discharge, that you had bought the Double H in the hope of regaining your health, that it had been the dream of your boyhood to own a ranch. I was wild with happiness to know you were alive. I thought, helping Dick back to normal living will be my war work from now on, and, here I am, darling."

Kit hoped her face had been as expressionless as her brother's as he listened to Lois Langley's explanation of her presence, that it hadn't shown her flaming resentment at that saccharine "darling." Memory had made the word precious to her, it hurt to hear it cheapened. Could he believe his ex-fiancée's phony line, knowing she had written him she was in love with an officer whom she intended to marry? The officer was in the room. She had acknowledged Dick's satiric introduction to him as if meeting him for the first time.

"I suspected I talked too much to that reporter after I left the hospital. Now I know it," Dick said lightly. "As for staying at the ranch, you'll have to put that up to Kit, Lois. She's the boss in the house."

He had neatly side-stepped the decision. Okay, she'd handle it her way, it might not be his, but if it wasn't, he had it coming to him.

"I'm sure you and your mother will be more comfortable at Mountain Lodge, Miss Langley. The Dude's Rest isn't equipped for housekeeping." Kit attempted a hint of amusement which didn't quite make the grade. "As for having your meals here, I can't picture you two lovely ladies sitting at a long table with the cowhands, smelling of horses, yellow soap and pomade, lined up on each side, who stack their dishes in the kitchen when they're through. You have to be prompt at meals, too, for, come hell or buzz bombs, the cook's schedule is geared to the minute to prevent loss of the men's time."

"Really, is that the way you live, Miss Marlowe? How cute, how terribly cute." Mrs. Langley's laugh tinkled. Her voice had a feline quality. Had she sharp, tearing claws to match? "Sounds like life in a Wild West novel and I adore Wild West novels and movies. Cowboys fascinate me. I'm crazy to meet one. It makes a place named Mountain Lodge seem terribly tame and uninteresting, doesn't it, Lois?"

"Then the name belies it." Rex Danton spoke for the first time since the two women entered. Kit had wondered how he was reacting to the way in which the girl he had snitched was throwing herself into the home and arms of her ex-fiancée. Now she knew. Of course he wanted her to stay at the Lodge where he was living.

"Outstanding personalities flock there from all over the country; in fact, they came from all over the world, before it flamed into war." His voice brought her thoughts back to the matter at hand. "Especially it's a Mecca for contract and gin-rummy experts."

"Really!" Mrs. Langley's eyes glowed green as Go Ahead lights. "Lois, we shouldn't intrude on Richard and his sister if there is a decent spot in which we can live. Is it far from here, Colonel?"

"Only twenty miles. It might seem far in New York, but this is the trackless West." Sally Carter's voice dripped friend-liness as she took over. "We're living there, Mrs. Langley. Is that your sedan at the gate? You can trail us. Ready, Mother?"

"*I'm* not ready, Miss Fixit." Lois's voice was sharp with an-noyance. "I don't know why you and officious Colonel Danton are butting into *our* arrangements."

Kit saw her brother's eyes widen with amazement, saw them flash to Rex Danton's impassive face, come back to Lois Langley. As hers met them she sprang up and tucked her hand under his arm.

"You want me to stay here with you, don't you, Dick, dar-ling?"

"I repeat, Kit is boss, Lois. Ask her."

Does he want the girl here or doesn't he? I could wring his neck for passing the buck, Kit thought furiously. As long as it is up to me I'll decide as I want it.

"As 'boss' I shall have to say 'no,' Miss Langley." If eyes could burn she would be a pile of gray ashes. "I'm too new at the job of ranching to dare enlarge the family. You'd die of boredom. You just happen to find charming people here today. It's the first time we've had guests since I arrived and I've been here two weeks that have seemed like two years."

"I'm not the bored type, Miss Marlowe. I can always adjust

myself happily to my surroundings," Lois Langley declared
The hint of superciliousness in her voice steeled Kit in her determination not to have them stay.

"Maybe so, but you haven't been tested on a mountain-
country ranch in winter. Joe Carr, our foreman, told me today
that often great drifts cover the gate and picket fence, sometimes in early November. We may be marooned here for days.
All signs point to a hard, cold winter. The crows have been
flocking for weeks. The mountain rats are already making
their nests and deer and elk are down from the high ridges
early. Contrast that prospect with the luxury of Mountain
Lodge, its music and dancing and cards, its guests, its smooth
all-weather highway to the city. Perhaps you don't know that
the county's returned hero, Colonel Danton, is staying at the
Lodge and at present is its outstanding attraction?"

Her tongue should be pulled out by the roots for that hateful thrust at a man who had flung his present and future into
the United Nations' effort to rid the world of brutes, Kit told
herself. She laid her hand against her hot cheek. No wonder
it burned, no wonder Mrs. Carter was regarding her in hurt
surprise.

"Sally, we'd better start for the Lodge." The woman's voice
broke what seemed to Kit's guilty mind a shocked silence.
"You know how your father worries until we get home. There
is a rumor that a mountain lion is prowling through the forest
and that an escaped enemy prisoner is on the loose somewhere,
has been for months. It is believed he is in this state. Which
would you prefer to meet, Mrs. Langley? I'd take a chance on
the lion. Also, there has been an epidemic of cattle highjacking
in the county. Those desperadoes don't care *what* they do."
She held out her hand to Kit.

"I am glad you are at the Double H, my dear, I'm sure

you'll love the life, cowhands and all. Captain Marlowe, bring your sister to the Lodge for dinner Saturday night, will you? We can offer a swarm of officers from the Fort, music and dancing as attractions."

Kit held her breath for Dick's reply. Would he accept?

"Thank you, Mrs. Carter. If you think we city slickers — I believe that term has succeeded 'tenderfoot' to describe out-landers — will be safe after dark from the escaped prisoner and desperadoes at large, not to mention the prowling lion, we'll be there with bells on." His voice was grave but Kit caught the twinkle of fun in his eyes and the responsive twitch of Mrs. Carter's lips.

"To make sure of your safety, be our guests for the week end, Captain. Come in time for tea so that we may invite some of your neighbors to meet you. As Sally said, there are plenty of rooms available. We have a church service Sunday morn-ing, attend it or not as you like."

"That's a super, but super, suggestion, Mom. Do plan to stay over, Captain. The music is out of this world and I'll bet you're an ace stepper."

"Sally, *dear*," her mother protested.

"Thanks a billion, Infant. I never could resist flattery. It's my Achilles' heel. We'll be there." Richard Marlowe held Mrs. Carter's black jacket while she slipped into it. "Your daughter is an expert saleswoman, madam."

"I'll agree to that, she's cute." Mrs. Langley's laugh tinkled. "Lois, I've decided we'd better go to Mountain Lodge. *Don't* protest. When I decide, I *decide*. Luckily our bags are in the car. We should not impose on dear Richard's hospitality if we can find a comfortable place in which to live."

"How can we impose on what has been refused, Mother? You've won, Miss Carter, *this* time. My coat, Dick, darling."

As Kit walked along the path toward the waiting cars, Sally Carter slipped an arm within hers.

"Pin a medal on me, Kit," she confided in a laughter-choked whisper. "Didn't I steer the she-wolf, tracking down her man, away from the Double H? I understand those tactics are being used in the present shortage of men on the home front, but I've never seen the huntress on the prowl before. Mother did her stunt with her crack about the escaped prisoner and the desperadoes. She's no slouch when it comes to intuition. You weren't too bad, yourself, your description of a winter here gave me the shivers. I'll be seeing you."

Sally would get a medal, figuratively speaking, from her, Kit thought, but what was Dick's reaction to having the girl he loved living in the same hotel with the officer for whom she had broken her engagement? It didn't need a psychiatrist to figure that Rex Denton wanted her there.

In the west, white-capped mountain peaks shone in the glow of the sunset like the russet gold of auburn hair. A canyon of purple haze shrouded their base. Rolling cloud masses burned pink, red and crimson from the flames of the sun which had dropped behind them. Somewhere a stallion screamed. The angry bellow of a steer accentuated the stillness and immensity of the country. A hawk perched on the roof of the poultry house in watchful waiting sent icy inchworms tobogganing down Kit's spine. Standing at the white gate beside her brother she watched the two cars till they were hidden beyond a clump of cottonwoods at a curve in the road.

"Danton turned the Mountain Lodge trick when he referred to the presence there of contract and gin-rummy experts," Dick Marlowe declared with satiric amusement. "Lois once told me that Mrs. Langley is a card hound. I'm going to the barn."

"Dick, you look all in. You're working too hard."

"Sure, I'm working hard." His tragic eyes snapped. She

heard the grit of his teeth. "It's an outlet for the hate which burns me up when I think of what the brutes did to — Sorry, didn't mean to let myself go, Kit. See you at supper," he added and turned away.

His face had been white and tense. Did it mean he would ride all night again? What was he thinking? What was he feeling? Did he still love Lois Langley? Was he puzzled, as she was, to know what had happened between his one-time fiancée and the man whom she had declared she intended to marry? Had he sensed the animosity between them?

As she walked toward the house a few notes of "Something to Remember Me By" drifted from an open window. Rex Danton was seated at the piano running his fingers over the keys when she entered the library. He rose and closed the window.

"I took the liberty of letting in some fresh air. The Langley ladies were drenched in perfume. I prefer the smell of burning cones. What was the stuff?"

" 'Suivez Moi' — Follow Me, in case your French is a bit rusty."

"How come you know? There must be dozens of scents?" He stood looking down at her perched on the arm of the wing chair. Firelight set the silver eagle on his shoulder glinting, sent fantastic shadows wavering across his tunic.

"My grandmother collects perfumes. It's her one personal extravagance, though she is a spendthrift when it comes to me. I've sniffed at the crystal flagons in her cabinet often enough to recognize the most potent. The scent was appropriate under the circumstances, wasn't it? Why didn't you follow? They were going your way."

"They were not going my way. Guess again." He looked at her with the hint of a smile that made her feel like an adolescent. "Now that the tumult and the shouting has died I can be heard. I'm not staying at the Lodge. I'm living at Rushing Creek Ranch."

"In that adorable stone house? I'll say the Langleys were lured to Mountain Lodge under false pretenses."

"By whom? By you, if you are implying that I would be an attraction. In your determination to be unfriendly you overshot the mark. Now that we are on the subject, just why are you unfriendly? Yesterday you took Skip Cane's word for it that I had 'gypped' your brother. When I arrived today you accused me of having 'stolen' his girl. You can't believe after the act Lois Langley put on this afternoon that she is in love with me?"

"That doesn't prove you're not in love with her. You admit her line was a cover-up?"

"I admit nothing. Have it your way. We can't seem to get on the same wave length. As I reminded you yesterday, I am fed up with fighting — and women."

"I'm not wholly responsible for the exodus of the Langleys to Mountain Lodge," Kit protested indignantly. "Mrs. Carter frightened them with her theatrical reference to a mountain lion, the escaped prisoner and the highjackers."

"It was more than good theater. The lion sounds like somebody's nightmare, but there *is* an escaped prisoner on the loose, two POWs to be exact. They have been missing from a lumber camp north of here for four months and highjacking cattle *is* a paying industry. Do you, like the others I have met since I came home, think that the European war is over but for the shouting? *Can* you believe that the Nazis have stopped the infiltration into this country of saboteurs? You're in for a shock. Agents are still being trained and sent here to create conditions which will further German attempts to seize world domination.

"Sorry I let myself go," he lightened his voice, "but I see red when I come up against the war-will-be-over-by-the-end-of-'44 apathy. We'll need all the manpower we can collect before we get the brutes licked. How many cowhands on the place?"

It took Kit a second to orient her mind to the quick change of subject.

"Ten."

"I judge from your brush-off to the Langleys that you and your brother have your meals with them?"

"We do. Isn't it the custom?"

"It needn't be. There is a family dining room."

"You're telling me as if I hadn't seen the adorable kitchenette and pantry connected with it. That's where I've parked the Marlowe heirlooms Grandmother insisted I bring with me."

"I wondered how come Ma Snell knew what to produce. Why don't you use the dining room?"

"Dick has views — garnered from Western movies and novels — on ranch living. He thinks that having me at one end of the long table and himself at the other is according to the custom of the country. I have a suspicion that the men would be much happier without us."

"It's an unwise arrangement here at present for more reasons than one. Cattle raising must go on. Ranch owners can't be choosy about the hands they hire. In years past Uncle Pete unknowingly has had law evaders on the pay roll, running the gamut of crime from an alimony dodger to a housebreaking jewel thief who murdered his man. Joe Carr, your brother's foreman, and I had a heart-to-heart while I was in the kitchen. He reported that two of the cowhands are feuding, that trouble between them may break out any minute."

"How exciting! Which ones?"

"That's off the record at present. Tell your brother you want more privacy in daily living, that you'd prefer your meals in the dining room. If you don't, I will."

"Having side-stepped the problems of the Double H, why take them on again? We really don't want your advice."

"No? Don't be reckless, gal, and throw away what you may need sometime. Isn't that a car stopping at the gate?" He crossed to the front window. "And still they come. Another guest. A man this time. Young, handsome as a movie headliner. He's striding toward the house as if heading for a grim military operation."

"Let me see," Kit demanded beside him. "Good heavens, it's Shep Trask."

"Ma Snell's Ouija certainly is on the job. Does the oncoming swain connote more company or more trouble?"

"Whichever it is, I can handle the situation without your help."

"Says you. Why isn't a man his age in uniform?"

"Someone has to stay behind to make the ammunition, doesn't he? Besides, he is definitely a political figure in our state." She crossed the room to answer a peremptory knock on the front door, stopped on the threshold.

"I'm sure Ma Snell would love to see you again before you leave."

"Relax, I'm taking off. You don't think I'd intrude at this love-is-heaven moment, do you? *I* got extra-sensory perception."

"I wish you'd take your ESP to the kitchen."

"I'm going, but *not* to the kitchen." He looked over his shoulder as he opened the door at the rear of the room.

"Keep your fingers crossed or I may come back."

VII

SHE DIDN'T believe in that silly Ouija board, Kit assured herself. It was curious, though, that guest after guest, the first since her arrival, had appeared at the Double H today to fulfill the "company" part of the "message." As for "trouble," the arrival of Lois Langley in the neighborhood was bound to mean heartache for Dick. Shepherd Trask, at this moment approaching the house, meant a complication — if nothing more — for her. She opened the door in response to a second resounding knock.

"I warned you I'd trail along, Kit, and here I am," announced the tall, fair-haired, immaculately tailored and groomed man on the step. "May I come in?"

"Of course, Shep." She opened the door wide. "I was so surprised to see you that my manners failed me. Enter, my lord." She realized from the sharpening of his green-flecked hazel eyes that her light touch didn't quite come off.

She waited for him to remove his topcoat and led the way to the library. Had Rex Danton come back as he had implied he might? Nothing moving in the long room but the dancing shadows on the beamed ceiling, walls and furniture, cast by the scarlet, blue and gold flames leaping and writhing in the great fireplace from which came the resinous smell of pine cones.

"Quite an outfit you have here, Kit," Shepherd Trask observed with a hint of condescension in his approval. His eyes swept her from head to foot. "What's the idea wearing slacks at this time in the afternoon?" Without waiting for an answer he moved hurriedly away from the front of the fire and stood at one end of the long mantel. "Whew, that's hot. Why the conflagration?"

"This room is drafty. Dick likes heat and plenty." She looked up at him from the depths of a wing chair. The implied criticism of her appearance was so characteristic. She was sure his love for her was sincere but he never used the build-up approach.

"With General Eisenhower's impassioned plea for more and still more ammunition to speed the gigantic drive on the Western Front, how did you square leaving the plant with your conscience, Shep?"

"The superintendents in charge are competent and eager to push production. Outside my job of helping to provide what it takes to win the war, you're the most important factor in my life, have been since you were a small girl."

"Please don't resume that saga, Shep."

"Why not? Haven't I traveled halfway across the country, being bumped off planes for buck privates on a hurry-up call, even when I had priorities, to ask you again to marry me? I'm used to your quick turns of mood. You're as changeable as a weather vane. I decided I'd be Johnny on the spot if or when you whirled in my direction. Before you left the East you told me you liked me tremendously — that was your word — tremendously."

"I told you, also, that while I have been fond of you practically all my life, I do *not* love you."

"How do you know that a 'tremendous' liking isn't love? Never been in love, have you?"

"What a question to ask a girl who has lived to the advanced age of twenty-three. Tactless, I calls it."

"Quit kidding. Besides the manufacture of ammunition I am up to my ears in politics. The coming election is incomparably momentous. I side-stepped my responsibilities to see you. I'm not in the mood for merry persiflage."

Merry persiflage. Kit swallowed a nervous chuckle. How like him. He had been the big boy next door from the time she was a little girl. Dick called him a stuffed shirt; he wasn't, he was really a dear, at heart, if he didn't believe in praising anyone and did indulge in sulk fests. He was born when his inventor father and his scientific-minded mother were middle-aged, had been in the infant-prodigy line-up at college, on graduation had been railroaded into a plant manufacturing his father's inventions, never had been really young. How could he help being a trifle on the ponderous side?

"When you put it that way, Shep, I'm not in the mood for love, and believe it or not, when I do love I won't be changeable as a weather vane, I'll be as fixed as Bunker Hill Monument. The evening before I left home I told you I was coming here to be with Dick as long as he needed me."

"I hope he didn't sink your small inheritance with his in this gamble. Why in heaven's name did he elect to live on a ranch because a girl jilted him? There are other richer and more rewarding ways of getting away from it all — if that's his objective."

"Perhaps, but ranching is a productive industry of enormous significance in the history and life of the nation." She was quoting Rex Danton word for word, but Shep wouldn't know that. "Just to keep the record straight, 'my small inheritance' is intact. I'm here to stay for the duration of Dick's need of me. That, as they say in the newspapers, is to end the discussion." The front door closed with a force which rattled the brass fire irons at one side of the hearth.

"Here he is now. Don't mention his wounds, Shep, he's terribly sensitive."

"Why? He should consider them a badge of honor. Gosh, wouldn't I welcome the chance to fight and get a few nicks, instead of battling to keep men on the job who care for nothing but their pay?"

"See who's here," Richard Marlowe exclaimed as he entered with right hand extended; the other was thrust into the pocket of his gray coat. "What brought you out to the wide open spaces, Shep?"

"A succession of planes." Kit was thankful that she wasn't named as the lodestar. "Thought I'd step off the home treadmill and get a change of outlook."

"You'll get it here, all right. I'll tell one of the boys to start a fire in the Dude's Rest, the guest house to you. Fires there mean what Ma Snell calls 'company.' Where's your luggage?"

"In the cab which brought me from the city. I told the driver to wait at the gate till I knew I had the right place and would be welcome."

"Sure you're welcome and you have the right place. Kit, make up a bed for Shep, will you?"

"Does *she* have to do that?"

"And who else? You're out where the West begins, fella, and where, judging from my experience at hiring it, domestic service ends. Come along, we'll pick up your bags and send the driver round to the kitchen for a snack before he starts the long trek back. Oh, by the way, Shep, we don't dress for dinner here."

He laughed. He was quipping like his before-the-war self.

Today's "company" had made a dent in his depression. Looked as if the Ouija had been off the beam when it had spelled "trouble."

After the two men left for the guest house Kit carried the tea things to the kitchen.

"Mind if I wash the china and silver here, Ma Snell?" she asked the woman who was counting out eggs from a large basket. It wasn't necessary to explain she wanted a chance to talk about Rex Danton. "May I borrow your apron? I was brought up to wear an apron in the kitchen."

"Sure, take the red-poppy one Rex used. I made him put it on. I'm sold on having you round in your pretty clothes — though I can't say much for the pants you wear — you're lots of company, Kit. I like men, but Christmas, they're sort of monotonous. Except Rex — you never can tell what that hombre'll do next. I'm surprised he didn't bring one of them grass-skirt dancers home as a wife."

"He wasn't in that part of the war." Kit concentrated on the careful drying of a paper-thin cup. "Has he always had a lot of — of love affairs?"

Hands on stalwart hips Ma Snell frowned at her.

"He's never had none — the on-again-off-again kind, you mean by your voice. I've seen a lot of young men come an' go in the years I've worked at the Double H, college fellas an' cowhands — an' a sprinklin' of criminals — we didn't know they was criminals though till the sheriff come an' picked 'em up. Rex was friendly to 'em all, an' him the apple of the Old Boss's eyes, but he's had principles, I reckon you'd call 'em, an' he's never let 'em down. He's clean as the wind from the Divide. He's grade A quality. An' — "

She dropped into a chair beside the table with its green and white checked cloth. Her face was drawn and aged.

"What is it, Ma Snell? Are you faint, dear?" Kit laid her hand gently on the woman's shoulder.

"Now that was sweet of you to call me 'dear,' Kit, just as if I belonged. Never fainted in my life. It's a kind of spell of pain that catches me sometimes, when I get excited, but I've never before let on. I don't intend to have the cowhands on this ranch gossiping over my innards."

"Have you consulted a doctor about the attacks?"

"Sure, you don't think I'm fool enough to let myself die if I can help it, do you? Livin', even in these awful times, can be fun. Don't look so troubled. It's easin' up now. It's nothin' serious." She tapped the Ouija board beside the heaped-up mending basket on the table. "This'll warn me when it is."

"Do you *really* believe that, Ma Snell?"

"Sure. Didn't it write 'company' an' didn't we have company today?"

"I'll say we did. That wasn't just company, it was a deluge."

"Christmas, you have a pretty laugh, Kit, it's like music. First time I've heard it."

"I haven't been doing much laughing lately, Ma Snell. I'm a little out of practice. Why don't you go to bed and rest?"

"Me? Go to bed? Get hep to yourself. Who'd cook the supper?"

"I'll cook it."

"You cook? How come?"

"I was brought up in the old-fashioned way. A girl who doesn't know how to cook is not a really educated woman, is not capable of managing a house, Grandmother believes."

"I didn't know rich folks trained their girls like that. I don't need your help. I'm all right now. If ever I do, will you come?"

"Of course, Ma Snell, but where?"

"Forget it. That was just what the Old Boss used to call a figger of speech. To my fourth weddin', perhaps. Run along an' get dolled up for that fella I saw walkin' across to the guest house with Dick. I don't need the Ouija to tell me he didn't come all this way to see your brother."

Later, in a cherry-red frock with a moderate V neck and elbow sleeves, a dog collar of three strings of lustrous pearls about her throat, Kit sat at one end of a long table covered with black and white marbleized oilcloth in the pine-walled room. She watched Shepherd Trask seated at her right, as the cowhands filed in, said "Good evenin', ma'am," and slid into their seats. Their bronzed faces, middle-aged, mostly, shone from scrubbing, their hair glistened with pomade, black ties were knotted neatly at the collars of their gay plaid shirts.

The appetizing smell from platters of pink ham, its fat crisped till it curled, filled the room. Each slice was topped with an egg, its center yellow as a gold nugget, its white firm with a brown lacy edge. Stout dishes of fluffy mashed potato, of orange-color squash, were passed from hand to hand.

What was Shep thinking of this way of living, she wondered, as Ma Snell entered with a plate piled high with wheat cakes dripping with melted butter, rich with brown sugar, in each hand. Her hair had been freshly touched up, her lips and cheeks reddened. Kit's eyes met her brother's alight with their before-the-war twinkle. Had he been watching for Shep's reaction also? If he were as amused at the situation as his expression indicated, seeing Lois Langley couldn't have torn his heart to shreds, could it?

"What breed of cattle do you raise at the Double H?" Shepherd Trask inquired in his top-drawer manner of Swede Olsen, the cowhand with hair the color and texture of straw, seated across the table.

"Black Herefords. They iss wery goot for this country, they iss."

"They bring a high price, I understand."

"Yah. But that iss all right since they iss goot cows, mister."

"Like your job?"

Oh, dear, why doesn't Shep speak to Olsen as man to man, not like a professor to a moronic pupil, Kit thought.

"Yah. It iss a goot job. Like yours?" The curt question sent a wave of red surging under Shepherd Trask's fair skin.

"Yes. I like mine," he answered with dignity and turned to Kit. "Most of the new plays are being tried out in our home town before going on to Broadway. I have become a confirmed first-nighter. I go alone," he added hurriedly as if to assure her that she had no rival.

She felt as if he were talking of a world she had known in her dreams, so far away her life in the East seemed. He told of the incredible prices asked — and being paid — for clothing, regal furs and jewels, plus 20 per cent tax; of crowded first nights at the theater; of the mounting intensity of the battle for the election of a President; of preparations for the greatest Community War Fund drive in history; of the rumor that the enemy intended to pepper the Eastern coast of the U.S.A. with buzz bombs, the new V-3's; of the majority opinion that war in the European Theater would be over by Christmas.

"Do you see many officers in this part of the country? I know your passion for uniforms," he concluded with a hint of bitterness.

"I have seen one only since I arrived two weeks ago, in spite of the fact that there is a military post and a replacement center adjacent to our nearest city." It wasn't necessary to add that she had seen that uniform for the second time today.

As the men at the table stacked the plates they had used and filed out to the kitchen with them, Shepherd Trask's critical eyes followed and came back to her.

"What goes on, Kit?"

"Hold everything, Shep. It's a Double H custom. Some of them will help Ma Snell with the dishes. She's a queen in her department and can grant favors in the way of favorite eats. You won't have to do it. We'll have our coffee home-style in the library. Follow Dick and I will bring in the tray."

The gate-legged table in the softly lighted room in the precise spot where it had been standing when she served tea reminded Kit of the events of the afternoon. What had Dick felt and thought when he had seen Lois Langley, she wondered again.

"Give me that." Shepherd Trask relieved her of the large silver tray and set it on the table. "I recognize the Marlowe silver and Spode coffee cups I've seen for years. Now I begin to feel at home." He sank into a deep chair and lighted a cigar.

"Sugar, Shep?" Kit held the silver tongs suspended.

"You *know* I like it black and strong and straight."

She ignored the reproach in his voice and handed him the delicate cup.

"This is strong enough to walk off with the coffeepot and dark as a blackout home street at midnight. I have a horrible suspicion that Ma Snell brews a day's supply in the morning and lets it simmer till dark. She's the cook, in case you care."

"Can't say I do. I wish you'd stop trying to make conversation and listen to me."

"Listen! What else did I do through supper? I felt as if I had tuned in on a news broadcast."

"Sorry if I bored you."

"Don't be sulky, Shep. You didn't bore me. I loved every minute of it. It transported me back to civilization. It seems a lifetime since I left it."

"You're as out of place in this wilderness as a Dresden figurine would be in a Five and Ten."

"I don't like your comparison. I'm not the Dresden figurine type and I'm not out of place here. I'm listening and learning. I've changed my style of riding from the home variety to one better adapted to this country. I now speak casually of a 'slug of hay' and I can hear Dick called 'Dick' by the cowhands without blinking an eyelash. That's progress, my lad."

"If you're not out of place your pearls are. It isn't safe to wear them here."

"Don't be absurd, Shep. I love them. I remember seeing them around Mother's throat; wearing her wedding pearls seems to bring her very near. I'm just a little sentimentalist at heart. Who but you and Dick know they are anything more than wax beads?"

"That Swede cowhand who sat opposite me at table knows that they are three strings of perfectly matched Oriental pearls."

Kit's hand caught her collar in a frightened clutch. "Law evaders on the pay roll — a housebreaking jewel thief who murdered his man," Rex Danton had said.

"Why do you think that?" she asked breathlessly.

"I saw him look at them. I know greed in a man's eyes when I see it. Where do you keep the pearls when you're not wearing them?"

"In a jewel case in my room."

"Give the collar to Dick to put in his safe, he has one in his office, hasn't he? If you don't want trouble here, better send it home to your bank by me when I go."

Trouble. Ma Snell had prophesied: —

"Company and trouble was the message I got. But today's ain't so awful as the mess of trouble that's coming here later."

Silly, she flouted herself, as if a piece of wood could foretell the future.

"Thanks for the offer, Shep, but I'll keep my pearls. Who knows, they may start excitement and believe me, life on this ranch can stand a little pepping up."

He caught her hands and drew her to her feet.

"I've come a long way, Kit. How about a kiss of welcome?"

She shook her head.

"Sorry, Shep. You know how I feel about — "

"Sure, I know. I've heard you say it often enough. You wise-crack about not wanting to smooch your lipstick and the next minute declare you are keeping your kisses for the man you love. I'm mad about you, but I've kissed plenty of girls."

"What does that prove?"

"Okay, laugh. I've seen you kiss men in your stag line before they went overseas."

"Of course I kissed them." Memory tightened her throat. "And each kiss was a little prayer for their safety, Shep."

"Looks as if I'd have to join the service to get what I want." He cleared his rough voice. "How about a little game of gin rummy?"

VIII

NICE PLACE you've got here, Rex. Glad you didn't let Rushing Creek Ranch go. Your uncle would have been fit to tie if he'd thought you hadn't some foothold on this property he left you."

Joe Carr, foreman of the Double H, tall, thin, seated on a corner of a broad, flat desk in the large, pine-walled room of the stone house, brushed back a drooping iron-gray forelock and produced the makings of a cigarette. He was wearing dark green cowboy pants, a scarlet vest over a blue and white checked shirt and high russet boots. The broad brim of a black Stetson clapped on the back of his head made a frame for his weather-beaten face with its hawklike nose and prominent cheekbones.

He nodded toward the portrait of a gray-haired, keen-eyed man above the mantel.

"Heck, the Old Boss looks easygoin' an' kinder smilin', but try to put one over on him an' his eyes would turn to steel. You're growin' to look like him, Rex."

"I wish I could *be* like him. He was a great organizer."

"Sure was, always made me think of one of them circus fellas, ridin' bareback holdin' the reins of six horses in his hands an' everything under control. Seems as if I could see him now a-comin' in that door." Dancing flames in the stone fireplace revealed the hint of nostalgia in his dark eyes.

"He taught me all I know. The Old Boss sure knew cows. I come to the Double H when I was twenty-one an' except for an occasional vacation, I've been handlin' cattle here since. Forty years is a long time to stick in one job."

Rex Danton turned from the window through which he had been watching an arrogant bluejay balanced on the telephone wire which bound the ranch to the outside world, jeering raucously at the brown and white calico horse hitched to a post outside the iron gate. He could hear the tumble and rush of the creek which cut through the smooth green lawn a hundred yards from the house below the terrace.

"You've done a grand job, Joe. I miss Uncle Pete like the dickens. I've been here two days. Each time I've entered this room I've felt a curious silence. Not just the stillness of an unoccupied house, but a vibrating silence as if someone beyond a veil were waiting to speak."

"That sounds spooky. Do you suppose he is waitin' to put you wise to somethin'? Heck, don't you go to gettin' ghost notions an' infectin' me with 'em, young fella." A wide smile appeared to cut his lean, cadaverous face in two. "It's bad enough to have Ma Snell everlastin'ly sniffin' an' shakin' her head over them messages she claims to get from that wacky Ouija board of hers without you goin' haywire." His heavy black eyebrows met in a frown. "Cripes, sometimes they come true. Now she's seein' a mess of trouble ahead."

"What kind of trouble?"

"She don't say. Claims she don't know. Guess the message got kinder gummed up comin' through."

Rex dropped into a capacious crimson chair opposite the desk, draped his long legs over one arm, drew a package from the breast pocket of his khaki shirt, shook out a cigarette and prepared to listen. Joe Carr was a quiet man who attended strictly to his own business and didn't say much unless he was stirred up. He hadn't dropped in for a neighborly call. He had come for a purpose. What had happened during the two days which had passed, days which had seemed like weeks, since they had talked together in the kitchen of the Double H?

"Trouble is what you came about, isn't it, Joe? Give."

"I suppose 'tisn't your business any longer, what goes at the Double H, but I had a feelin' you'd oughta be told."

"Is it Captain Marlowe? Does he antagonize the hands?"

"Heck, no. He's a swell guy. He's got what it takes to make a real stockman." Carr grinned. "That is, when we've peeled off some of the wacky notions he's lifted from Wild West yarns and movies about ranchin'. I guess he thought he'd live the life of Riley on the Double H. He's found it ain't like that, but he's puttin' all he's got into the job. It's the girl who worries me. She's a mighty good-looker, ain't she?"

Rex swung his feet to the floor and stood up. He poked the fire which, in response, shot up leaping, lapping, blue, crimson, gold tongues of flames as if to demonstrate indignantly it didn't need poking.

"Do you mean Miss Kit, Joe? What's happened to her?"

"Nothin'. Nothin' will so long as that city slicker who's bedded down in the Dude's Rest stays and rides with her."

"Shepherd Trask?"

"That's the fella. Queer guy. I suppose 'tisn't his fault that he was dealt a ramrod for a spine when he was born. Rich as he is, there's something about his mouth makes me willin' to bet he's savin' as all get out. He tries to be friendly with the boys, dropped in at the bunkhouse last evenin', but he just don't know how to let go. They've been laughin' at him behind his back, but they weren't laughin' near so hard after he cleaned 'em out at a little game of Red Dog. He peeled the shirts off their backs, fig'ratively speakin'."

"Commando tactics. What has all that to do with Miss Kit's safety?"

"I'm comin' to that. She and him go ridin' together in the mountains, but it's after he leaves what's troublin' me."

"Perhaps she'll go East with him — as his wife."

"Mebbe so, this bein' a marryin' as well as a killin' war." Joe Carr became absorbed in rolling a cigarette. "Can't figger out why you never married, Rex. Your sister Barbie used to have terrible pretty girls visitin' her in this very house, an' they trailed you as if you were King of the Range. Them youngsters sure had a good time. Remember how they used to keep the phonograph in the corner a-goin' for dancin'? When 'twa'n't that they was poundin' out — an' I mean poundin' — the latest songs on the piana. We had college-trained men in the bunkhouse then, men knowin' the up-to-the-minute details of breedin' range cattle, but the Army and Navy has swallowed every mother's son of 'em."

Rex's eyes were on the gorgeous crimson *rebozo* from Old Mexico flung across the end of the grand piano while memory re-created a group of men and girls gathered about it singing "Night and Day."

"I've often wondered why I never fell in love sufficiently to ask a girl to marry me, Joe. Lucky now I didn't. These last years have been heartbreakers for women with men in the service. Why are you anxious about Miss Kit?"

"Before this guy Trask came she went ridin' off alone, long rides, an' — "

"Has Skip Cane been to the Double H again?" Rex inquired sharply.

"What made you think of him? Not since he come to get a job an' Dick turned him down. But, I hear he's apt to be hangin' round the post office when one of our hands goes in for the mail. Happens too often to be just accidental. He asks a lot of questions about how we're doin', an' what we're sellin', an' when we're shippin', an' are you hangin' round the ranch — he's sure sore at you because you give him his time, Rex. Our boys are wise to him. I reckon they fill him up with a lot of dope that ain't true."

"He'll bear watching. Why don't you tell Miss Kit not to ride alone?"

"Me? She wouldn't listen. What she needs is a good dawg for company. There are dawgs on the ranch but she ought to have a special. That's one of the things I come to ask your advice about. A bunch of French Canucks at Two Forks are raisin' Airedales. They're friendly fellas at home but terrible fighters. I've seen a cougar run from an Airedale half his size."

"You're not implying that Miss Kit is in danger from a cougar in this region, are you? You've gone haywire. One hasn't been seen in the neighborhood for years."

"We've had a dry summer. No knowin' what critter would steal down from the mountains and when. The other day I saw a shadder sneak through the trees, I'll swear it was a long, gray mountain lion. I've seen a wolf prowlin' round a calf pen with teeth sharp as a set of daggers, an' last year, a mad coyote went barkin', howlin' an' snappin' along this creek foamin' at the lips. Besides, all the lions an' cougars an' wolves an' coyotes don't go on four legs, if you get what I mean. Gives me the willies even to think of what might happen to her." He grinned.

"Sounds if I'd fallen hard for a girl, don't it? Perhaps I have. Ma Snell thinks she's tops an' Ma Snell knows human

nature, if she did guess wrong about one husband. I'm teachin'
Miss Kit to shoot — she's good. I reckon an Airedale will fill
the rest of the bill for protection. I'll dig down for cash and
buy one for her."

"I will provide the cash. You select the best dog they have
at Two Forks and give it to her."

"That's not such a hot arrangement. Why not take it to the
Double H yourself, Rex?"

"It would look better coming from the foreman than from
the former owner of the ranch. What goes in the bunkhouse?
A couple of days ago you told me Michigan Murphy and Texas
Smith were feuding. Are they at it still?"

"They are. It's my guess that Tex suspects Mich of being
mixed up with highjackers, but ain't found no proof. Swipin'
a truckload of cattle's gettin' to be sort of a habit in these parts.
Swede Olsen an' Mich don't hit it off, either. Mich is a smooth,
bossy fella, don't say much, but he rides Olsen an' I kin see
the glitter of knives in the Swede's eyes sometimes when he
looks at him."

"How long has Mich been at the ranch?"

"Lemme think. He signed up in May. Swede Olsen came
along about the last of June."

The last of June. The strip of paper he had found in the
stove sticking to the piece of blue denim at the line rider's
camp had been dated August 15.

"Tex Smith blew in the first of this month."

September. He might have had a New York paper of August
date.

"Where did he come from?"

"You're askin' me. He said Texas."

"Aren't you watching Mich Murphy?"

"Sure I'm watching him an' Olsen, who's settin' in the

kitchen tootin' his harmonica every chance he can get. That Swede's soft-soapin' Ma Snell to beat the band. She laps it up like cattle at a salt lick. What's he aimin' to get from her? Money? She's got plenty. I've been figurin' on givin' Olsen his time, I don't cotton to him, but, heck, he's a good worker, competent, except for handlin' cattle — sometimes I think he's never seen the critters before — an' we need workers so terrible bad, I've kept him on. I'm watchin' 'em *all*, but I ain't lettin' on I am. I guess it's what you call in the Army 'a tactical delayin' action.' We've got a queer bunch of cowhands, but we take what we can get these days and don't burrow deep into what they've left behind 'em. The Army must have beef."

"What are the prospects of a supply of beef cattle at the Double H, Joe?"

"Good. With feed grain abundant they'll get their last-minute feast. That means tender, juicy steaks. Not so much utility beef. We've been building up our herd for years. I didn't let down after your uncle went. There'll be fifty head of Hereford cows in the next shipment, weighin' approximately seven hundred pounds each. They ought to bring top price, which has been about $15.25 per hundredweight. There's twenty steers ready averagin' 1270 pounds each which ought to bring $16.26. They'd be a rich haul for a bunch of highjackers."

"Does that mean you suspect there is a plot hatching to steal them?"

"You got your rope on the right pair of horns, Rex. They won't get 'em, now that we've been — what's that word they use in the Army?"

"Alerted?"

"That's it. We'll get 'em to market — if we have to shoot our way there. It's my guess this lot will sell without a cutback.

Our brand has an A 1 reputation. I hear the armed forces keep agents combing the packing houses to mark all top-grade meat for the fighters. They'll get it when they buy the Double H brand."

"Our men know they get the best, they know that the American Army is the best fed, best clothed, best equipped and the best provided with medical care of any army in history. What they are not sure of is whether the people at home realize the size of the job they have on their hands and will let up in their effort to keep supplies going to the front. It gives them the willies when they read in our papers that the war will be over by the end of '44. They know darned well it won't."

"Is that so? I've had the feelin' that 'twas 'bout over in Europe except for moppin' up."

"You, and *thousands* like you." Rex flung a cigarette into the fire with the force he might use in flinging a grenade. "It gives me the shivers when I read the opinions of even high-up military men that the date of the collapse of the Reich fighting force will be October fifteen of this year. Get that? This *year*. I've been up against the devils and I know they still have terrible weapons and powerful forces to marshal against us. We're in for days of trial and tragedy the extent of which we cannot even guess. In the language of the GI, 'Things is tough all over.' "

"That's puttin' it straight. Perhaps Gen'ral Ike was givin' the optimists on the home front a right to the jaw when he sent out that D Day message, 'I call upon all who love freedom to stand with us.' "

"That's the idea."

"Heck, when I see the news picture of them grinning, clean-cut young fellas, just wiped out because a lot of human coyotes was allowed to cut loose, it makes me sick at my stomach to think I'm too old to carry a gun."

"You're doing your part in making sure that the boys who are fighting have meat. I'm glad there's such a bright outlook for an income from the Double H. You believe, don't you, that Captain Marlowe got a square deal when he bought the ranch?"

"If what they're whisperin' he paid for it is true, he got a bargain. Cripes, has anyone been sayin' he was *cheated?*"

"Hold everything, Joe. I just wanted to know how you felt about it."

"Now you know." Carr swung off the desk. "I guess I've filled you up with forebodin's that will make Ma Snell's 'messages' sound like angels of light, but I savvy you ought to be put wise to what's goin' on an' what's threatenin'. You might be able to advise the new Boss. He's kinder young, only twenty-eight."

"You make me feel like an old-timer stroking a long white beard."

"It's sure fine to see that grin of yours again, Rex. I know you're jest thirty, but your eyes look forty. I guess what you've seen aged 'em an' put that white in your hair. Drop in at the bunkhouse an' size up the situation. Perhaps I've got it all wrong. Perhaps Mich and Tex and Swede Olsen are just grown-up Boy Scouts. Perhaps I'm so rarin' mad every time I see the red scar on the Boss's face an' that stiff arm, to think that hundreds of the fellas his age are whole an' sound, gripin' at their pay an' wantin' more for extra hours while he was gettin' hell in the Pacific, that I ain't a fair judge. So long, Rex."

"Stop in the kitchen and ask Chang Loo for a drink, Joe."

"Heck, you got that Chinee back again?"

"And was he glad to come. 'Everycling alla fine now,' he said when he arrived. He looks as if he hadn't had enough to eat in spite of the fact that Uncle Pete left him a generous pension."

"Probably savin' the cash to go home to China. I'll be seein' you."

Rex watched him as with the wide, rocking gate of a man who has spent most of his life on the back of a horse he crossed the room. His voice had been rough with feeling when he spoke of Dick Marlowe's wounds. "Swell guy," he had said. What had been the "swell guy's" reaction when he had seen Lois Langley enter the library of his home? "War hysteria," she had characterized her engagement to her ex-fiancé for whose hospitality she had made a bid. Why think of her? Now that she had run down Marlowe, he, himself, could write Finis to the episode.

He lifted the lid of the phonograph and started the needle on a record already in place. Had his uncle left it there? The opening orchestral notes of the "Habanera" from *Carmen* flooded the still room. Came a woman's voice, low-toned, throaty, somnolent. Emma Calvé's. It had been his uncle's favorite. He visualized the big, kindly man in his favorite chair beside the fire with his pipe. "Do you suppose he is waitin' to put you wise to somethin'?" Joe had asked. Was the spirit of Peter Danton lingering near in the hope of getting across a message?

"Boy, oh, boy, now I'm going cockeyed, must be the music," he told himself and stopped the needle. Even after the phonograph was shut off the beautiful voice seemed to drift in the air.

Cigarette in one hand, the other thrust into a pocket of his trousers, he paced the long room thinking of what Joe Carr had told him. Was the possible highjacking of the Double H cattle the real reason back of his call? The man wasn't an alarmist. He must be genuinely troubled as to Kit's safety, plus the feud between Mich and Tex, plus distrust of Olsen, to come to him. Had one of the three burned a betraying garment at the line rider's camp? Why suspect a cowhand? Any person traveling through the country was welcome to use the camp.

He stopped at the window attracted by the roar of motors. Nine fighter planes, flying low in echelons of three, were passing overhead on their way to the airfield. Even here, beyond the sound of guns, the war was present. The roar dwindled to a faint purr and vanished.

His thoughts returned to Kit and her safety. What could he do about it? She distrusted him, disliked him because she believed her brother had been "gypped" into buying the ranch. Marlowe hated him because of Lois Langley. He recalled the expression of her eyes as they had met his across the luncheon table. "I hate as intensely as I love," she had threatened.

So what? Plenty. She would doubtless give Marlowe and, if the opportunity presented, his sister a detailed account of Rex Danton's *alleged* pursuit of her in England. She would lay on emotional effects with a heavy hand. With her ex-fiancé and Kit at Mountain Lodge this week end she would have a field day to plant her trouble mines. Would she? She would not. He'd be there to stop her. How? He laughed. He could trust his hunch when the time came.

"It's the water which keeps moving if only a little which gets to the sea."

The words he had heard his Uncle Pete quote scores of times echoed through the corridors of memory. He looked over his shoulder, said aloud: —

"You've said it, Old Boss. It's time I moved."

IX

FOLLOWING Joe Carr's suggestion to drop in at the bunkhouse and size up the situation, Rex stopped at the Double H on his way to Mountain Lodge late Saturday afternoon. He had planned to start earlier in the hope of meeting Dick Marlowe before he left for the week end, but a long-distance Government call had detained him. Much as he disliked going when the Boss was not present, Joe's uneasiness about a threat of danger to Kit Marlowe had communicated itself to him. The menace of the feuding cowhands and theft of the cattle could be left to the foreman to handle.

The sun had dropped behind a purple mountain leaving it a dark cutout against a gorgeous crimson sky, when Joe grinned a welcome at the door of the bunkhouse.

"Come in an' meet the boys, Rex. They're just washin' up for supper. Mich, Tex an' Olsen are takin' the truck to the city for supplies an' are aimin' to get twenty-four hours' whoopee as a perq. You'll know 'em by their outfits. They're dressed to kill an' loaded with dough."

Bing Crosby's voice singing "Don't Fence Me In" was coming over the radio when they entered the long, lighted room. Emotion tightened Rex's throat. Three years since he had seen it, three years packed with excitement and tragedy. He felt ages older but the place hadn't changed. The hot smell from the potbellied stoves at each end; the huge black bear pelts in front of them; the blanketed bunks; the tables for games with spilled cards and dominoes; even the figure shaving before a mirror on the smoky wall and another astride a chair in a green and red plaid shirt, thumbing through a dog-eared catalogue, were the same, though the persons were different.

"Here's the nephew of the Old Boss come to say 'Howdy,' boys," Joe Carr announced.

Nine men looked up and nodded. The man astride the chair sprang to his feet as if the sight of the uniform had snapped him to attention, then hurriedly departed by a rear door. Was he a discharged service man, not too honorably discharged? Could be he was a deserter?

"This place seems like home to me," Rex said. "I was a kid of four when Joe put me on a horse out in that corral for the first time."

There was a slight mumble in response before the men again became absorbed in what they were doing at his entrance. His face reddened, his little speech had laid an egg.

"Tex Smith is the gent in the red satin shirt and green pants dollin' up before the mirror, Rex." Joe Carr had taken over as master of ceremonies. "Michigan Murphy is claspin' that silver belt round his middle, an' Olsen was aimin' to order another outfit from that catalogue he was studyin' when you come in. Don't know why he beat it."

The man who had been tugging at an ornate filigree clasp looked up and ran his fingers through a mop of bristling red hair.

"Howdy," he said. His grin revealed a set of remarkably perfect teeth. "Very glad to meet you, Colonel. Hot stuff where you came from, yes?"

The record had flopped over. A woman's husky voice singing "Together" drifted through the long room. One of the men picked up a guitar and strummed a soft accompaniment.

"Very hot stuff," Rex replied curtly as he contrasted the colorful tawdriness of the clothing and sleek curves of the cheeks of these cowhands with the bloodstained, mud-splashed uniforms, the strained faces of the men he had left on the other side. A distant, soft-toned bell had an immediate effect. Each man sprang into action and started for the door.

"Well, what d'you think of them three?" Joe Carr asked when he and Rex were alone. "I tried to tip you off as to which was which."

"You got it across. Olsen was out of the room before I had a chance to see what he looked like. Why? Maybe he's expecting an M.P. on his trail. I'll bet he's been in the service. He'll bear watching. You said he wasn't handy with the cattle, so whatever he's here for I don't believe it's highjacking a truckload. Tex was the guy shaving, wasn't he? I'll bet once he gets an idea into that bullet-shaped head you couldn't pry it out. If he thinks he has the lowdown on that redhead Mich, he'll hang on like a bulldog till he proves it. That's the way I figured out the situation, Joe. Better let the Boss in on your hunch. He would resent a suggestion from me. Did you get the dog?"

"Sure. Miss Kit's crazy about him."

"How much do I owe you?"

"Nothin'. I'm makin' my pin-up girl a present." Joe's grin split his face. "You don't need to be jealous of me, though, you keep your eye on the Trask guy."

When Rex reached Mountain Lodge dinner was over, dancing had started and from the ballroom drifted the music of strings and brasses beating out the "Victory Polka."

"Tst! Tst! See who's here," Collens exclaimed as he entered the lounge. "Had your dinner, Colonel?"

"No. Send up something to my room, will you? I'll eat while I'm changing."

"Sure. Say, who do you think are here? The new owner of the Double H and his sister. The Carters invited the neighboring ranchers to meet them at tea, this afternoon. Jeepers, is she a knockout! Cal Smiley registered for a Saturday through Sunday stay. You'd think by his what-a-big-boy-am-I strut across the lounge with Miss Marlowe he'd brought her into the world."

"He did, didn't he, into this particular world, when he sold her brother the Double H?"

"If he did he needn't go Little Jack Horner on us. I had more to do with their coming than he. Captain Marlowe wrote to the Chamber of Commerce inquiring if there was a ranch for sale, said since he was a boy he'd had a yen for this state. I happened to be in the secretary's office when the inquiry came. I'd just had a letter from you giving directions about Mountain Lodge and you added that you'd told Smiley to sell the Double H. I passed the information along to the secretary. He got in touch with Cal. It was as simple as that. There's a mother and daughter here who've got what it takes — Langley, is their name."

Collens was right, Kit Marlowe was a knockout, Rex agreed, as later he stood on the threshold of the ballroom. A green comb sparkled in the dark waves of her hair, clips of the same color glittered at the corners of the square neck of her white frock. A collar of pearls accentuated the golden tan of her skin. Officers and their gayly dressed partners formed a kaleidoscope of varicolored patterns which changed with each beat of the music.

The scarlet-coated orchestra was playing, "I'll Walk Alone" when Rex touched the sleeve of the Lieutenant of Infantry with whom Kit was dancing. The slim young officer glanced at the insignia on his shoulder and hastily removed his arm from her waist with a respectful, "Yes, sir."

"He needn't treat me as if I were Father Time," Rex protested as he fell into step with the girl. "Long time no see, Kit. Don't mind if I call you Kit, do you?"

"Why not? Most of the cowhands call me that."

He controlled an intense desire to shake her out of her cool indifference and laughed.

"Now that we have that little matter settled to our mutual satisfaction, mind if I tell you you step like a dance maestro's dream? That was what is known as a rhetorical question. No answer required. How are things shaping up at the Double H?"

"If one can believe my pal Joe Carr, foreman, we're doin' fine. What do you think?" She was no longer indifferent, she was smiling, eager. "He has lend-leased me the most adorable Airedale. It belonged to his brother, who has just been drafted. He wanted a good home for his pet while he was in the Army."

Rex controlled a grin. Joe had gone subtle. His brother would be too old for the service — if he had a brother — which he hadn't.

"Like dogs?"

"I adore them."

"What's the Airedale's name?"

"*Le Grand Charlie*. He was born the day General de Gaulle returned to liberated France. I call him *Charlie*. Joe said he would miss his master at first and that he hoped I'd take him with me when I rode and let the dog sleep in my room till he had adapted himself to the change."

What was behind that request? Had Joe discovered a two-legged coyote menacing the girl? If so, why hadn't he spoken of it while they were together in the bunkhouse? A chill that wasn't occasioned by a draft stole along his nerves.

"Do you?"

"You ask that with the fierce voice you might use cross-examining a witness at a court-martial, Colonel. Do I what?"

"Take the dog when you ride? Keep him in your room?"

"Oh, that. You were off the conversation beam so long, I had forgotten what we were talking about. I do. From now on, he's my steady."

"Who's your steady, Kit?" Shepherd Trask in dinner clothes demanded jealously as he touched Rex's sleeve. "Cut. You're violating the anti-monopoly law, Colonel Danton."

"But, it's been such a short monopoly," Rex protested as he withdrew his arm.

"You've been heavy-handed with the lipstick, Kit," he heard Trask say in an annoyed voice, as he turned away. Sounded as if the boy from home was the nagging type.

From the side lines he looked for Sally Carter. In a lime-green frock which intensified the gold in her auburn hair, she was dancing and talking with Dick Marlowe who was grinning broadly as he listened. She was bringing back life and laughter to his face. Why break up the twosome?

"Colonel Danton, how surprising to see you here. Lois said she had heard you were the hermit type." Mrs. Langley floated toward him in a wave of perfume. Still "Suivez Moi"? He wouldn't know. Her aqua lamé frock shimmered with silver sequins. She tucked her hand under his arm and looked up with appealing eyes. "I'm an excellent dancer, if I am the mother of a great big girl."

"Okay, prove it." He slipped his arm about her. Strings, flutes and horns were playing "Too-Ra-Loo-Ra-Loo-Ral" with zest and zing.

"Excellent? Why so modest? You're great," he approved as they danced in perfect unison to the music. "You are even better than your daughter." Thunderation, why had he mentioned her?

"Lois! Where have you danced with her, Colonel? I thought you met for the first time at the Marlowe ranch."

Was her surprise genuine or was she putting on an act? Was it probable that Lois hadn't mentioned him in her letters or since her return?

"I've been watching her rumba with Cal Smiley. He's tops. When I was a kid I used to see him dancing with my sister and wonder how he did it."

"He must be ages older than you."

"Only eighteen years, that isn't much."

"To look at him and hear him speak I wouldn't think that you two came from — from, well, the same side of the track. He seems so, to put it mildly, ordinary."

"Wrong air wave, Mrs. Langley. Cal's great-great-great and my ditto were pioneers in this state. He is probably one of the richest men in the city. He's high-power stuff in politics. He'll be governor some day, and he's a maverick."

"What is a maverick, Colonel?"

"An unbranded calf. In other words a bachelor."

"How cute. Anyone could tell he hasn't a wife. No woman with pride in her man would let him out of the house in evening clothes till he'd taken that row of fountain pens out of the left pocket of his waistcoat."

"I'll bet you an orchid no woman could separate Cal from his fountain pens."

"Is that a challenge, Colonel? I accept it."

"Good. Here's your chance to begin. He's making a bee line for you. Trust him to recognize perfection when he sees it."

"Colonel, you're irresistible, you say the *cutest* things."
Her laugh tinkled. "If I hadn't a grown-up daughter — "
What she would do in such a case was left to his imagination
as Smiley cut in.

"This is a party, Rex," Mrs. Carter reminded as he joined
her in a spot as far removed from the music as possible. "You
look troubled." She caught her breath in a frightened gasp.
"Have they buzz-bombed our coast?"

"No. *No*, Aunt S'rena. I'm suffering a twinge of conscience.
I was thinking that I had purposely started a little fire which
might spread to startling proportions."

"A fire! In this wooded country. Are you crazy?"

He couldn't explain that his statement to Mrs. Langley
about Smiley's wealth was the "little fire" he had started, nor
the surety that she would set her daughter, possibly herself, on
his trail was the spread to which he referred.

"Relax, Aunt S'rena. That word 'fire' was a mere figure of
speech."

"And I was taking you literally. Charge it up to war nerves.
I've invited the Marlowes and their guest, Shepherd Trask,
the Langleys and Cal Smiley to our sitting room for a snack.
Mind coming with me now, Rex, to prepare for the party?"

"Mind? It's just my dish. This is the first time I've danced
since I left the hospital. A chair will look good to me."

The living room of the Carter suite was charming with the
touches that turn a hotel room into a home: flowers, photographs, curious little silver boxes, two lamps with rose-color
shades and a small blaze in the fireplace. A lace-covered table
held glasses, cups and saucers and plates of paper-thin sandwiches and cakes.

"Call this a snack? I'd say it was a gorge," Rex observed.
He lifted a silver-framed photograph from the mantel and

looked at the clean-cut, smiling face. Serena Carter slipped her hand under his arm and rested her white head against his sleeve.

"It is just like Seth, Jr., isn't it? When I look at it I can hear him say, 'Hi, Mom.' " She brushed her fingers across her lashes. "I'm ashamed of these tears. I had him twenty-five years, a devoted, tender, splendid son, and then he gave his life for his country. His father is braver than I. Answer the knock, Rex, please."

A boy entered and placed a large silver urn over a small, lighted alcohol lamp and departed. She sank into a chair by the fire and looked up at Rex standing with his arm on the mantel.

"Rex, dear, you know that I am genuinely fond of you, don't you?"

"I do. You've no idea how the certainty of your affection warms my heart."

"Then you will believe that I am not trying to butt into your personal affairs when I warn you against Lois Langley."

"At what target was that remark beamed? Shoot."

"Yesterday, Sally and I met her at the swimming pool. She began by saying she wanted my advice in a complicated situation. She couldn't consult her mother, who knew nothing about it. She went on to explain that she had been stunned when she met you at the Double H, that you had shadowed her in London, had begged her to break her engagement to a man in the Pacific Theater to whom she was engaged, whom she loved devotedly; that, swept off her feet by your ardor, she had done so."

"Did she mention the man's name?"

"No, but after the afternoon at the Double H, I put two and two together; the result, Captain Marlowe. Right?"

"So I had been informed just before she arrived that epoch-making afternoon. Here's my version of the story."

He told of their meeting in London, touched lightly on the girl's attraction toward him as a far-from-home reaction.

"We understand each other now. That's all there is to it."

"I'm afraid it isn't, Rex. To quote Sally, whose argot I deplore but adopt at times, '*There's* a dame on the prowl.' If you should by any chance lose your heart to a girl, tell her the truth before Lois gets in her poisonous work. That's all about that. Ma Snell told me something of conditions at the Double H the afternoon I was there. It seems that Richard Marlowe has black spells of depression. The first time he left the house at midnight for a wild ride, his sister ran to Ma Snell's room to ask what she should do.

" 'Don't do nothin', dearie,' Ma Snell said she answered. 'He'll come back and don't let him know you missed him.' "

"A tough situation for a girl, Aunt S'rena."

"That isn't all. Evening after evening he slumps in the big chair in the library while Kit reads to him, or plays and sings. Occasionally they play cards. Sometimes at night he walks the floor of his room and Kit goes in and talks to him till he quiets down. At first I tried to stop Ma Snell's confidences, then decided that by listening I might be able to help. That was one reason I planned this week end, to give that child a change. Even under the present emotional strain one feels her physical, and mental, aliveness. It's a pity Captain Marlowe can't, or won't, pull himself out of his depression for her sake. From what I have heard, you had experiences as tragic as his; your spirit hasn't been crushed, Rex."

"As tragic perhaps, but different, Aunt S'rena. Wherever I was I had the warm certainty that others were coming to my rescue, perhaps overhead or hurrying up from the rear, and always I had the companionship of men with whom I could talk. Richard Marlowe was alone for days. Very big the Pacific Ocean. The sea is heavy. Very small a rubber boat in its waves and troughs."

"I understand now. One can always count on you for warmth and perception, Rex. Kit Marlowe is a lovely person, isn't she?"

"She's beautiful, vivid, tender as a woman should be and desirable." He laughed. " 'Nuff said, Aunt S'rena?"

"Enough to relieve my mind of the fear that you might go off the deep end — Sally's argot again — about this Langley girl. If you can bear to talk about it, tell me something of D Day. No military operation to date has equaled the Invasion for boldness of conception or force of execution. It is one of the great achievements of history. What stands out in your memory of your Normandy experience?"

He couldn't tell her that the outstanding nightmare for him had been obeying orders to blow in a tunnel and to bury alive a company of the enemy which had been stealing out to snipe for days, getting their man, or men, with each shot. It had to be done to stop the slaughter. It had been done, but he winced away from the thought that he had worked out the plan for the demolition. Because there was danger in throwing the plunger he had insisted upon doing it. He had planned the job. If he had made a mistake he was the one to take the consequences. It had been instantaneously effective. He remembered that when he had confided his regrets to his superior, the officer had said : —

"That job is done, Major. Finished. Train yourself not to look back."

"Is it a military secret? Shouldn't I have asked the question, Rex?" Serena Carter's voice brought him back to the softly lighted room.

"Sure you should ask it. You want to know something of D Day?" A laugh bubbled from the spring of memory. "It was a small thing, but I'll never forget it. Came the order to disembark. The engineers and medics went first, the engineers to establish a beachhead and to prepare the way for an invading army, the medics to care for the wounded, both later to fight side by side with the infantry and artillery. A young lieutenant sprang beside me from the ramp of an LST into the water on that dark, epoch-making morning. As we waded toward shore under heavy fire, he sobbed, 'Boy, oh boy, Major. My feet are getting wet. I'll take an awful cold.'

"Fear of getting wet feet was so funny when I thought of the hell-swept beach for which we were headed, that I chuckled. It relieved my tension. I'm sure he hadn't the slightest idea what he was saying to relieve his. I remember seeing him later directing bulldozers as coolly as if he were a traffic man on a pleasure highway, instead of under ceaseless fire as the enemy laid down a big pattern."

There were voices and laughter in the corridor before Sally flung open the door. The Langleys, mother and daughter, Dick Marlowe and Kit, Shepherd Trask and Cal Smiley followed her into the room.

"So, this is where you are, Rex!" Sally Carter exclaimed. "We've been combing the ballroom for you. Okay, Mom?" She looked quickly at her mother who smiled as she met her daughter's anxious eyes.

"Clear skies, Sally. Rex has been telling me of an amusing wartime experience."

"Amusing! Can there be such a thing in this fiendish war?"

"Sure, Infant," Dick Marlowe's light voice answered. "That's what keeps the GI's going."

"Don't forget the contributions the Red Cross girls and their doughnuts make to their comfort and morale, darling," Lois Langley reminded.

"I'm not likely to forget them or the nurses. Those last are only a little lower if not on a par with the angels. Let me pass the coffee, Sally. I have one sturdy hand."

"You'll have two before you know it," the girl assured earnestly. She smiled at Kit Marlowe to whom Rex was offering a plate of sandwiches. "Something tells me that *you* don't have to be Red Cross or a nurse to make a soldier happy, Kit."

Why the dickens had Sally said that? It's fuse to dynamite, Rex protested to himself as Lois's eyes flashed to his, then to the girl beside him.

"Perhaps that's the reason Miss Marlowe isn't in the service," she drawled. "It's so much *safer* cheering the boys on the home front."

Rex opened his lips in angry protest. Before he could speak Kit laid her hand on his arm.

"Safety first? I hadn't thought of it just that way, perhaps that is the reason I didn't enlist, Miss Langley. Rex, *darling,* shall we tell her that I shall continue my safe job of cheering soldiers, that I'm going with you when your leave ends?"

X

IN ALL her after life would she be haunted by the nightmarish memory of the tense silence which followed her flippant announcement? The blood seemed to have drained from Kit's head leaving an empty space big as New York Grand Central, through which her sugary "Rex, *darling*" reverberated like a voice over a public address system.

Why had she allowed Lois Langley's taunt to infuriate her? Why had she been instantaneously certain that no retaliation for the slurring voice would be so effective as to claim Rex Danton? Lois had written Dick that she loved Rex and intended to marry him. Something had happened between the two that had roused her anger. She had ignored him with insolent indifference that afternoon at the Double H. When she entered the room a few moments ago her blue eyes had unsheathed little daggers of hate.

"She-wolf tracking down her man," Sally had said of Lois. What would she say of Kit Marlowe's tactics? Why didn't someone move? Why didn't someone say something? Had each person staring at her as if hypnotized been struck dumb?

The muscles of the arm she was clutching tensed. The line about Rex's mouth was even whiter than when he had been so furious at Skip Cane in the line rider's cabin. Was he about to declare that she had gone cockeyed? That tonight was only the third time they had met? She rated it. He gently shook off her hold and laid his arm about her shoulders.

"There's no accounting for the vagaries of women," he said lightly. "I've been begging Kit to tell you we were that way about each other. She wouldn't. She claimed that it was too quick to be credible — she hasn't seen love strike like lightning as I have. Now, she knocks the breath out of me with the sudden capitulation to my wishes. I know you think I'm a lucky guy, Aunt S'rena."

The effect of his slightly hoarsened voice was like an electric switch which set a roomful of wax figures in motion. Mrs. Carter blinked her lashes and nodded like a Mandarin. Dick Marlowe took an impetuous step toward his sister, Sally linked her arm in his and stopped him. Shepherd Trask's eyes burned like spotlights as they interrogated Kit's. Cal Smiley's mouth hung open from surprise. Mrs. Langley, beside him, giggled nervously. Lois adjusted the pink rose at the low V of her black sequin frock.

"Your buzz bomb was effective, Miss Marlowe." Her laugh was a masterpiece of innuendo. "Even Rex, in spite of his chivalrous ad libbing, if his expression is to be believed, was knocked out by the news that he is the victim of a matrimonial holdup. I congratulate you on a brand-new approach. It must be his fatal charm that makes girls lose their heads."

"Skip it, Lois." The color mounted in an angry surge to Rex Danton's hair. He removed his arm from Kit's shoulders and stepped toward the taunting girl. Before he could speak Mrs. Carter slipped between them.

"Kit, dear. Now that you're practically one of the family — we Carters have adopted Rex — knock at the door of your Uncle Seth's study at the right and tell him we want his company." Determination succeeded nervousness in her voice. "Rex, place a chair at the end of the table. Mrs. Langley, will you preside at the coffee urn? Dick, pour the sherry, please.

Cal, you and Mr. Trask get busy with the sandwiches and cakes. We girls will relax and let you men wait on us."

She sank into a deep chair. Sally perched on a moss-green pouffe, Lois snuggled into the curved end of a rose-color sofa. Kit opened a door in response to a gruff "Come in" and closed it behind her.

"Time you appeared, Seth," Serena Carter exclaimed a few minutes later as her husband entered the room. "Where's Kit?"

"From the window she caught a glimpse of the white-topped mountains and asked if she might go out on the balcony for just five minutes. She won't stay long. It's a cold night, even for September."

"She'll freeze in that thin white frock, I'll get her." Shepherd Trask started across the room. Rex laid a detaining hand on his arm.

"That's my job, Trask," he reminded. For an instant the two men stood tense as fighters waiting in the ring for the sharp, imperative bell. Then Trask turned in response to a question from Serena Carter and Rex opened the study door.

As he crossed the room he could see a slender figure, white in the moonlight, leaning against the balcony rail. He caught up an afghan from the couch and opened the long window.

"What's it all about, Kit?" he asked as he closed it behind him. He laid the wrap over her shoulders. "No sense committing suicide from pneumonia because you've gotten yourself into a mess."

"Pneumonia, with my face burning like a red stoplight?" She laid a hand against her right cheek before she drew the woolly thing across her breast. The green comb in her hair glistened, her dark eyes glittered with angry tears as she looked up at him.

"Mess. You've said it," she agreed passionately. "I've

always been incurably interested in the motives that make people do what they do. I have been here five minutes asking myself why *I* went haywire and why, if and when I d-did, I d-dragged y-you into it."

"Forget me. Lois went all out to get you. She rated a healthy swat. Pity you didn't let her have it instead of that phony yarn. Your teeth are chattering. You're cold. Come back into the house."

"I deserve to freeze. It isn't c-cold that m-makes me shiver. It's fury that I could be such a dumbbell as to swallow Lois Langley's taunt, line, hook and sinker. Knowing how she had double-crossed Dick, each time she called him 'darling' my endurance almost reached the snapping point. A psychiatrist would have a reason for it. The word means a lot to me. The last time I saw my mother and father together I was ten. She had come down the stairs, I can see her now in a white frock frosted with silver, these pearls about her throat, a diamond star in her dark hair. As she reached the lower step Dad caught her in his arms.

" 'You are very lovely tonight, my darling,' he said.

"His tender, unsteady voice sent queer tingles through my veins and I thought, 'Will someone say that to me sometime?' Darling has been a precious word to me since. I'm sorry. I didn't mean to bore you with my memories."

"I'm not bored." Rex cleared his gruff voice. "There was another reason for your outburst, wasn't there?"

"Yes. When Lois started to bait me, something snapped. It's a long, sharp splinter in my heart that I haven't gone overseas to serve there. What will I tell my children when they ask me what I did to help in the World War? I couldn't square it with my conscience to leave Grandmother while Dick was away, then he came and needed me. All the sting and ache and disappointment came to a surging boil when she hurled that safety-first grenade. If I had to make someone the goat why didn't I take Shep? I'll probably marry him eventually."

"Eventually. What a cold, detached way to speak of a prospective husband. It gives me the creeps. In my creed, marriage is synonymous with love. If that is Eastern-states style I'll side-step the region when looking for the woman in my life."

"Nobody asked you to find a bride there. Sorry. That's a dumb crack after the spot I've landed you in. I don't understand my burst of romanticism to the brain. Sounds like a scenario for a B movie, doesn't it? Perhaps I haven't a brain. Perhaps that's the answer."

"I wouldn't be too sure of that, or, while we're still on the subject, that you'll marry Trask. Let's go back to the beginning and work up to the late climax."

"*Don't* make a joke of it."

"*I'm* not making a joke of it. You sent that 'Rex darling' flaming into my life like a rocket bomb. The crash may prove disastrous."

"Don't you know that that is what is troubling me? Don't you *know* that I would give these, much as I love them," she touched the pearls about her throat, "if I could take back the last half hour? A scientist has declared that the human brain is capable of holding three billion ideas and I can't rake up one to meet this situation."

"Take it easy, Kit. I can't think straight when you look at me through tears and this is the time for straight thinking. Your brother told you that Lois broke her engagement to him because I asked her to marry me, right?"

"Right."

"That isn't true. I had her briefed at our second meeting. I never loved her. Never felt an urge to kiss her. Never asked her to marry me. Never wanted her for my wife."

"So you say. She and Dick say differently."

"Okay. If that's the way you feel about it, we'll play it your way. Now, come in before you freeze to death."

"Come in! Just like that. We must plan here and now how I am to tell them it isn't true, that I was just trying to be funny."

"How can we plan anything when you doubt my word? There's no foundation of trust to build on and trust will salvage many a situation which seems hopeless. Why tell them? Why not let it stand that you'll marry me when my leave is up?"

"Marry you! I didn't say we were to be married. I — I just said I was going with you."

"No? That was what I inferred, you — being you, it didn't enter my mind that you would go with me except as my wife."

"Oh, darn, it gets worse and worse. Of course I wouldn't go with you — any way. We've got to straighten this mess out. Of what use is your engineer training if you can't figure out a way?" His grin, his eyes, sent the blood to her cheeks again.

"We had electric generators at our command post. Why not have light? We had water-purifying units, so, we had pure water to drink. We knew how to build a waterproof billet, so we had those, but when it comes to figuring out this sort of problem it wasn't provided for in the curriculum. As I suggested before, let it stand as is until the excitement blows over. Then you can break the engagement, it's being done." He leaned his arms on the balcony rail and looked up.

"Corking night, isn't it? Looks as if there were millions of stars, but I have it on good astronomical authority that we see only a few thousands."

"Stars! How can you talk about stars when I am on the verge of a nervous breakdown to know what to do?"

"I've told you. I committed myself when I backed you up.

I don't welsh. We'll let it stand. You're cold. This time you are coming in." He drew her to the long window. "Even a newly engaged couple shouldn't ignore the hostess. Look at me. Okay, no sign of tears. Remember, you've got to go forward in life, you *can't* go back. We learn that in the Army — and how."

The room was rosy with lamplight, murmurous with voices and laughter, the soft radioed strains of piano and orchestra and a man's voice singing "Swinging on a Star" when they entered. Apparently the party was hitting on all cylinders. What had been a nerve-racking experience to her already had receded into the background of the minds of these persons, or they were putting up a convincing bluff. Kit had the sensation of having been reprieved from prison. Rex Danton was right when he said it would blow over. She met his eyes. "You see," they seemed to say, "already it has ceased to be a front-page story." He picked up cup and saucer.

"I'm sold on that coffee you're pouring, Mrs. Langley. The aroma is something out of this world."

Kit perched on the arm of the broad couch beside Seth Carter.

"I'm literally st-starving." Maddening that her voice should be unsteady. She tried again. "Shep, coffee please."

He brought a cup and offered it without looking at her. Mr. Carter rose to answer a question of Smiley's.

"Sure, Cal, I believe with Governor Bricker that America possesses a reservoir of fresh leadership which never has been tapped."

"How tall these mountain men are," Kit exclaimed as he crossed the room.

"And how you've fallen for them," Shepherd Trask accused bitterly.

"Don't sulk, please, Shep."

"Sulk! Is that your name for it? I call it righteous indignation. Didn't I come halfway across the continent to see you — and in return you flippantly announce your engagement to Danton."

"I'm *not* engaged. I can't explain now. It was just one of those quick turns you accuse me of making. I lost my temper and — you know the rest."

"What do you mean, 'I know the rest'? I don't know what you and Danton were doing on that balcony for the last hour. Did he kiss you?"

"I've told you before my reaction to being kissed. He did *not* and it wasn't an hour. I've known you all my life, Shep, I like you tremendously — "

"So I've heard before. Where's that getting me?"

"Wire for Mr. Shepherd Trask," a boy in scarlet livery announced at the door. "It was rerouted from the Double H." Conversation and laughter stopped as Trask read the message.

"Not bad news, Shep?" Kit asked anxiously.

"No. A business tangle that requires my immediate attention at home. Good night, Mrs. Carter, and thanks for your hospitality. I'll get my bag and make arrangements at the desk downstairs to get to the airport. As it is Government business, I ought to get a priority on the next plane."

"I'll drive you to the city, Shep," Dick Marlowe proposed.

"Dick, *darling,* you shouldn't with your poor arm," Lois Langley objected.

Kit opened her lips in furious protest at the reference to her brother's disablement, closed them as she met the "hold-everything" warning in Rex Danton's eyes.

"I must be in the city in the early morning to meet my sister," he said. "She'll stop over an hour on her way to the Coast. Captain Marlowe, I will drive Trask in."

"Will you, *darling?*" Kit said with Lois Langley's inflection on the endearing word and promptly hated herself. She certainly was a glutton for trouble.

Later in her room she could remember nothing of her good-by to Shepherd Trask. She could remember only Rex Danton's eyes as he had drawn her apart from the others and warned: —

"*You* haven't extra-sensory perception, have you? If **you** call me 'darling' again in that voice, prepare to take the consequences, and I mean consequences, Miss Marlowe."

XI

IN THE LIBRARY at the Double H Kit listened intently to the virile, lovable voice of a presidential candidate as it came from the radio. Politics, she thought, has become a personal matter to millions who before have hardly known the first letter of the word and millions of people have become a matter of personal concern to the politicians.

At the close of the forceful speech she tuned in on another station. First came dire hints of a return to stringent rationing. Followed bulletins of air raids, bombed ships, trapped troops, torture and awful slaughter. When the commentator went off the air she snapped off the radio and crossed to the window. *Charlie,* the Airedale, who had been stretched on his side before the fire, sprang up, shook himself and trailed her.

The second week in October. Gorgeous afternoon after twenty-four hours of rain. Perhaps life was like that. Storm, tears and despair followed by the sunshine of hope and joy and courage. Practicality routed reflection. Thank goodness the storm hadn't been snow, which wouldn't have been unusual at this time of year. The quaking aspens on the mountainside were flames of gold. The slanting sun had turned the telephone wires to ruby ropes. It was incredible that the horrors to which she had been listening could be happening in this same beautiful world.

Why, why, couldn't a way be found to stop war forever?

Killing, maiming of human beings, destruction of homes and property was such a senseless way to settle a dispute. Why didn't women, billions strong, *do* something about the wholesale slaughter of children they had brought into the world? Suppose they devoted the brains and time they spent in hospitals, Red Cross, canteens, relief units, bond drives, to working out a way to put a permanent stop to war, to bring a lasting peace? Working at the idea twenty-four hours of the twenty-four, couldn't they accomplish it? When it came down to cases, what was she doing to stop it? Answer, nothing.

She clasped one hand over the other and flinched. Ooch, the long burn that ran from the top of the little finger beyond the knuckle of her left wrist hurt like the dickens. That was what she was doing to help win the war, wasn't it? Springing out of bed when the rising bell sounded at five-thirty. Getting breakfast for the cowboys so that cattle could be raised to supply our fighting men with the meat they needed. In between, writing to her friends in the service, caring for the poultry, setting the house in order, cooking noon dinner and, before she had a chance to turn around, preparing supper; pinch-hitting for Ma Snell in the kitchen while she took a well-earned week off in the city to buy a trousseau for her fourth honeymoon. It wasn't enough. The Government was pleading for help in hospitals. What was wrong that it had to plead?

A wall mirror reflected her pink and white striped frock as she passed on her way to the chair in front of the fire. "Lucky I brought a few cottons, *n'est-ce pas, Charlie?*" Lucky she knew how to cook even if she wasn't used to the wholesale preparation of food. That word "lucky" went double for being too occupied during the day with the house, cheering Dick in the evening and too dead to the world when she dropped into bed at night to dwell on the mess into which she had plunged

Rex Danton, to say nothing of herself, at Mountain Lodge.

Eyes on the darting flames she pondered the cause of her outbreak. There was the long strain of watching a world being beaten and tortured by the Powers of Evil, the demons Hitler and Hirohito. There was the anxiety about her friends in the service, and the ceaseless alternation between hope and despair while Dick was missing. There was the shock of the change in him; the certainty that it was a mistake for him to give up the profession he knew for a business experiment. There was the ceaseless effort to lift, lift, *lift* him out of the black fog of depression. There was the gnawing regret that she wasn't doing more to help. It added up to a brand-new self who had flung that retort at Lois Langley, not the person she had thought she was, but a girl she didn't know, a girl of whom she was a little afraid.

Only four weeks since she had landed herself in that hot spot? It seemed like a year. She snuggled deeper into the chair and rested her head against the back. She was tired, bone tired. At home she had kept at her different jobs from early morning, sometimes through the evening. She would be all in at night, but not this dead-to-the-world muscular tiredness, the spiritual weariness that came from her aching desire to help Dick.

Dusk deepened in the corners. The fire whispered and snapped. Leaping flames flung grotesque shadows on the walls. A plane droned overhead. The tall clock in the corner ticked away time. A red log dropped apart noisily.

The sound sent the startled dog into her lap. He circled a few times and settled down with a "Whoof!" of content. The heat from the fire burned her cheeks, set the long dark mark on her hand smarting. Perhaps the smart was what brought tears to her eyes, not fury that she could have made such a break. She hadn't seen Rex since. Shep hadn't written, though he had sent a gift. The Carters hadn't called again, why should they? On the way back from the week end at Mountain Lodge Dick had demanded furiously: —

"What gives? Did you have a brainstorm when you implied you were engaged to Danton, Kit? Of all men in the world why pick that guy with whom to put on an act? It was an act, wasn't it? Were you blocking Shep Trask?"

"Good heavens, no, I'm not that subtle. He didn't enter my mind. Of course it was an act and a dumb one. I was so furious at Lois Langley's treatment of you that I struck at her, sensing that nothing would hurt as much as the threat of losing Rex Danton."

"Do you think she still loves him?"

She remembered that she had tucked her hand under his arm before she admitted: —

"I'm sure she wants him. I doubt if she can really love anyone."

"She can make a darn convincing bluff at loving," he replied gruffly and left it at that.

Since then he had been moodily absorbed in ranch business. He had told her that he had been at the Circle Q several times to look at improvements being made in the cattle barns. Did the presence of Lois at Mountain Lodge contribute to his gloom? Was he seeing her? Why had he not realized that she was cruel and heartless when he met her first? How could a girl like her attract men?

Why think of her? She wasn't worth it. The words of the clergyman at the Sunday morning service at Mountain Lodge echoed along the sound track of memory. Again she was looking through the great window at a clear, cold, turquoise sky, patched with drifting, silvery clouds. The crags of towering mountains stood black against it. Again she heard the warm colorful voice reading Paul's words to the Philippians : —

> "Whatsoever things are just, whatsoever things are pure, whatsoever things are lovely, whatsoever things are of good report . . . think on these things . . . and the God of peace shall be with you."

She closed her eyes and sleepily drifted into the past. She was in her grandmother's living room. A mirrored wall reflected the Burgundy-rose hangings, Louis XV chairs covered with petit point and two consoles, each topped with a porcelain bowl filled with pink tulips. From the long window she looked out at the Basin. It was the time of day she loved. A blue sky turning pink and violet beyond the Technology Buildings, an east wind rippling the green water into meringue-topped wavelets, the slanting sun turning windows to plates of gold. Her grandmother breezed in.

"Pour the tea, Kit, then tell me — "

The fire snapped loudly, the dog in her lap stirred. The vision faded. She was back in the library at the Double H. The dream, if it had been a dream, was very real. So real that she wondered what her grandmother had been about to ask her. She was wide-awake now. From the distance came the excited yelping of the ranch dogs. With a growl the Airedale jumped to the floor, each hair bristling.

" 'Scuse me, ma'am," a man's voice said.

The words and the dog's angry bark startled Kit to her feet. Swede Olsen, wearing a purple and white striped satin shirt, cowboy pants of Kelly green, and sensational high red boots, was standing on the threshold. A long, straw-colored lock of hair dangled over his forehead. Why was he here? She was alone in the house. Her heart went into a crash dive. Shep had said this man's greedy eyes had appraised her pearls. Instinctively her hand went to her throat. Thank goodness she wasn't wearing them now, they were safe in her room, no longer in her jewel case, but hidden where no one would think of finding them.

"What do you want, Olsen?"

"I brought this box from the post office, ma'am." He held out a large package. "It iss marked Special Handlin'. There iss a letter pasted on top. I tank it was goot you have it if 'twas wery important. I left the mail bag at the Boss's office."

"Thank you. Put it here, please." She cleared a space on the large table loaded with copies of the *American Hereford Journal* and current magazines. He suggested: —

"Maybe you like better for me to carry it to your room, yah?"

"I will open it here. That is all, Olsen. Why are you waiting? Anything you wished to speak about?"

"Yah, ma'am. I was goin' to ask if you put in a goot word for me with Joe Carr. He like you fine. He washes supper dishes for you, some of the rest of the hands would be wery pleased to do so, but he say, 'No.' I tank he don't like me."

His eyes had a curious intensity as if he were probing her mind's reaction to his suggestion.

"I know nothing about the ranch business, Olsen, I never make suggestions."

"I tank it may be you do it this time, ma'am. I like the job fine, but a man can't do goot work when he iss wond'ring if he iss goin' to be given his time any day, now. If I didn't like the Boss much, I wouldn't stand for Joe's accusin' me of stallin' — "

"Don't say any more, Olsen. I've told you that I know nothing of ranch business."

"Sorry, ma'am." He glanced around the room. His eyes came back to her. "I tank you'd be goin' to town for the rodeo tomorrow, ma'am?"

If he had not expected to see her, why had he brought the box?

"I can't leave home with Ma Snell away."

"Yah, yah, that iss right. Most of the hands iss goin', it iss a goot show, they tell me. I'm goin' myself. It's wery pretty here," his eyes pointed the words at her, "with the fire and flowers."

What was it all about, Kit asked herself as a door closed in the distance. Why had he asked her to intercede for him with Joe Carr? Why hadn't he gone to Dick? Each time his intent eyes had met hers a creeping-up-of-mystery tingle had vibrated along her nerves.

"What did he mean by looking at me as if he were paying me a compliment when he said, 'It's wery pretty here,' *Charlie?* Why did he suggest he carry the box to my room? To find out where it is?" The dog, squatting on his haunches on the threshold, watching the front door, only whined in answer.

She detached the letter on the package and broke a nail trying to unknot the string before she seized the ornate scissors on the secretary desk and snipped it.

"It's from Grandmother. Curious that I should have dreamed she spoke to me. Now what?"

She lifted the box cover. Sniffed. Her grandmother's favorite scent of the score she owned. Reams of white tissue. "No paper shortage where you came from," she said aloud as she raised sheet after sheet.

"O-o-o, you lovely thing," she crooned and lifted a snowy ermine lumber jacket from its tissue cocoon. Beneath it was a white fur bandeau with a border of fuchsia beads. She laid it on her dark hair and nodded approval at the looking-glass girl before she opened the letter.

> Darling Kit — You're a sweet child. I miss you frightfully, but it lifts a load of anxiety from my mind to know you are keeping up Dick's courage. That's your most important war job at present.
>
> I saw these in a shop window and couldn't resist. I could see how lovely you will look in them when you run out to a neighbor's in the evening. You . . .

Laughter choked Kit's voice, laughter denatured with a sob. It was too absurd. "Run out to a neighbor's in the evening," just like that. A thirty-mile run. She hadn't been away from the Double H since the week end at Mountain Lodge, a month ago. If only her grandmother could see her two hours from now "dishing up" supper for the cowhands — it — it was too — too f-funny.

She tucked the letter into her pocket and sank into a chair, flung her arms across the soft coat on the table, dropped her head on them and laughed and cried. She was so darned tired and — and ashamed, ashamed to be complaining of her present job, when men and girls she knew were suffering in cold and mud under fire. Ashamed of the lie she had told about herself and Rex, achingly aware that she was not doing her share to help win this horrible war. The dog whined and laid his nose against her knee, sprang up with a sharp, short bark as a voice demanded: —

"Hey, what goes on?"

XII

STOP THAT, Kit, or you'll have hysterics." The hand on her shoulder administered a light shake. "Go lie down, Charles. I can handle this situation without your assistance."

She looked up at Rex Danton as if she were seeing a ghost. He loomed. She rubbed her eyes. He was in gray tweeds that accentuated the breadth of his shoulders.

"W-where did you — c-come from? Where is y-your uniform?" The sentences were punctuated by quick-drawn breaths.

"Never mind that. What goes on? Is this a fancy-dress party? What's that becoming thing on your head? I saw a cowhand dolled up to the nines leaving the house. What was he doing here? Why are you crying? Did he frighten you?"

"I'm n-not f-frightened. I'm n — not crying. I've been on a sort of sorry-for-myself binge. I'm really l — laughing."

"Okay, you're laughing. What's the joke?" His stern eyes and voice steadied her.

"Grandmother sent me this and the bandeau, that's the 'becoming thing' on my head. Shall I model the jacket for you, sir? It's the last word in furs. I'm sure your wife would be crazy about it," she drawled.

She slipped on the coat, walked across the room and back with the measured tempo, grace and style of a professional model. Arms half lifted to show the cut of the sleeves. The glance over her shoulder. Turned to the right, to the left.

Smiled a bright, meaningless smile. She floated away from him, came back. He thrust his hands hard into his coat pockets. She heard his long, deep breath.

"How'm I doing?"

"I'm sold, on more than the coat. Where did you learn all that?"

"The technique is simple. Smile. Sway. Turn. I've modeled at dozens of fashion shows for charity. Clothes go to my head like laughing gas."

"You're a city gal, you belong in the center of the fashion belt, don't you? I can't see you living in the big open spaces. The chap who said, 'Oh, East is East, and West is West, and never the twain shall meet,' hit the jackpot as far as you're concerned." He cleared his gruff voice. "What's the gorgeousness for? Your trousseau? Getting ready to marry Trask?"

"Certainly not. They are for me to wear when I run across to a neighbor's in the evening. 'Run.' Get it? Imagine that with the nearest neighbor thirty miles away." Her chuckle verged on the hysterical.

"I'm a neighbor. Rushing Creek is only four miles from here. You could do that easily — perhaps not run, but in a car. What is there about your grandmother's suggestion to inspire wild laughter?"

She ignored the reference to his ranch.

"Because the ermine jacket must have cost a small fortune — I remember seeing one like it illustrated in *Vogue* — and — then I visualized myself in the kitchen cooking dozens of pork chops and frying bushels of potatoes — 'just a good plain cook, that's me' — and — and — it struck me being so fun — " A laugh that was half sob ended the sentence.

"Stop that. What have you done to your hand?" He caught her left wrist gently.

"Just a first-degree burn. The Nurses' Aide in me speaking."

"*First* degree! Why is it so dark?"

"I dabbed tea on it."

"My dear, my *dear*." He bent his head. She pulled her hand free. Silly, for one breathless minute she had thought he intended to press his lips to it.

"Hold everything. I shan't cross the chalk line." Did his grin mean that he had read her mind? "How did you get the burn? What d'you mean you're *cooking*? Has Ma Snell walked out on you?"

"Only temporarily, I hope. Haven't you heard that Cupid staged an arrow-shooting party at the Double H? She is preparing to wed her fourth. 'The fourth husband at sixty-five,' says she, and I twenty-three without one, says I. Tragic, I calls it."

She was being flippant to control an insane urge to cry it out against his shoulder. No man in what Shep had called her stag line had inspired that desire. "Nothing so strong as gentleness. Nothing so gentle as real strength." Her grandmother's favorite quote from Saint Francis de Sales echoed through her mind.

"We'll take up the matter of your lack of a husband later. I'll drop that problem into what the psychologists call 'the deep mind.' According to their theory it should pop up solved. At present I'm more interested in Ma Snell's fourth. She likes men but this speed doesn't seem up her alley. Where did she meet him? Better take off the jacket or you'll melt in this hot room. Let me help so you won't brush it against the burn."

He lifted the ermine coat carefully from her shoulders and laid it in the box. She drew off the bandeau and folded it on top.

"The Cinderella from splendor-to-kitchen motif." She

sighed with exaggerated regret as she adjusted the cover. "Exit the fairy godmother's elegance."

"I don't like to talk about myself, but you still have the Prince on the job, meaning me," he reminded with mock modesty. "Why do you look at me as if I were a stranger you'd never seen before?"

"You are. I've never met this civilian in superbly tailored gray tweeds."

"Glad you approve the clothes if you are not sold on the man inside them." Laughter disappeared from his eyes and voice. "Where did Ma Snell meet her fourth candidate?"

"Olsen, Mich and Tex brought him back from the city the week end we were at Mountain Lodge. They said he was a range rider and an expert blacksmith, who wanted a job. As we are temporarily out of blacksmiths, Joe Carr advised Dick to snap him up. Dick snapped. He is a Maine man, he says."

"No kidding. What's his name?"

"Ezra Dodge. That's New Englandish enough."

"How old is he?"

"If Ma Snell is sixty-five — as she claims — I'd say he was in the late fifties. Apparently he fell for her charms at once. He's a fast worker. Four weeks later she is shopping for lovelies. She planned the trip to take in the rodeo tomorrow that is being staged for funds for the local USO. There will be riders from all the ranches within miles. That's why the cowhand you saw leaving the house was 'dolled up to the nines.' He's going." She was tempted to tell him of the Swede's complaint about Joe Carr. Why bother him with the Marlowe ranch business?

"Boy, does that come tomorrow? Ever seen one?"

"No."

"It's four-star entertainment. Want to go?"

"Crazy to but I can't. Let's skip it or I may burst into tears of disappointment. What happened to Ezra's three predecessors?"

"Number one died. Number two disappeared and Ma Snell was granted a divorce for desertion. Number three was trampled to death by a Hereford steer when he tried to bulldog it. What do you think of the present candidate?"

"Something tells me he's not what he pretends to be. I wouldn't trust him as far as I could see him."

"Does Ma Snell know you don't trust Dodge?"

"She suspects it. I asked her how she dared marry a man she had known for such a short time. She came back with, 'Don't you read the papers and the love stories? If you believe them, girls marry soldiers they've met only three times. Compared with that, four weeks is pretty slow goin'.' Joe Carr is terribly upset about it. Has she money?"

"A tidy little fortune. Savings from her wages which have been high. Insurance from the two departed and to make sure she had enough to last her through a long life, Uncle Pete left her a pension. She couldn't buy many outfits like that," he indicated the box on the table, "but the income will afford a comfortable living. Uncle Pete was her adviser and the job has descended to me."

"Can't you prevent her marrying this man who has come from goodness knows where? He's tall and big, has the weathered cowboy look. His name may be New Englandish, but he appears Western to me. She is staying with her sister, Mrs. Singley, in the city."

"I can't stop her. She's free, white and twenty-one, in her right mind and in full possession of her money. When is she coming back?"

"Saturday and this is Thursday. She promised me she

would be married here. Joe Carr is a Justice of the Peace. Now that I know she has money, I'm scared stiff for fear the amorous Ezra will slip off to town, marry her there, get her small fortune and disappear. She's a fine woman with a heart of gold under that absurd make-up."

"You're telling me. Perhaps Ezra, also, has discovered that. Perhaps he really has fallen for her?"

"In four weeks? It's absurd!"

"Sure of that? I've known it to happen at the third meeting."

The quizzical light in his eyes sent a surge of warm blood to her cheeks.

"You're referring to my lunatic announcement at the Carter party, I assume. You haven't forgotten it? Then it is true? At about two A.M. my super-ego, conscience to you, gets busy and keeps me awake. I try to convince myself that my world-beating idea was nothing but a wacky dream. Where have you been? What have you been doing these interminable weeks that you haven't been here to help me wipe it off the slate?"

"First, to our oil fields to look over conditions there; to the hospital for a check-up; then to Washington to get my honorable discharge from the Army. My front-line fighting days ended when that machine gun peppered my leg. I had my choice between office work at the Pentagon or carrying on Uncle Pete's oil interests. This year about twenty-four thousand wells were opened. The goal for 1945 is twenty-seven thousand. Our head engineer isn't equal to increased responsibility. I was told that on a short cruise a battleship will consume in the neighborhood of a million gallons of oil. That fact settled the question of where I am needed most."

"A million gallons! And that is only one ship. No wonder gas for civilians has to be rationed."

"And a battleship is only one of the hundreds of thousands of armored vehicles and ships that are drawing on this country for their fuel supply. Much as I hated to leave the service I can be of more use to the Government here than hanging round Washington. As that was the consensus among the brass hats, meet Rex Danton, engineer, with an office in the city."

"And with a D.S.C. ribbon in the buttonhole of his coat lapel. Now that surprise is wearing off, I'm beginning to take in the details of your snappy get-up."

"Glad you like it. I strive to please."

"Do you mean that? Then, why haven't you told the Carters that my announcement that night at Mountain Lodge was a joke? A dumb joke, I'll admit, but a joke."

He drew a package of cigarettes from the pocket of his gray coat, frowned at it and slipped it back unopened.

"I'm keeping my powder dry. I figured that if we let the 'dumb joke' slide — your words, not mine — for a while, we might decide to let it stand."

"Let it stand. You mean that I — "

"Quote. 'I'm going with you when your leave ends.' Unquote. Right?"

"Wrong with a capital W. I wouldn't marry you if you were the last man in the world. I don't like you. Your 'fatal charm' hasn't worked with me."

"We've traveled a long way from Ma Snell and her matrimonial gamble, Kit." His light voice, as if her theatrical taunt amused him, set her cheeks burning again. "Let's get back to her."

The Airedale, stretched flat in front of the fire, roused, ears pricked, listened. With short, upswept tail wagging he ran to the door.

"Hiya, young fella," a voice called before Joe Carr appeared in the doorway. He pulled off his black Stetson and stared as if doubting his eyes.

"Heck, I didn't recognize you fer a minute in them store clothes, Rex. What d'you know. Out of the Army. Ever since the manager of the Old Boss's oil interests quit, folks has been sayin' you ought to come home an' take over, but you're such a natural-born fighter, I didn't tell ya fer fear you'd get mad."

"Home is the fighter, home from the war. I'm here to stay, Joe. What's on your mind?"

"Seein' you in them clothes I almost clean forgot. I'm glad you're here, too, Kit. We got to work fast. Dodge, the black-smith, he's an ex-range-rider too, Rex, borrowed the ranch jalopy. I was out with the Boss, most of the cowhands went off in the trucks with their hosses to the rodeo, or he wouldn't a got it."

"Where has he gone?"

Kit knew what was coming by the little ice shivers that coasted along her veins.

"To the city. Told Tex he'd arranged to marry Ma Snell there, tomorrow after the rodeo."

XIII

SHE WON'T marry him there, she promised me she would be married at the Double H. I'm sure she won't renege."

Kit's excited declaration of faith rang through the still room. Joe Carr scratched his head before he shook it negatively.

"I ain't so certain you can rely on that sort of a promise, Kit. Dodge is a smooth number. I sure ought to have given him his time when I savvied what he was aimin' for, hangin' round the kitchen, washin' dishes evenin's an' freezin' all the other hands out. Olsen is sore about it. Dodge knows I'm dead set against Ma Snell's marryin' him. He's planning to pull a fast one."

Rex Danton glanced at his wrist watch. "What time did he start?"

"About three, Tex said."

"It's now four-thirty. Are you sure, Kit, that Ma Snell intends to stay with her sister?"

"That was her plan. She added that Jane would be terrible mad with her for marrying again, that if she made it too hot, she would go to the hotel — she didn't intend to be bossed by anyone. Can't you do something to stop her, Rex?"

"Sure, I'm going for her. If Ezra doesn't beat me to it, I may be able to knock a little common sense into the head under that blond wig."

"I ain't so sure 'bout you puttin' it across alone, Rex," Joe Carr observed doubtfully, "but Kit could. Ma Snell thinks a powerful lot of what she says. She better go along with you."

"Just like that!" Kit's exclamation was breathless. "Why make me Ma Snell's keeper? How can I go? Who'll get supper for the hands and breakfast and the other meals? Besides, where would I stay?"

"You've the right idea, Joe." The foreman's wide mouth, which had opened to answer the volley of questions, snapped shut as Rex spoke. "I'll get Chang Loo at Rushing Creek. He'll take over the kitchen. It will give him something to do. I can get there and back while you are dressing and packing a bag, Kit. You'll stay tonight with Ma Snell, wherever she is, and I'll bring you home after the rodeo tomorrow. Change to something warmer and take an extra coat."

Kit's pulses broke into double-quick. Her eyes went starry with excitement. A rodeo! What fun it would be. What *fun!* She seized the box with the ermine lumber jacket. Halfway in her impetuous dash to the door she stopped.

"We've forgotten Dick. He won't like it."

"I'll straighten it out with him. Is he goin' to like it better if he loses Ma Snell for good?" Joe Carr demanded. "House-keepers like her ain't raised any more. You could eat off her kitchen floor it's so clean. If the Dodge fella succeeds in gettin' legal hold of her an' her dough, it's my guess we never see her again."

"You don't mean he would mur — " The horrible word caught in Kit's throat.

"I don't mean nothin' except somethin's wrong. If he wa'n't double-timin' us, he wouldn't sneak off, would he?"

"That's right," Rex Danton agreed. "Going my way, Kit?"

"Going! Going! Gone!" She dashed into the hall with the the dog at her heels.

"It's like a movie," she thought, as in the room which had once been Peter Danton's, with its great canopied bed and worn chintzes liberally sprinkled with birds of paradise, she buttoned the big gold discs on her one-piece frock of soft tangerine-color wool. "Only kidnaped heroines aren't usually in the sixty-five-year class," she added as she touched her throat with perfume and clipped on earrings that matched the buttons. Kidnaped. Ezra Dodge wouldn't dare.

She wrote a note to her brother and propped it in a conspicuous place on the desk in his room. Returned and packed a week-end case before she crushed a beige beret with a sparkling star on her dark hair and slipped into a shag coat which matched her frock. Her shoes were of the same beige alligator as her large shoulder bag in which she tucked her grandmother's letter. She would finish reading it tonight.

Gloves in one hand, suitcase in the other, long nutria coat over her left arm, she paused on the threshold. Had she better take her pearls? No. They would be safer here where she kept them hidden tied in one of her fine handkerchiefs, tucked into the toe of a gold sandal in the huge old-fashioned mahogany wardrobe. The rodeo would attract pickpockets and sneak thieves.

She unlocked the wardrobe door and left it ajar. That would suggest there was nothing valuable within. Shep had declared that Swede Olsen knew the pearls were real. He might have told some of the other hands, and not all of them were going to the rodeo.

Pulses quick-stepping from pleasurable excitement, she reached the threshold of the library. Rex Danton in gray topcoat was talking to the foreman.

"The ranch cook is all set for her afternoon off," she announced and pirouetted. "The American Look. Have I captured it?"

"I've seen you in riding togs, slack outfit, evening dress and that striped cotton you had on a few minutes ago; I'll have to get acquainted all over with this citified gal."

"Sorry to interrupt the build-up, Rex," Joe Carr interrupted dryly. "Don't forget what I told you, there's a patch on the right rear tire of the jalopy."

"I'll remember. Chang Loo is in the kitchen 'alla ticklee pinkee' to be where he will have company — he has been alone for four weeks — so drop the ranch commissary from your mind, Kit. Give me that suitcase and coat. Let's go."

"Please don't look so dejected, *Charlie,* I can't take you with me." Kit swooped and hugged the Airedale who was gazing up at her with wistful eyes. "Take him to the kitchen and give him a cookie, please, Joe, and keep him at your cottage while I'm away so he won't miss me. His eyes make me feel as if I were abandoning my own baby on a strange doorstep." She dashed through the doorway, down the path to the roadster.

Ahead, a rim of the sun like a red-gold halo poised on the purple top of a mountain. The glow set a near-by little cloud blushing. Behind them a man's voice sang with quavering pathos, "Home on the Range." As Rex drove away from the white gate, two horsemen were coming down the hill toward the west.

"There's Dick," Kit exclaimed. "He's been riding fences to make sure there are no places where the animals can break through. As if you needed that explained to you. I'm so accustomed to describing the A B C of ranching in my letters to Grandmother and my men friends in the service that I've acquired the habit. I left a note for him. Will he understand? The whole situation seems so improbable."

"You'd be surprised how many important happenings have seemed improbable — before they were definitely listed as dangerous."

"Dangerous." Feathery chills scooted along her veins. "You don't think Ezra Dodge's pursuit of Ma Snell possibly can be enemy-inspired, do you?"

They passed the clump of cottonwoods and had a clear view of the purple mountain top which had lost its halo and looked bleak and lonely against the glow. The blushing cloud had faded to violet. Crows flitted across the crimson sky like lost souls above the fires of Hades.

"Do you?" she repeated.

"I've learned not to take chances. A small cave-in can change the course of a mountain stream. A trifle may change the course of a life. The fact that Dodge took the jalopy without leave seems a trifle. It may develop into a major threat unless we are able to block it. Mind you, I say *may*. Joe Carr says Dodge is a lazy devil. There's a chance that he is merely pursuing a meal ticket for his old age."

"Do you really believe that?"

"No. But I'm not infallible. See the gorge between the two white-capped mountains ahead? There's a legend that about sixty years ago a solitary horseman, a 'dead tough' in the slang of the day, who packed looted gold, rode into that gorge with a posse a mile behind on his trail. A horseshoe had been picked up in front of a robbed bank. The light snow showed the imprints of three shod hoofs and one unshod of a mountain pony. The sheriff and his men knew by that they were on the right trail, but in the very middle of the gorge it stopped. No sign of the hoofprints ahead or on either side."

"I'm all gooseflesh from suspense. Was there no indication of a struggle as if man and horse had fallen into a crevasse?"

"No. If it happened today we might figure that they — plus loot — had been snatched into the air by towrope and hook from a hovering plane, but they didn't have them in those days."

"Were the horse and rider found?"

"No. Nor hide nor hair of them. The posse hung around through the night and the next day without solving the mystery. The following morning the sheriff, watching through his glasses, saw two buzzards hovering above the spot."

"How gruesome. Did they ever discover what happened?"

"No. The place was named Mystery Gorge. Not very original, there must be dozens by that name in the mountain states. There are herds of elk and spotted deer there, but they remain unmolested. Hunters give the place a wide berth. Suppose we get away from mystery and tune in on another station." He turned the dial of a radio.

"Watch your weight," a woman's voice warned. "This year's gal will show lots of skin — "

"Want to hear it, Kit?"

"Love to. I'm fashion-minded."

"Pedal pants, neither shorts nor trousers, but something in between that tapers below the knee," the voice went on. "Black, even in play clothes. Long jackets sleeked to the figger. Rounded shoulders instead of square, mannish ones. No relaxing of L-85 but a swing away from the slim silhouette to slender curves. The pretty-lady sort of evening frock. Chignons designed for your romantic moments. Longer skirts to balance larger hats. Undies gone feminine — definitely with lots of — "

Kit snapped off the connection.

"It's a crime to ask you to listen to more of that. Better for me not to, she makes clothes so alluring. Tune in an hour from now and a man's grave voice will remind: —

" 'The Government asks you *not* to spend money for what you do *not* need. Dangerous dollars. Buy a bond. Keep it. Put it away and see it grow.' I don't *need* anything, but, boy, how I'd like a whole new spring outfit."

"Love of clothes is part of being a woman, isn't it?"

"It's a part of being this woman, but thank goodness, she has enough strength of character to resist — in spots, if her grandmother hasn't. Smell the sage and pine and spruce. It's a heavenly blend."

"I can smell your perfume. What is it?"

" 'Je Reviens.' I Will Return. Shep sent it. Pretty subtle for him. Like it?"

"*No.*"

"That's because you're sold on 'Suivez Moi.' Wonder if my soot-conditioned lungs appreciate the freshness of this air? The world is so alive. Every twig is dancing, every dry leaf is shimmying to the tune of the breeze. It's exciting. It sets me a-tingle. You prophesied that I would love this country. I do."

"But not so much as you love the East?"

"I love the East for different reasons. My forbears helped build its foundation. I love my church, it recharges the batteries of my spirit, the theater, opera, the companionship of friends who talk my language, but if only I could be of more use to the Government — and — and forget that lie I told about you and me, I'd be slap-happy here."

"We'll relegate that last to the Department of Unfinished Business. Remember the sermon at Mountain Lodge?

" 'Whatsoever things are just — ' "

His rich voice repeating the words sent a surge of tears to her eyes.

" 'Think on these things — and the God of peace shall be

with you,' " he concluded. "There are times when the horrors I have seen and been part of get an octopus grip on my mind. That sermon has helped me. I repeat the admonition, 'Think on these things and the God of peace shall be with you' and He is."

"I didn't know you were at the service."

"Sure I was there. Barbie's west-bound train left at sunup and I started for Mountain Lodge. The clergyman who was to preach was a pal of Uncle Pete's. I knew he would expect to see me. I had said all there was to say to you the night before, anything more would be anticlimax, so I kept out of your way."

"You know your Saint Paul, don't you?"

"And that isn't all. I was raised to think that knowing the Scriptures — Grandmother called them — was an important part of a man's education. She belonged to an 'Open Bible Society,' the members of which agreed to keep the Good Book open on the living-room table. Not a bad idea. I never visited her that I didn't stop to read a verse. Often when I was in a hot spot in the deafening fury of battle, memory would broadcast a line or two from the Book. It gave me a sense of power, invincibility, led to enduring faith. I've heard other men confess to the same feeling. Sorry, didn't mean to bore you with my confession, it just surged up."

"You haven't bored me. I — I feel as if I had been permitted a glimpse into your Holy of Holies. My grandfather used to quote, 'The alert men in all walks of life are men of faith.' How do you think I would have lived through the nerve-torturing period while Dick was missing if I hadn't held tight to a faith which showed me the way when the path was dark?" She cleared her husky voice. "Now *I'm* sorry I opened my heart."

"Don't be. It's a very lovely heart. To return to the present.

You said you would be slap-happy if you could be of more use to the Government, didn't you?"

"My very words, mister." She spoke lightly to crowd back the memories her confidence had set swarming.

"You are of use at the Double H, aren't you? To keep on keeping on after your enthusiasm has burned out is being a soldier, isn't it?"

"My enthusiasm to help Dick hasn't burned out. I am beginning to wonder if he wouldn't pull himself back to normal faster without me."

"Does that mean you are thinking of going home?"

"No. I wouldn't go so far from him. But I have been wondering — "

"Just a minute." Rex stopped the roadster and jumped out. He examined a muddy spot left by yesterday's heavy rain at the junction of two roads.

"Our Romeo made the left-hand turn," he said as he slipped back behind the wheel.

"How do you know?"

"Joe said that the right rear wheel of the jalopy was patched. The rut to the left shows a dent made by that."

"Then the road to the city and Ma Snell's sister's house is the left-hand road?"

"Something tells me that meeting Ma Snell tonight was Ezra's little red herring drawn across his trail. The road he has taken leads to Mystery Gorge."

XIV

IT SEEMED hours to Kit that Rex bent forward over the wheel, his keen eyes narrowed as they scanned the road that turned sharply to the left between cottonwoods and hackberrys. The world was so still she could hear the stir of unseen life in the leafless shrubs, the swish of pines in the light breeze. The piercing cry of a flitting nighthawk split the air and roused him from his absorption.

"Let's go," he said, threw in the clutch and swung the roadster to the right.

"Why aren't we following Ezra Dodge?"

"Because we're after the person we set out to save from the peril of a plunge into matrimony. Right?"

"The perils of a fourth plunge," she corrected. "I wouldn't dare interfere with a first."

"Even if you saw only trouble ahead for one you loved?"

She thought of Dick and Lois Langley. Could she keep from saying, "Don't"? Better to leave his question unanswered.

Swathes of crimson and violet and green streaked the western horizon. Snowy mountain peaks turned pink. Russian thistle and tumbleweed rolled across a field to pile against a zigzag fence. A single star pricked through the sky. A heron winged its way up creek. A cottontail skurried across the road. The beady eyes of a sage chicken peered from a clump of rabbit brush. Rusty hinges creaked. The battered door of a tarpaper shack swung back and forth. Spruce, hemlock and cedar scented the light breeze. A plane hummed overhead. The clock on the instrument board ticked away the minutes.

The highway. Black, shining like a patent-leather belt. Clear air. A hint of frost. Lights of cars. Suck of tires. Shriek of a distant train whistle. The glow from the city a gold rim on the horizon. Log cabins. Well-built modern houses. More stars. The Big Dipper. Near enough to touch.

"Asleep?" Rex asked.

"No. Wide-awake. Preparing to reach for a bunch of those twinkling stars to set in my bonnie brown hair. It isn't brown but it expresses what I mean."

"I have it on the same excellent authority that stars do not twinkle, but we'll let it go. We are nearing our objective. Lucky I've been at the home of Ma Snell's sister before. We'd better get together on our line of action, work out what one of the presidential candidates has called 'a durable cohesion.' Question one. Why did we break out in the late afternoon to locate Ma Snell? You take the first crack at it."

"Can't we tell the truth, that we suspect that Ezra Dodge is after her money?"

"That's out. Definitely."

Had the tire marks turning to the left instead of toward the city prompted his emphatic "definitely"? She let her mind turn back a few hours. To Joe's entrance into the library at the Double H. Heard him say: —

"Told Tex he'd arranged to marry Ma Snell there tomorrow after the rodeo." *After the rodeo*.

"I have it." She sat erect in her eagerness. "I *have* it!"

"Have what? If you grab my arm like that, we'll land in the ditch."

"Sorry." She thrust her hand into her coat pocket. "Remember Joe said they were to be married at the close of the rodeo? Here's my answer to Question One — I've never seen a rodeo. Crazy to. Want to be in the city the night before to see the crowd and the cowboys gather. Dick wouldn't let me come alone. Flash! Ma Snell. Take her to the hotel with me as that prehistoric creature — a chaperone."

"Your eyes glow like spotlights. It's a super solution. Where do I come in?"

"You — let's see. You were coming to town to join the Langleys — quote, 'for your romantic moments' — and the Carters, so played the Good Samaritan and brought me along. How's that?"

"Not too bad. We'll let the quip about romantic moments slide for the present. If the Carters were coming, why didn't you plan to join them, if you wanted to see the show?"

"They invited us to be their guests. I was substituting for Ma Snell — how could I leave? You juggled Chang Loo out of your hat and presto, here I am. Dick wouldn't leave the ranch, so many of the cowhands were going to the rodeo. There is lots of work to be done to prepare for his first shipment of cattle next week. Two truckloads. Perhaps I shouldn't have left him. He's terribly low in his mind."

"You can't carry him and his moods on your shoulders for the rest of his life, Kit. He's got to pull himself out of the slough of depression."

"He will. I know he will. I am just helping him tide over a tough time. If only Lois — "

"Don't stop. What about Lois Langley? Believe it or not, it doesn't disturb me to hear her name mentioned."

"Why should it? In spite of the act she put on that evening at Mountain Lodge — " Kit could feel the blood burn to her hair. Why, *why* had she reminded him of that night and her own stupendous break?

"Getting into deep water — Miss Marlowe?" She knew from his laugh that he divined what she was thinking.

"I'm not in deep water. I was about to say that if she would hurry up and marry you, Dick would stop thinking about her."

"Would he? I wonder. I've known cases where it hasn't worked that way. However, it might be a solution. We'll have to see what can be done about it. Here we are." He stopped the roadster in a street lined on each side with stucco houses with blue slate roofs, as alike as a row of peas except that peas aren't the same size and the houses were.

"Nice little hangout, Ma Snell owns it," Rex explained. "Sister Jane occupies it sans rent. We'll get one hundred per cent co-operation from the aforementioned Jane if she suspects we are here to prevent the marriage. We won't put her wise yet. Go ahead. Open the campaign on the I'm-here-for-the-rodeo line." He stepped out and opened the door for her.

"Aren't you coming with me?"

"Your voice sounds scared. You're not afraid of Ma Snell, are you?"

"I'm not afraid of anything." She turned her back and approached the house in what she fondly hoped was the grand manner even while she reminded herself that her boast wasn't true, she had been afraid of Skip Cane the day of the storm.

A woman in a print frock with a design of black hounds pursuing red rabbits over a yellow ground opened the door in response to Kit's ring. Her brown hair was twisted into the tight curls of an unbrushed permanent. Fine lines fanned from the corners of her slaty eyes; a small girl in a beautifully smocked red dress clung to her skirt. She was without exception the coldest, most unresponsive person she had met in her life, Kit decided.

"What do you want?" she demanded.

"I am looking for Ma — Mrs. Snell. She told me she would spend the night here."

"Well she won't. She's gone to the swellest hotel in town. Trust Hetty for hitting the high spots. Silly old thing. Her with a chronic appendix and a Ouija board runnin' round with a boy."

A boy. Even this disillusioned woman wouldn't call Ezra Dodge a boy. Kit had the sensation of being whirled in a cage at the Funny House.

"What's this about a boy?" inquired Rex Danton behind her. "How are you, Mrs. Jane? Is that Alicia? Golly, but she's grown."

"Rex! Rex Danton." His voice had worked a miracle. The woman had come warmly alive. "Why aren't you in your uniform? I've been crazy to see it. I could cry. Hetty said you'd come back, handsomer than ever an' all dolled up with ribbons. She didn't let on, though, you'd brought a wife with you. Picked a beauty, didn't you?" Her gray eyes, no longer slaty, swept Kit from the beige beret to the alligator shoes. "Snazzy dresser. Lots of what the movies call 'oomph,' hasn't she?"

"I'm not — "

"Switch to another station, Jane," Rex interrupted Kit's hurried denial. "This is Miss Marlowe, sister of the Captain who bought the Double H."

"Good land, I did make a break, didn't I? Perhaps it wasn't a break, though. Perhaps I'm just a little ahead of the parade." Her smile revealed prominent white teeth. "Won't you two come in? Excuse my hair. I've just had a permanent. Getting ready for the big time tomorrow."

"Will Jack ride?"

"Sure he'll ride, Rex. There are some big prizes up for bulldogging. He thinks he's a trifle old for it, but I told him to go ahead and be a sport. We need a little extra money awful bad. 'Licia here's got to have her teeth straightened. The kettle's boiling, stop for tea, won't you?"

"Thanks no, Mrs. Singley," Kit declined. "I must locate your sister. I had planned to stay at the hotel with her."

"You'll prob'bly find her and her boy friend at the hotel bar, though I will say Hetty never takes anything stronger than beer and stops at one."

"What was the boy like? It may help to find them if we know."

"He had on some sort of a uniform, Miss Marlowe."

"Uniform?" Two exclamations synchronized to a note.

"Perhaps not uniform exactly. He came for her in a car."

"Thanks a lot, Mrs. Jane. We'll find her. Perhaps we will meet at the show tomorrow. Good luck to Jack. Come on, Kit."

"Just where do we go from here?" Kit inquired as in the roadster beside her he started the engine. "Can you locate the 'swellest' hotel? Would Ma Snell be likely to go there or was she throwing sand in the gear of sister Jane's curiosity?"

"Sure, she might go there. Why not? She's a respectable woman, her family goes back to pioneer days — " he chuckled — "there were pioneers and pioneers. There were fine men among the first settlers, the leadership of these had an effect, but by and large, the average mountain man was a tough hombre when the Colt .45 was the law of the land. Had to be to survive. I can't figure out the 'boy' in the case. Some sort of a uniform, Jane Singley said."

"When she opened the door I thought she had the hardest face I've ever seen. When you appeared she positively melted."

"I got charm, believe it or not." A frown followed his light reply. "Her husband, John, Jack to everyone, was a cowhand at the Double H when I was a boy. He was ambitious to be his own boss. Uncle Pete staked him to a small stable of horses to breed as racers. He has made good, partly due to his wife, who has ambitions and an itching palm. He was right. He is too old to bulldog. The streets are packed. Always this way the night before a rodeo."

He drove slowly through a highway crowded with cars and horse-drawn vehicles, lined on each side with lighted shops, gay with color, gay with laughter, gay with the spirit of antici-pation. Men and women singly, in pairs, in groups, thronged the sidewalks. Six-gallon hats, leather belts, satin shirts, cow-boy pants and high-heeled boots on the cowboys, the women equally spectacular.

Lighted shop windows displayed Stetson hats, shirts of blinding brilliance, spurs and boots. A door opened and let out the aroma of coffee. From another came the acrid smell of liquor. Drifts of radioed music. A scrap of "I'll Be Seeing You." A few notes from "Going My Way." Uniforms, blue, olive drab and Marine green. A colossal Indian in a towering feather war bonnet. Civilian clothes in smart texture and cut.

"What fun!" Kit exclaimed. "Ma Snell was right. 'Livin' even in wartime can be fun.' I'd like to do that."

"Do what?"

"Didn't you see the girl in cowboy outfit on the wooden broncho having her picture taken? I'll do it tomorrow. I'll smother my conscience and buy a costume like hers. Have the snapshots mounted and send them to my friends overseas."

"Are there many of them?"

"Too many." The gaiety had left her voice.

"Any special?"

"No." She thought of the four men who had begged her to marry them before they left, the men she had sent away with a kiss and a prayer. Two of the voices she never would hear again. "No. Sometimes I think I haven't it in me to love a man enough to marry him."

"Don't be downhearted about it. You'll make an attractive spinister. A career, *Le Grand Charlie* and a couple of cats will round out your life, nicely. Here we are at the hotel. You'd better go in alone and inquire for Ma Snell."

Kit mounted the steps in a wave of color and laughter, was whirled round and round in a revolving door before she could make her escape. At the desk she waited in a line of men, uncomfortably aware of the glances cast at her.

"I was to meet Mrs. Hetty Snell here," she told the clerk. "Will you have her paged, please?"

He was short and flurried, but the eyes that gazed at her through thick lenses were kindly, as after fingering through cards and consulting the tall, lank man beside him, he said: —

"Sorry, miss. No person of that name has registered."

XV

NOT HERE?" Kit was aware that she stared at the clerk incredulously. A hand seized her elbow.

"For Pete's sake, move, Kit, you're holding up the line," a voice reminded.

"Shep! Where did you come from?" she demanded as propelled by him she left the desk. His mouth was set in grim disapproval.

"I was on my way to the Double H. Had to see you. Got to take a plane back Sunday night. Couldn't get anyone here to drive me out. They're all crazy about that confounded rodeo tomorrow."

"So am I. That's why I'm here."

"*Alone?*"

"Of course not. The Carters are here."

"Sure? You looked as if you'd been knocked on the head when the clerk answered your question."

"Oh, that. I was inquiring for the housekeeper at the Double H. She's been on furlough for a few days. Her sister told me she was here."

"Why should you want to see her? Don't you get enough of her at the ranch? What have you done to your hand? What's that long dark mark? Gosh, Kit, it looks as if you had hired out by the day to scrub. Why are you so careless? Darn this ranch phobia you've picked up."

She thought of Rex Danton's tender "My dear, my *dear*," when he had seen the burn and then she thought, "Of course, it's just his line."

"Hullo, there's Danton!"

"Where, Shep?"

"Shaking hands with the woman in the mink coat and red hat. He's in civvies. When did he get out of the service? Boy, perhaps now I'll get a line on his politics. Couldn't sound him out at Mountain Lodge. There's a soldier-vote act that makes it a criminal offense to ask a man in U.S. uniform how he intends to vote. Did you know he was coming?"

"You don't know much about this country, do you, Shep? This 'confounded rodeo' is for the benefit of the local USO. Everybody who can ride, walk or crawl will come." She wasn't too sure of that but she had to say something. Rex had seen her. His eyes narrowed as he approached.

"Glad to see you back, Trask," he welcomed. "Sally's waiting in the room you are to share with her, Kit. Better make it fast. Some of the ranchers invited to meet you and Dick at Mountain Lodge are having tea and drinks in the Carters' sitting room and you and she are expected. I've sent up your suitcase. This way."

"Join the party at the Carters', Shep, they'll love to have you," she called over her shoulder. "Split-second timing I call your arrival, Colonel. I was about to be put through the third degree. I feel as if I were being jet-propelled," she protested as he hurried her across the lounge. "Have you seen Sally? Am I really to share a room with her?"

"What do you think I was doing while you and Trask were heart-to-hearting? What's he back for?"

"To see me, probably."

"Sure, 'Je Reviens.' I Will Return. I had forgotten. I looked up Mrs. Carter and told her you were here. She was delighted. Is Ma Snell registered?"

"No."

"I had a hunch she wouldn't be. That's why I contacted the Carters p.d.q."

"Where can she be? Was she in that jalopy with Ezra? Perhaps they are married already. Perhaps he is taking her to Mystery Gorge to mur — "

"You have imagination, plus, haven't you? You've gone white. These people waiting for the elevator will think I'm your husband, that we are quarreling — "

"Here's one person who won't," Kit interrupted as Lois Langley approached. Her light blue eyes swept over them, her eyebrows arched.

"See who's here," she exclaimed. "My word, something tells me this may be a honeymoon."

"Not yet, but soon," Rex corrected in the voice of a man whose dearest wish was about to be granted. "Here's the elevator, Kit. Room 444. Tell Aunt S'rena I'll join her party in fifteen minutes."

Before the car shot up Kit saw Lois tuck her hand under his arm, saw her lips move as she looked up at him, saw them walk away together. Was he telling *her* she'd make an attractive spinster? Not a chance. He had appeared very sure that Kit Marlowe was cut out for a career woman.

"Forget it," she told herself impatiently and forced her thoughts to Ma Snell. Where was she? Vague doubts as to the wisdom of her rush to the rescue of a three-times married woman, who certainly knew her way round, began to crystallize into the conviction that Joe Carr might not be a wise adviser.

The next few hours were a flashing kaleidoscope of impressions. The eagerness of Sally's welcome dimming a little when she found that Dick was not coming. The ranchers and their wives greeting her as if she were one of them. Surprise that she was ravenously hungry for tea and delectable sandwiches and cakes. Snatches of music each time the door opened to admit more guests. The boisterous welcome accorded Rex, when they saw him in civvies. The shake of his head in answer to her whispered, "Found her?" Shep Trask's suspicious surveillance. The Langleys going all out to be charming to the men. The mother's tinkle when Cal Smiley entered. The daughter's watchful eyes on Rex. Mrs. Carter and Sally smilingly declining to spend the evening at a movie. The surprising quiet of the room after the guests had departed. The telephone bell ringing sharply. Serena Carter's answer.

"Yes. Yes." A long pause as she listened. "I understand. I hope it's nothing serious. I'll tell her." The click of the phone in the cradle.

"Rex wants you to go out with him, Kit." The terrified pound of her heart.

"Nothing serious, you said. Is it — Dick?"

"No, child, no. Take your warm coat."

Rex Danton was waiting for her when she stepped from the elevator. Her relief when he smiled made her realize that she hadn't fully believed that bad news about Dick wasn't imminent, that taking her warm coat didn't mean a drive to the Double H.

"What is it?" she whispered.

"Nothing to make you look like a ghost girl. I have a hunch I've found her."

"Ma Snell! *Where?*"

"I'll tell you when we are in the car. Quick. Let's beat it before I am held up by more enthusiastic friends assuring me

I can be of more use here at home than in the fight. Maybe I can, maybe jacking up the oil supply for planes and tanks will be my way of paying my debt to the men I saw slaughtered. There's plenty of grinding work ahead, but it hurts like the dickens to get out of the service."

"It must, but remember you are helping where you are most needed. That is the rock of comfort to which I cling."

She hadn't realized that she had been tense with anxiety until, beside him in the roadster, she relaxed with a long, unsteady breath.

"What's the matter, Kit? I felt you slump. Thought for a minute you had fainted."

"No. My slump, as you unromantically dubbed it, was Joy with a capital J. Mrs. Carter was so mysterious about your message I thought something had happened to Dick. Now that I know he's okay, 'God's in his heaven: All's right with the world.' Forgive that mad burst into song."

"I suspected you had a singing voice. Now I know it. You are on top of the world, aren't you?"

"Forget me. Where did you find Ma Snell?"

"Haven't found her yet but — "

"Old Man Mystery coming up. Go on. Go on."

"I suspect she's in the hospital."

"The hospital! 'A sort of uniform' her sister said. Would that be an interne with whom she drove away?"

"Could be I'm all wet, but, that's the way I figure it."

"Is she very ill? What is the matter? I know. I *know*. Jane Singley said, "Silly old thing. Her with a chronic appendix and a Ouija board, runnin' round with a boy.' "

He laughed as she had not heard a man laugh since December 7, 1941.

"A chronic appendix and — a Ouija board — " his repetition was punctuated by chuckles — "suppose they will operate for both?"

"Then you think they will operate?"

"I don't know. I'm not even sure she is at the hospital. The desk wouldn't give me any information when I phoned. I came for you planning that we would attack together."

"What made you suspect she was there?"

"Jane's 'sort of a uniform' kept bobbing up in my mind. She would have recognized that of any branch of the service. I had a hunch — "

"Old extra-sensory perception doing its stuff?"

"Getting your sparkle back, aren't you?"

"The change from the Double H kitchen to the bright lights of the city has infused my spirit with a champagne bubble."

"You had me scared when you stepped from the elevator. As I was saying when so rudely interrupted, I had a hunch the 'boy' might be a hospital interne, that Ma Snell knew she was ill. I telephoned Joe to check on phone calls from the ranch. Half an hour ago he reported that twice during the last ten days she had called the hospital in this city, and that soon after we left this afternoon there was a long-distance call from that same hospital for you."

"For me? Now, I'm sure we've found her." Kit told of Ma Snell's sudden attack of pain the afternoon she had washed the tea things in the kitchen, of the conversation that followed.

"She assured me that she had consulted a doctor, that she wasn't fool enough to let herself die — that living even in these awful times can be fun — that it was nothing serious, tapped the Ouija board and said, 'This'll warn me when it is.' I believe all her talk about marrying Ezra was a cover-up to get to the city without any of us suspecting why she was going. She told me she didn't intend to have the cowhands 'gossiping about her innards.' "

"That ties it. If we can get information at the hospital, we're all set."

"We'll get it. Ma Snell asked me that same afternoon if I would come to her if she needed me. That explains the long-distance call to the Double H."

"I know some of the doctors. Uncle Pete was on the Board of Directors. We'll put it across."

It wasn't difficult. Opposition melted when Kit gave her name. Ma Snell was there for an appendectomy. She had instructed them to phone the ranch to ask Miss Marlowe to come. The nurse's small birdlike eyes glowed with excitement as she explained.

"Have they operated?" Kit inquired.

"Not yet. She begged us to wait until she had seen you. The old girl has something terribly important on her mind, or thinks she has. She doesn't want her presence here known."

"I'll wait. Tell Ma Snell I am here, ready to help her in any way I can, Kit."

She nodded. Tall, straight, strong, for a tense second Rex Danton seemed to her to be the only dependable thing in the war-shattered world. She resisted the urge to hold tight to his hand and followed the nurse whose starched white creaked as she moved along a cool, disinfectant-scented corridor. Its snowy walls were broken on one side by a desk at which a red-headed, blue-uniformed nurse bent over a report chart, while a white-frocked, black-haired interne leaned over her. Through partly open doorways came the fragrance of flowers, low voices, sleepy laughter.

From the window of a waiting room at the end she looked out at the glittering panorama of the sky. Stars in clusters, stars in patterns, stars in rows, stars solo, shed a glow on rooftops and chimneys. Too early for the moon. Gorgeous night. Were men she knew and liked, perhaps at this moment, digging into foxholes, flying on bombing missions, under this same sky?

"Ready, Miss Marlowe," the nurse announced from the corridor.

"Now, it was sweet of you to come, dearie." The weak, drowsy voice came from a white bed.

Kit's eagerly opened lips closed. The nurse had made a mistake. This gray-faced woman with short white curls wasn't curvaceous, highly colored Ma Snell. Her eyes swept the room, lingered on a mass of gilt-blond hair on the dresser. It was Ma Snell, sans make-up, sans transformation. She laid her hand tenderly on the work-roughened fingers.

"I told you I would come when you needed me."

"Draw up a chair so we can speak low."

The hint of mystery in the weak voice sent little chills feathering along Kit's veins.

"Does anyone know you're here?" the woman whispered.

"Only Rex."

"O — K — I — I — fooled Jane. I said I was go — ing to the hotel. Didn't want her — boss — ing round — here. She — she tells everything — she knows. I'm dragging you and Rex into danger, but I must — tell someone." She closed her eyes as if too weary to force her voice through her blue lips.

Kit knelt beside the bed.

"Forget about danger, Ma Snell. Rex and I can take it. What must you tell us?"

"Marrying Ezra was just — cover-up." It was an increasing effort to talk. "Ouija had warned trouble, terrible trouble.

The minute I laid eyes on him I knew he was mixed — up — in — it."

"What kind of trouble?"

"I don't know. That's for you — and Rex to find out. Be careful. Watch Olsen — too. He was — always givin' me the old oil. There's more than one — in the scheme. If they suspect you've seen me — they may try to get you — both — " Her eyes closed.

"Ma Snell! Ma Snell!" Kit whispered, "Who — who are the others?" The heavy lids lifted.

"One of the — "

"One of the — what? Go on, tell me. *Tell* me."

"Look — out — for — J — Jack — "

"Keep awake, please — *please,* just a minute, Ma Snell."

There was no movement of eyes or lips in response to the passionate plea.

XVI

WHY THE hush-hush about Ma Snell's presence at the hospital? Why the under-cover departure from her sister's house? Was Ezra Dodge, apparently headed for Mystery Gorge, connected with it?

Rex turned the questions over and over as he paced the floor of the square white-walled reception room. Had the red carnation-sprinkled hangings and chair covers been intended to be a note of cheer for anxious waiters? They did their stuff. Footsteps. Quick, running footsteps along the corridor. He met Kit at the threshold.

"What's happened? You're white. Has she — gone? Dead?"

"No." She put up her hand as if to loosen her tight throat. "For a minute I thought she was. I rang for the nurse. She said it was sleep, something they had given to quiet her. To be expected."

"Come here." He drew her into the room and held her with an arm about her shoulders. "Stop and get your breath. Your voice sounds as if you had been terribly frightened."

"I was. Not because I thought Ma Snell had slipped away. In my Nurses' Aide service I have seen death too many times to be afraid of that — it was her warning."

"Warning! Good Lord, has she been at the Ouija again — *here?*"

"It wasn't that. Bend your head."

Standing close, speaking low, she repeated what the woman had told her.

"Pretending she would marry Ezra was a cover-up?" he repeated incredulously. "Ouija warned trouble and she knew he was mixed up in it? I don't get it. If she felt that way about him, why didn't she tell me?"

"You've been away, no one knew where."

"That's right. 'Watch Olsen too' — it would take more than the hundred eyes of Argus to watch all her suspects."

"How can you joke about it?"

"That's just the light touch, honey, to relieve your tension. Her last words were, 'Watch out — J — Jack'?" he repeated.

She nodded.

"Jack. Could she have meant Jack Singley? Unless he's changed mightily in the last three years, he wouldn't need 'watching.' And she feared they would try to 'get' you and me. Just what does that add up to? Sounds like an old-time melodrammer. Sure she wasn't delirious from dope?"

"She seemed rational and terribly anxious."

"Does the nurse think she will come out of the operation okay?"

"I didn't ask. I fairly flew here to tell you. I am sure Ma Snell knew what she was saying, that something is frightfully wrong. 'You'd be surprised how many important happenings have seemed improbable — before they were definitely listed as dangerous.' Colonel Rex Danton speaking."

"If you remember everything I say as well as you have those words of profound wisdom, we'll get along. We'd better figure out our next move."

"I have figured mine. I will stay here and help. This hospital is tragically short of nurses, what hospital isn't? They'll have a uniform I can wear. What will you do?"

"Don't have me on your mind. I've been out after dark before." To relieve her tension he spoke more lightly than he felt. "I will meet you at the rodeo tomorrow morning at ten-thirty."

"I had forgotten the rodeo. Is it safe for us to go after Ma Snell's warning? Besides, she may need me."

"All the more reason to carry out our plans. After all, she isn't so near and dear that you must take her presence here as a personal tragedy. I'll return to the hotel and tell Sally that you are staying at the hospital tonight."

"Thanks. She knows I am a registered Nurses' Aide, that I have been hoping I could help somewhere. Now I will report for duty. Good night."

He waited till her quick footsteps faded into the distance. A man and woman talking in low tones went down the steps to the exit. He followed them. His roadster was parked in a side street. Would he find it? This part of the city was weirdly quiet. He was still in the hospital zone. His footsteps echoed eerily.

The car was where he had left it. He gave a short grunt of self-annoyance. He and Kit had been alerted to danger by a woman who was doped against pain. Ma Snell was fond of Jack Singley. His fool determination to try bulldogging for a prize might have been on the top of her mind.

Mrs. Langley and her daughter were in the Carters' sitting room at the hotel when he entered.

"Where's Kit?" Sally demanded.

"She seen her duty an' she done it," he answered lightly. "She has had helping at the hospital on her New England conscience since we passed it on our sight-seeing tour. She phoned to ask if she was needed. I could hear the line crackle from the excitement of the acceptance. I took her over and the receptionist fairly fell on her neck."

"Will she miss the rodeo?"

"No. She'll show up there in the morning, Sal. She plans to phone her brother and if he says okay, she'll put in a couple of days of service."

"A couple of days of service," Lois Langley repeated. "It is cruel to leave Dick alone so long, with his helplessness and memories."

"Jeepers, cut out the sob-sister stuff, Lois," Sally protested. "You should have seen our late Captain of Marines hold down a wild filly I had looped at the Circle Q. She was all set to bite through his hand but he administered two hefty cracks on her nose that set her thinking of other things and how."

"You're a great champion of the disabled, aren't you, Sally? You must seem terribly young to Richard Marlowe. No wonder he calls you 'Infant.'"

"Oh, shut up, Lois."

"*Sally!*"

"I don't care, Mom. How can I be 'young' as she means it, with a heart which feels as if it had been put through a wringer? She's always stabbing with that poison tongue of hers. Makes me think of the toy adder with the quivering fangs I once owned."

"If that's the way Sally feels about me, I'm *persona non grata,*" Lois Langley suggested lightly. "Thanks for your hospitality, Mrs. Carter. Oh, I know you don't approve of your daughter's — " she hesitated and laughed — "shall we be polite and call it frankness? Come Mother. We are to join Cal Smiley in the bar. He promised to produce a real cowboy for us to meet." She lingered on the threshold to add, "We won't use the seats you reserved for us at the rodeo. We have other plans."

"Sally, Sally, why did you do it?" her mother deplored as the door closed behind the two women. "Why make enemies, child? You can't fight Dick Marlowe's battles for him."

"I wasn't fighting for him. That cat makes me see red. Why didn't you get in a lick, Rex? She declares you went off your head about her, tried to break her engagement to Dick Marlowe."

"To answer your question, I thought you were doing very well without help, Miss Carter, *very* well."

"Okay, grin. You may not think it's so funny later. I didn't like that crack of hers about the *cruelty* of leaving Dick alone. I wonder what that dame has up her sleeve?"

It was a day to make one forget for an instant there was a war on, Rex thought the next morning as he left the hotel with Kit's nutria coat on his arm. Cloudless blue sky above majestic white-capped mountains. Brilliant sunshine. A slight breeze, pine-scented.

Horses everywhere. Cowboys and cowgirls, amateur and professional, ranchers and their families, town dignitaries, business men and women, soldiers and sailors and aviators, were milling outside the arena, a crowd which for a few hours was playing at forgetting care and heartbreaking anxiety. The bray of a mule. The bellows of long-horned steers mixed with the shouts of hawkers and the beat and throb of the military band from the Fort.

A fanfare of trumpets. The parade had started. His pulses picked up as they had when he was a boy at his first rodeo. This was going to be a riot. Where was Kit? They were to meet here at ten-thirty. Couldn't be that anxiety for Ma Snell was keeping her. He had telephoned the hospital. The patient had come through the operation well.

"Stars and Stripes Forever" — the burst of music from the Fort band passing in a truck brought his attention back to the present and to the impressive Grand Marshal on a white horse carrying the Flag. Followed the Queen surrounded by her ladies of the court in resplendent riding costumes, on horses culled from the finest in the county. That would go for the girls, too. The dark-haired rider looked like Kit. Boy, it was Kit on a thoroughbred. The bay sidled and pranced as if aware that he was carrying the top of the pick. She saw him, laughed, waved and called: —

" 'High lights in the world of sports.' "

She was a person he never had seen before. A spirit out of captivity. His eyes stung. Besides maiming, killing, torturing men and turning cities and towns into shambles the brutes on the warpath were trampling the hearts of women. For an instant the colorful parade turned into broken, smashed trees beside a road, thrown into relief against a dark sky by the spotlights of bulldozers as they shoved and turned and pulled. Fountains of soft earth spurted up as a shell exploded.

Impatiently he flung off the spell of memory. Had Kit passed? There she was. His eyes followed her. Where had she acquired the fringed chaps, short green skirt, orange satin blouse? Her Stetson had a silver band and her fringed gloves were as white as her hat. That color scheme would make an indelible impression on anyone who saw it.

She was out of sight before he realized that he had been too stunned with surprise at her presence in the parade to return her wave. Men riders in broad-brimmed hats, coiled ropes at saddle forks, followed the women. A satin-skinned gray reared and backed out of place at a strident blat from the school band behind.

"Ride 'em cowboy!" the crowd shouted. The horseman waved his Stetson in a theatrical flourish in response. His triumphant eyes met Rex's. Skip Cane.

No reason in the world why he shouldn't be here, and every reason that he should, Rex assured himself to counteract the sense of apprehension the cowhand's presence caused.

"Skip's ridin' high, wide an' handsome, ain't he?" a voice drawled behind him.

"What fer? That's what I'd like to know," a second voice answered. "Every job he's had since he got his time from the Double H he's been told to roll his bed an' git down the road after a couple of weeks. He ain't been drinkin' hard lately. That means somethin' with that tough hombre. It's my guess he's gettin' ready to pull a fast one. Come on, let's give a look at the cows before the show starts."

"Jest a minute, here come the kids on their ponies. Ain't they cute all dolled up in red, white an' blue?"

Rex's eyes rested unseeingly on the children on their shaggy mounts. His mind was busy tying up the look of triumph in Skip Cane's eyes with the conversation he had overheard. He was pulling a "fast one," the speaker had conjectured. Would the fast one have repercussions at the Double H?

"Her last words were 'Watch out — J — Jack — '" Kit's whispered report of Ma Snell's warning slipped into the pattern of his thoughts. Were Skip and Ezra Dodge working together? Was Jack Singley in the combine? If so, where did Ma Snell fit into the scheme?

"Quite a show. Quite a show," Seth Carter wheezed beside him. "Notice the mare Miss Marlowe was riding? That's our Sunny San, that bay is going places as a Blue Ribbon winner."

"Both girl and horse are tops. What took Kit into the parade?"

"Sally's friend who was to ride our entry lost her nerve at the last minute. Sally got in touch with Miss Marlowe at the hospital last night, thought it would give her a big kick to be part of the show, fixed her up this morning with her own cowgirl regalia so she could take the welsher's place. We're going back to the Circle Q tomorrow. I've given the Doc's prescription a fair trial, now I want to go home. Come on, let's go look over the cattle."

Kit was leaning with arms on the rail of a pen in which a wild-eyed cayuse was pawing the ground when he finally caught up with her. Her cheeks were pink, her eyes glowed with excitement, she was laughing as she looked up at — Rex blinked and looked again. Right the first time. The man in the red and green plaid shirt, blue pants and spurred high tan leather boots was Skip Cane.

"See who's here?" the cowboy said and clapped on his Stetson at a rakish angle. "Howdy, Rex. Out of the Army, I see. Going to put on your bulldogging specialty today?"

Rex caught the flash of warning in the girl's eyes before she laughed.

"If you are not, Mr. Cane is staging a show, especially for me, aren't you?" she demanded.

"Sure." The cowhand swaggered. "What's more, I'll divvy the prize I win with you, even if I did half promise it to Lois last evenin'."

"Lois L — " Kit swallowed the rest of the name. "Give all of it to her, I don't want it. What's the shouting?"

"The announcer is calling the riders. Watch me do my stuff, ma'am." Cane dodged and pushed his way through the crowd and disappeared.

"What's it all about?" Rex demanded of the girl beside him. "Did Skip have the nerve to speak to you?"

"I spoke to him. What did he mean by referring to Lois as if he had known her for ages?"

"He must be the cowhand Cal Smiley promised the Langleys he would introduce to them last evening. Why did you speak to him? For the love of Mike, why stir up that snake?"

"Because he is a snake. Because when I saw Ma Snell this morning at the hospital for a minute she opened her eyes, whispered, 'Watch Skip— He—' Then she drifted off again."

"First Ezra, next Jack, then Skip Cane. She must have something pretty serious on her mind to carry it through her unconsciousness like that. Anything more about the mysterious Jack?"

"No. I hated to leave her but I was on duty all night in one of the wards and the Head insisted that I come here. Said I needed the change. Is that my coat on your arm?"

"You left it at the Carters'. You'll need it before the show is over so I brought it. I couldn't believe my eyes when I saw you in the parade."

"I don't wonder. In this outfit of what the current stylists call 'courageous colors,' I'm something to write home about. The bugle! What does it mean?"

"That the Show is on. Let's go. Why are you waiting?" Her dark eyes seemed enormous as they met his. The blood had drained from her face.

"I — I — just saw Swede Olsen staring at me as if — if — I shouldn't be here. Didn't you notice the cowhand in the purple and white satin shirt?"

"No. I saw Olsen for a moment in the bunkhouse, he beat it before I could see his face."

"His eyes gave me the queerest feeling. It — it sneaked up on me and tightened my throat."

"That cockeyed Ouija-board prophecy of Ma Snell's is getting in on all of us." He slipped his hand under her arm. "Come on. We're sitting with the Carters. And as for that queer feeling, forget it. 'Trouble' will have to crawl over my dead body to touch you."

XVII

THEY passed chutes and catch pens on their way to the grandstand on one side of the arena.

"How gay it is. Everyone seems on top of the world. The place b-blazes with color. All right, laugh. I'll admit that catch in my voice was pure excitement," Kit conceded gaily.

"My laugh was relief that your depression of a few minutes ago had vanished. It's a treat to see someone keyed to concert pitch about what is old hat to me."

"It may be old hat, mister, but you're loving it, aren't you?"

"That's right. Here we are."

The Carters, Shep Trask and Bob Trent, a young lieutenant from the Fort, were already in their seats when Rex and Kit joined them, as were a few hundreds more, ranchers, their families and friends. They snuggled in warm coats for while the sun beat down on them a chilling breeze blew from the snow-capped mountains.

Something like a slightly denatured bedlam of immeasurable decibels stilled as a roar from the loud-speaker announced the first event on the program. A blare of music and the show was on.

Rex's eyes were on the two rope spinners but his mind was busy with the significance of Ma Snell's warning. Could it be tied up in any way with that scorched piece of blue denim he had pulled out of the stove in the line rider's camp? What had Blaney done about that? Had he decided it wasn't worth following up?

Where did Skip Cane fit in? That he would be mixed up in deviltry went without saying, but the Ezra Dodge angle pulled all calculations out of focus. Why had the range-rider-blacksmith induced Ma Snell to say she would marry him this afternoon? Why the rush? To give him a certain standing for what he intended to do? Was the prospective bridegroom here? The news that Ma Snell was about to take a fourth husband had been so surprising he hadn't thought to ask Kit to describe the man. "The minute she laid eyes on him she knew he was mixed up in 'terrible trouble,'" Ma Snell had said. Was that same "trouble" taking him to Mystery Gorge?

Her mention of "Jack" made the rest of her warning seem part of a fevered dream induced by pain and narcotics. Jack Singley was as straight as they come. Why concentrate on him? Why assume she referred to her brother-in-law? There were other Jacks in the world. Might be one among the hands at the Double H.

"He's a trifle old for it but we need a little extra money awful bad." Jane Singley's acid voice echoed through his memory. Before this, men straight as Jack had been tempted by "extra money" but what form had the lure taken for him, if it were he, was the sixty-four-dollar question.

"They are like acrobats in cowboy costume with tap-dancing feet." Kit's eager comment recalled his attention to the colorful arena. "What are they doing now?"

"Back flips. Watch those leaps. They are making the butterfly and wedding-ring loops. Boy, they're good."

"Good. They're sensational. They seem young. How come they escaped the draft?"

"A cowhand gets many serious knockouts in his work. Many

of the men here today are what they call 'stove-up inside' and are unfit for Army service. They may do some wild stunts occasionally but it gets them."

"What's coming now?"

"Saddle bronc riding. The first entry is from the Circle Q. Here he is." Rex was on his feet as a wild-eyed, bucking, kicking cayuse with a rider clinging to his back catapulted into the arena, leaving a trail of dust. "Boy, that's a vicious brute he's picked."

"He's been thrown. He'll be trampled if — " Shouts and groans from the crowd drowned the end of the sentence.

"Take it easy, Kit. Let's sit down." Rex laughed and touched her arm lightly. "You ain't seen nothin' yet."

"I know it. Is my face red. Your city-slicker guest is on her knees in apology. He went so high and so far I thought his back would be broken when he crashed. In the same instant I remembered you saying, 'You may even find a use here for your hospital training' and I thought, 'This is it.'

"Thank heaven, he's on his feet and grinning. If I were he, I'd wring the necks of those three cowboys on the fence harmonizing 'Yi Yi Yoopy Yay' as he hobbles out. From now on watch the gal from the effete East. She'll take the spills and like them. Hard-boiled Kathryn, that's me."

She wasn't. She flinched each time a rider flew over his mount's head and crashed, sending up a spout of dust and earth. Her long sigh registered relief when the event was over. Calf roping following with fierce competition between local cowhands and contestants from outside the state.

"Skip Cane told me he had entered this event and here he is," Kit observed as the tall, lithe figure in gay cowboy regalia swaggered into the arena.

"He's good and knows it," Rex replied as he watched Cane

expertly rope his calf. When announced the winner he swept off his dark blue Stetson and impressively bowed to the grandstand.

"My word, he beamed that acknowledgment straight at the Langleys, Kit," Sally Carter, beside her, confided in what she intended to be a whisper, but was loud enough to reach Rex. "Theatrical, what? Hollywood should be that cowhand's home."

"Where are the Langleys? Thought they were to sit with you."

"Lois and I exchanged a few poison-gas bombs — verbal — last evening, and she and her mother walked out on us. Gave me a chance to invite Bob Kent and Shep to sit here. Perhaps I was pretty rough, but she rated it."

"Where are they now?"

"In the front row with Cal Smiley. I saw them before the parade. Something tells me that the tentacles of Mother L. are gently closing round woman-proof Cal. Skip Cane completed the foursome. Lois slipped her hand under the cowboy's arm and they walked away. I bet she appears later with the silver band of his Stetson, if she doesn't get his gold tooth. That gal's an opportunist. The desk clerk at the hotel said they were checking out after lunch. I wonder — "

"What?" Kit demanded.

"I'll tell you later. It would take too much time now."

They had noon dinner at a chuck wagon in a grove of cottonwoods. The Carters with the Lieutenant, Kit and Shep Trask sat at a long plank table where they were served juicy, thick broiled steaks, mealy baked potatoes, fluffy red-gold squash on paper plates. At an adjacent table sat Cal Smiley entirely surrounded by Langleys.

"Is it a mirage or do I really see steak?" Kit demanded. "The smell of that broiling meat makes me ravenous." She was seated between Seth Carter and Shep Trask. "Aren't you hungry?" she asked Rex, who stood behind her.

"I am, but I've just spotted an old friend of Uncle Pete's, Sam Ruthven. I'll eat with him and bone up on state politics et al.," he answered before he turned away. He wouldn't explain that the grim set of Trask's lips and the glint in his eyes gave assurance that he intended to keep his place beside her.

What was Lois's idea flattering Skip Cane? Hadn't she sense enough to know he was dynamite, he wondered, as he turned away. Last evening when she had tucked her arm under his in the hotel lounge she had begged him to take her to the rodeo. His curt "Nothing doing" had gotten across. The expression of her eyes, even in retrospect, sent a shiver along his nerves.

"Glad to see you back, Rex." Tall, heavy Sam Ruthven wrung his hand in a grip which threatened to crush the bones. "And from your civvies, looks like you've come to stay. Eat at this table for two with me, unless you have a girl in tow."

"I'm a free lance for the present, sir." Rex drew out the wooden chair and faced the ruddy-faced, gray-haired man across the table. He was a great rancher who bought and sold many heads of cattle each year. A man of education, executive ability, upon whose judgment one could depend. Perhaps he could supply a clue to Ma Snell's warning.

"Sorry you felt you must sell the Double H." Rex was becoming accustomed to that expression of regret. His uncle's old friends said it as soon as they saw him. "Hate to see you young fellas giving up ranching."

"A young man has bought it. 'A swell guy, the making of a real stockman,' Joe Carr says. Richard Marlowe was a lawyer before he became a flyer. He can be a help in Washington."

"I've met him and sized him up. That sister of his is something to write home about, what? He may be just what we need. We've got a ceiling price on live cattle to fight and there's the Jackson Hole controversy, not settled yet — but soon. I'll sound him out. If he's okay we could push him along when we reach the fight on the allocation of the waters of the Colorado River. That's when we'll need all our top engineers, Rex, so thank God you're back whole — and I hope to stay."

"I'm glad you feel I can be of use here if I'm not a rancher. Everything I had or have came from this state, I figure it's up to me to put something back into it in return. Uncle Pete knew I wouldn't be a cattleman. He approved of the engineering course."

"Sure, I know. I reckon you both had the right idea. With this state becoming one of the great oil reservoirs, we need engineers. The mountain states lead the nation in the production of expert scientists and professional men, but, hang it all, they don't stay, they beat it for the East. Now they are caught up in this global cataclysm. So are we stockmen, with 11,676,-000 acres of grazing land in military use where bombs whiz down on bombing ranges, artillery fire screams on artillery ranges, planes take off from airfields and troops slug and squirm through basic training on some of the best grazing land in the world. War is hell in other ways than slaughter and material destruction, my boy."

"You've said it. It also starts a gigantic crime wave. The black markets here and abroad are a sample. This steak is done to a turn. The blood follows the knife, as Uncle Pete liked it. I had forgotten potatoes could be so white and fluffy. Seen any indications of it here, sir? I mean the crime wave, not black markets."

"Plenty. There's a lot of petty thieving — rationing accounts for that, probably, and two truckloads of my cattle on the way to the city to be shipped to Chicago were highjacked."

"Hi — jack!"

"Why the excitement? Have you never before heard the word? It's getting to be quite an industry in these parts."

"Sure, I've heard of it." Rex swallowed his heart which had zoomed to his throat as the word "jacked" clicked into the vacant space in a pattern. "I remember now, Joe Carr told me there had been an outbreak here. Any trace of your cattle?"

"Not even a hoofprint. They have vanished as completely as the legendary 'dead tough' who disappeared in Mystery Gorge with loot and pony."

The vision of a tire track with a dent flashed on the screen of Rex's memory.

"You haven't thought they might be hidden there, have you?"

"In Mystery Gorge? If they are, the thieves were from out of the state; there isn't a man within hundreds of miles who would venture there if the bribe was piled to the sky. The belief that somewhere in the Gorge bottom is a huge crack through which they might disappear makes them Stop, Look, Listen. Crazy idea, but it persists."

"I was so impressed by the horror of the story as a boy that the place was out of bounds for me. There's the bugle. The first afternoon event will be the relay races. We mustn't miss them. It has been great to see you, sir."

"The same here. Take care of yourself, boy. You're one of the state's assets, remember."

A man's voice singing "Home on the Range" was coming through the loud-speaker when Rex reached the arena. Apparently no one was listening. The babble of voices punctuated by excited laughter was deafening. The crowd had lunched well, if not too wisely, and was in the mood to take anything and everything in its stride. In the afternoon session the high tide of daring and danger would be climaxed by bulldogging.

In the grandstand Cal Smiley and Lieutenant Kent were with Sally, Trask was seated beside Kit. That settled it. He wouldn't be the spare in that combine. He watched the show from an empty space outside the fence on which perched the three singing cowboys. Relay races were followed by trick and fancy riding by girls who traveled from rodeo to rodeo putting on their show. They were good, but Sally Carter was adept in most of their stuff.

A deafening blare of music announced the last event on the program. The crowd went wild with excitement as two men on stocky horses rode into the arena. An enormous steer tore out of the chute, kicking up clouds of dust, to be greeted by shouts and hand-clapping. One of the riders kept pace with it.

With dismay, which had nothing to do with Ma Snell's warning, Rex recognized him. Jack Singley was the dogger, whose stunt was to jump from the back of his galloping horse to the horns of the steer and attempt to throw him while the hazer on the other side kept the animal from ducking away.

"Jack's too old, he's too heavy, he's too slow." Rex didn't realize he was protesting aloud till one of the cowboys on the fence grinned at him.

"You don't need tell him, mister. He's goin' to be shown, an' how," he prophesied gleefully.

The arena was still enough now, the crowd was holding its collective breath. The hazer rode on the fence side of the steer to prevent it from ducking as Jack made his leap. The singing cowboy swore colorfully.

"The hazer's hoss is too slow. He can't keep up."

"Boy, oh, boy, Jack can't make it," Rex exclaimed as the steer, unguarded by the hazer, ducked back just as Singley made his wild leap. He sailed over the animal's head and struck the earth with a splintering crash. A woman screamed. The crowd roared. Groaned. The terrified steer plunged round and round the arena till a rope settled on its horns and jerked it toward an open gate.

"Heck, I reckon that guy's through bulldoggin' fer life," one of the cowboys on the fence prophesied audibly in the tense silence which held the crowd in a spell of horror.

The motionless figure on the ground was carried out on a stretcher borne by two hospital internes. The second rider followed leading the two horses by their bridles. State troopers appeared as if conjured from the air by a magician. The singing cowboys chanted "Empty Saddles." Silently the crowd moved from the arena. The rodeo was over.

"Was — he — was he killed?" a low breathless voice beside Rex inquired.

"Kit." He could feel her shiver. "How did you get here through that crowd? You're white. Come on, let's get out."

"I tried to get to him to help, but a doctor from the ambulance was doing what needed to be done. I had to find you. The dogger was Jack Singley, Sally told me. If he's the 'Jack' Ma Snell was warning us about — "

"Here's half the prize I promised you, ma'am." Skip Cane, hatless, smiling, blocked their way.

"Miss Marlowe told you she didn't want the money, Skip, that settles it."

"An' who do you think you are, mixin' into my private business, Danton? You keep out of this."

Rex opened his lips, snapped them shut as Kit's hand gripped his right sleeve.

"You'll both keep out of it. I told you I didn't want half of your prize money, Cane. I always mean what I say."

"Is that so? They're sayin' round town you bulldogged Rex

into agreeing he would marry you, when he was all set with another dame. Looks like he was the guy who don't mean what — "

"I'm not in uniform now."

A fist shot out. The blow cracked like a pistol shot. Cane went down.

"Another redman bit the dust," Rex said through grim lips. "Come on, Kit." He seized her arm and hurried her along. "Cane is getting up. Can't stop to knock him down again. We must reach Ma Snell before she hears what happened to Jack."

"Where did he pick up that gossip about you and me? Are they saying round town that I — "

"Don't you know where that came from? You heard Sally say that Lois was walking with Skip Cane, didn't you? They both have it in for me. Forget it."

"I wish I could. I — " She clutched his sleeve. "Don't look now, but in a minute turn around," she whispered. "The tall man with the weathered cowboy look, in fringed chaps, black and white checked shirt and green plaid waistcoat and the huge white Stetson, hurrying across the arena toward us, is the happy bridegroom."

Rex wheeled. The man stopped as if he had been shot. Rex caught the flash of incredulity in small dark eyes.

"He's disappeared in the crowd," Kit exclaimed. "I was sure he was coming to ask me about Ma Snell."

"So that was Ezra Dodge!" Rex exclaimed. "*Ezra Dodge* from New England."

"Have you ever seen him before? I can't tell whether you are laughing or excited."

"Neither, gal, neither. I was thinking how surprised he'd be if he knew his love-making hadn't jelled, or would he? Come on, let's find Jane. She may need our help."

XVIII

WHAT shall we tell Jane Singley if she inquires for Ma Snell?" Kit asked on their way to the hospital in clear, frosty mountain air, under an indigo sky silver-gilt with stars.

"I doubt if she thinks of her. If she does, I'll answer," Rex replied.

He had been right. White and tense the woman stood at the window of the reception room staring unseeingly out into the night. Grief had obliterated any lesser anxiety.

"Nothing you can do for me, Rex," she replied to his offer of help. "Jack's gone. He didn't want to try bulldogging again, but — " She put her hand to her throat as if she were choking. "I'll never forgive myself. I prodded him into it. Hetty was furious, said I always had bossed the spirit out of him and I guess I had." A hard, dry sob followed the admission.

"Jack didn't feel that way about it, Jane. He was proud of your head for business, told me once that he wouldn't have made good without your advice."

"Did he say that really, Rex?" The woman's eagerness tightened Kit's throat.

"Those are exactly his words, Jane."

"Thank you. That helps. I'd better get back to 'Licia, now. She was crazy about her daddy. How — how *can* I tell her he won't come home again — ever?" She was sobbing under her breath as she left the room.

"Tough luck," Rex said. "I can't believe that Jack Singley was mixed up in a shady transaction as Ma Snell implied to you. Curtain on that, Kit, it is finished as far as you and I are concerned. Planning to stay here tonight?"

"Yes. I am needed."

"Then hop out of that cowgirl regalia. I will return it to Sally, bring your clothes here and leave the suitcase at the desk."

"You're a lightning-change artist," he approved, when she returned in a Nurses' Aide uniform ten minutes later. "Here's my office phone number. Report to me at once if Ma Snell is sufficiently conscious to explain her warning. The second number is my apartment where I will make my headquarters. Don't lose it. It isn't in the book. Give me a ring Saturday at the office. Sunday at the apartment. Remember I'm on call to drive you to the Double H when you are ready to go."

As she tucked the slip of paper into her apron pocket Kit had the breathless sense that she was being pushed adrift on a shoreless ocean in a tricky rubber boat.

"What's the matter?" His voice was rough with concern. He laid his arm about her shoulder.

"Nothing. I had forgotten for a minute that big girls don't get panicky. I must go. Good night."

At noon the next day a cadet nurse in gray uniform spoke to Kit.

"Phone call for you, Miss Marlowe."

She slipped the thermometer she had been cleaning into its case before she hurried along the corridor to the telephone. Who would call her here?

"Kathryn Marlowe speaking."

"Joe Carr at the Double H."

"Joe! *Joe!* What has happened? *Dick?*"

"Now don't you go bein' scared. Your brother's okay, Kit, but it's my guess he needs you terrible bad."

"I don't understand."

"You will when you get here. Don't ever tell him I phoned you, though. Why don't you answer?"

"I'm thinking how I can get home. I'll work it out."

"Be quick that's all. Come if you have to walk."

"Joe! Joe! Tell me *why* I am needed." A click at the other end of the line was the answer.

What did it mean? Rex had said he would drive her to the ranch when she was ready. Better try him first; after that, Sally. She dialed.

"Colonel Danton is out of town," a woman's voice replied to her question. "Any message?"

"Tell him Miss Marlowe phoned. That she has been called back to the Double H suddenly — *suddenly*. That's all."

Queer, he said he would be on call to take her home. He knew she had intended to stay until Sunday night and this was only Saturday, that was the answer. If she didn't have better luck with Sally, then what? It took time to get the hotel call through.

"Sally Carter speaking."

Kit explained.

"Jeepers, what do you think has happened? Has Dick been hurt? I just couldn't bear it."

"Joe said he was all right, but that he needed me 'terrible bad.' "

"I bet I know. I *bet* I know. Hurry. We want to be in at the finish."

"What finish? What do you mean, Sally?"

"Nothing. That was my sense of the dramatic getting in a lick. How soon can you be ready?"

"I have lunch trays to prepare, a couple of surgical beds to make and a date with the Blood Donor Center at two. As apparently Dick isn't suffering — I can't let them down here. Say three o'clock?"

"I'll come to the hospital. I'll bring Shep Trask if it's okay with you. He says you walked out on him last night and is he sore."

"Good heavens, while we were having lunch at the chuck wagon, I promised to dine with him. In the excitement of Jack Singley's accident and my eagerness to help here, I haven't thought of him since. He won't forgive that in a hurry. Thanks for giving me a chance to square myself with him — if I can. Hope I'm not upsetting your plans for the week end."

"Nope. The family is moving back to the Circle Q today. I'll be seeing you."

How could she have forgotten Shep so completely? The shock of Jack Singley's accident and the effect it might have on his sister-in-law was the answer.

Before she changed from her uniform Kit went to Ma Snell's room. The woman's big china-blue eyes were amazingly clear as they looked up at her while she deftly turned the pillows.

"You're awful cute in that light blue an' white rig an' the cap, dearie. Well, here I am, all my sufferin' behind me." Gone was the breathless tension of the night before last. Her voice was weak but not terrified as it had been then.

Kit knelt beside the bed.

"I'm happy that you feel so well, Ma Snell. Now — " she lowered her voice — "you'll be able to explain what you were trying so hard to tell me the night you came here. You were all mixed up about Ezra and Skip Cane and Jack and Rex and I being in danger. Did you mean Jack Singley, your brother-in-law?"

The big blue eyes narrowed, the large mouth twitched in a smile. Both were back to normal so quickly that Kit wondered if she had imagined the change.

"Well now, dearie, did I say all that? It was the dope they give me, mixed my ideas up, that an' knowin' Jack was a plumb fool at his age to try bulldoggin', an' realizin' my wedding to Ezra'd have to be postponed. Ouija didn't tip me off about that."

"But, Ma Snell, you said —"

"Now, now, you a Nurses' Aide an' not knowin' how folks' minds can get mixed up by fever. I was scared. My will's made but I was afraid I might step out of this world without havin' left a list of my things as I wanted them to go. I have another sister besides Jane. Christmas, how they'd fight over my belongin's. *Things* make a sight more trouble in families than money, remember that, dearie. Reckon I had bats in the belfry when I asked the nurse to send for you. See those pretty flowers someone sent me?" She nodded toward a tall vase of mammoth yellow chrysanthemums on the dresser. "They're awful cheerful, ain't they? You don't have to stay any longer. You'd better get back to the Double H. I don't need you and your brother does." She was too loquacious. The chatter about belongings and the flowers was a cover-up, Kit decided.

"What do you mean, my brother needs me, Ma Snell?"

"Christmas, I didn't mean to frighten you. You came to the Double H to be with him, didn't you?"

"I did." Kit rose from her knees and looked down at the pale, faintly smiling face on the pillow.

"I'm going." She laid her hand gently on the short white curls. "I don't know what it's all about, Ma Snell, but you haven't fooled me for a minute. You were desperately worried the night you came here. It wasn't *all* dope. Hurry up and come back to the ranch. The hands miss you. Something tells me that as a cook I haven't made such a hit."

Ready to leave, dressed in the tangerine outfit, with a patch of surgeon's tape on her left arm, Kit spoke to the nurse.

"Mrs. Snell appears to be bouncing back from the operation like a rubber ball, Miss Murdock."

"Lucky." The nurse's eyes were set in dark circles of fatigue. "We have to railroad patients out of here fast to make way for others."

"Does she know of the fatal accident to her brother-in-law?"

"Was the rodeo bulldogger her sister's husband? Glory be, tough as she is, that news might set her back. You didn't mention it, did you?"

"No. I wouldn't, until I knew if you thought it wise. We had other things to talk about. Remember the first night she was here, how anxious she was to see me?"

"Sure. She had us phone your ranch, made us promise we wouldn't operate until every chance of your coming was gone. I thought perhaps she was suffering from a guilty conscience."

"Do you think her mind was clear?"

"Clear as it could be with a lot of dope in her. She didn't ramble on, though, as many of them do. Seemed as if she were saving her strength for something special."

And I'm sure that "something special" was what she tried to tell me, Kit thought before the nurse added: —

"Isn't she a wonder? She insisted upon having that blond wig on an' her face made up before her beau came to see her."

"Her *beau?* Came *here?*"

"Sure, just before lunch. Didn't you see those outsize chrysanthemums he brought her? My, she was tickled. If it had been me, I'd rather have red roses, more class. He told the

Head they were to have been married after the rodeo yesterday. He'd been about crazy trying to locate her."

"And the Head fell for that?"

"Fell for it! What d'you mean, 'fell for it'? He was almost
her husband, wasn't he?"

"Yes, yes, I suppose he was. Were you impressed?"

"Not my type. Tall. Rather good-looking. Just another
middle-age cowboy. Kind of like a range rider in a Western,
fringed leather chaps, shirt like a checkerboard, under a green
waistcoat, the plaid so loud it would drown out a band. Think
of a woman her age getting a husband, to say nothing of one
like him. She told me she'd had three. Some folks have all the
luck. And was the guy anxious to see her. You'd have thought
he was a young soldier leaving his first girl to go to war. Sorry
you have to go, Miss Marlowe, your help was a godsend. Hope
the sudden call home doesn't mean trouble and that you'll find
everything fine at the ranch. Come again."

So, that is why Ma Snell changed her story, Kit thought as
she walked slowly along the corridor. Ezra Dodge had seen
her. Had he threatened her? Was Skip Cane mixed up in the
"terrible trouble"? Where had the cowboy picked up the story
of the crazy announcement about Rex and herself at Mountain
Lodge? That answer was easy. Hadn't Sally seen Lois turning on her charm as she walked with him? Rex had said, "Forget it." She'd better, pronto. There were important things to
be done. She must get word to him about Ma Snell's switch
from terror to complacency. She didn't know his address for a
letter. She would phone him from the ranch.

Shepherd Trask was standing beside Sally's roadster when
she reached it. Without speaking he took her week-end case
and placed it in the rumble. Sally, in a short mink jacket over

a navy frock and matching beret that set her hair shining like red-gold in contrast, winked at her.

"Storm warning. Cold wind blowing in from the Divide," she whispered. Aloud she said: —

"Sit next to me, Kit. Hop in beside her, Shep, this seat is plenty wide for three. All set? We're off."

Off to find what? From the corners of her eyes Kit glanced at the man at her right. His black Homburg was pulled down, his mouth was a grim line. "Storm warning" was right. Sorry as she was that she had forgotten him, she would wait for him to speak.

She drew a deep breath. An October afternoon. Air crystal-clear set her blood tingling. Faint violet cloud smudges like the matrix of a turquoise on the cold blue sky. Coppery brown foothills. Towering purple ranges with glinting patches which were lakes. Above them, seemingly near, but in reality miles away, loomed peak above snow-capped peak, colossal in their grandeur, like sentinels guarding the world below. If only she had reached Rex to report Ma Snell's contradiction of the warning she had muttered night before last, even with the uncertainty of the reason Joe Carr had called her home, she could enjoy every moment ahead.

The city and its highway left behind, the roadster sped swiftly along roads that wound through a sea of sagebrush, past acres of rich, dark soil freshly plowed — from which crows rose like a black cloud — cut by a creek rushing madly from the foothills. A cock pheasant, iridescent with color, skurried into the brush. Two cottontail rabbits in a field sat up on their haunches to see them pass. A little wind whispered among the cottonwoods and hackberry groves.

"Her head will drop off in a minute." Sally's laughing voice roused Kit from the Nirvana of peace into which she had slipped. "Better forget your mad and let her park it on your shoulder, Shep."

She sat erect with a start.

"Was I asleep? I wouldn't put it past me, I was on duty two nights at the hospital and this car runs smooth as cream. Good heavens, how long have I been in a comatose state? The sun has slipped behind the highest mountain peak and has streaked the west with color. Those streamers of crimson wave like Northern Lights."

"That's a rhetorical comeback for a gal who was lost to the world," Sally jibed. "Must have been the suggestion of your shoulder as a parking place which shocked her awake, Shep. My little pleasantry doesn't bring response from the gent at your right, Kit. As we appear to have reached a conversational bottleneck, how about music?" She twisted the dial of the radio.

"Let's plan a life together," a tenor voice pleaded.

"That's not so good either under the circumstances." Sally giggled and shut off the song. "Now what, Kit?"

"Let's talk. When I lapsed into a somnolent state I was try-ing to think what will be the outstanding memory of the rodeo in time to come, blacking-out the accidents and tragedy. The color and crowd or that delectable juicy steak? To what will you hand the Oscar, Shep? Come out of your foxhole of anger. I forgot my date with you. So what? It wasn't a crime, was it?"

"I came here to tell you something very important to me — Kit." He had spoken. That meant he was emerging from his hurt, little-boy sulk. She had been up against it before. She slipped her hand under his arm.

"I know you did, Shep. Sometime I'll tell you why I forgot and you'll understand, won't you? You always do understand me, don't you?"

Sally coughed.

"I'm still here, boys and girls of the radio audience."

Shepherd Trask laughed and Kit knew she was forgiven — this time.

"Sally, you haven't the mistaken idea you'd ever qualify for a mouse-in-the-wall role, have you?" he asked. "You fairly vibrate with life. Isn't that the Double H ahead?"

"It is. Large as life. I thought from Joe's hurry-up call, it might have burned to the ground." Kit leaned forward. "Are there two spirals of smoke rising from the guest house? Smoke denotes fires and fires there denote company. Ma Snell's Ouija prophesied it, but perhaps I'm still sleepy and just seeing things?"

"They're real, all right. Unless I miss my guess, smoke is not all that you'll see when you get there," Sally declared cryptically and shot the roadster ahead.

XIX

WITH A LOUD honk! honk! of the horn, Sally stopped the car at the gate in the white fence. As if he had been waiting for the signal Dick Marlowe dashed from the front door and down the path.

"Thank the Lord you've come, Kit," he greeted breathlessly. "Did you have a hunch I needed you? Hi, Infant! Where did you drop from, Shep? Pile out, all of you. I need your help. I'm trying to serve tea."

"What's it all about, Dick?" Kit asked as side by side they walked along the path. His right hand clutched her arm as if he feared she might break away. "For whom are you serving or trying to serve tea?"

"The Langleys. They moved into the guest house yesterday bag and baggage."

"The *Langleys!*" Kit whirled. "Did you know they were here?" she demanded of Sally Carter who was following with Shepherd Trask.

"My sixth sense suggested that they might have sped to the side of poor, lonely Richard," she answered and laughed.

"Cut out that 'poor, lonely stuff,' Infant," Dick flared.

"Yes, Captain," she said meekly and wrinkled her nose at him.

"Stop fencing with Sally, Dick," Kit protested impatiently. "In a minute we'll be at the door. Post me as to what happened, then I will know the line to take. Did you invite the Langleys to come while I was away?"

"For Pete's sake, do you think I'm a darn fool? What do I want of a couple of women hanging round with, 'Do ride with me this morning, *darling*.' 'A little game of gin rummy, Richard, it will rest your mind.' Rest my mind! Phooey. The only rest I want is to get those cattle ready for shipping." He was white with anger. The scar on his left cheek stood out like a fiery ring. "Do you think I'd double-cross you by inviting them while you were away, Kit?"

"I don't, Dick. I was so surprised I said the first thing that came into my mind. Did they explain why they came?"

"Said they knew you were to spend the week end at the hospital. They were sure I would be lonely. Lonely, my eye! They must think I'm a moron. Make Sally stay over Sunday, will you?"

"If I can. She and Lois are not very friendly. Your guests will doubtless be mad as the proverbial Hatter when they see me. Come in. Let's get it over."

What would she say, what line had she better take, Kit asked herself as her brother held open the front door for her. Dusk was stealing down from the mountains. Even though the two women had forced themselves in, it was too late in the afternoon now to suggest that they return to Mountain Lodge, that the guest house was needed for Shepherd Trask.

She stopped on the threshold of the living room. Lois in a turquoise wool frock, a band of the same color binding her blond hair, was seated at the low table. She looked up. A large diamond in a ring on her right hand, in which she had lifted the teapot, shot out a thousand rainbow sparks. The Marlowe silver reflected the quivering, leaping flames of the fireplace. Mrs. Langley, a lavender cardigan over her black dress, who was perched on the arm of the wing chair, smoking and scowling at the fire, sprang to her feet.

"Thank heaven you've come!" she exclaimed.

"Well, see who's here," Lois purred. "Just in time for the cup that cheers. I didn't know you expected a party, Dick," she added reproachfully as he followed his sister and Sally into the room with Shepherd Trask at his heels. "I hope Chang Loo won't mind this influx of guests, he didn't look too happy when he brought over our breakfast this morning. Tell him I'd like more of those delectable hot hors d'oeuvres at once, darling."

"The perfect hostess," Sally murmured in a tone designed to carry.

"Cut it, Infant," Dick growled *sotto voce*.

"Yes, Captain. Yes, sir," Sally agreed meekly and chuckled.

"Must have been thought transference that prompted you to have tea ready for us, Lois," Kit approved as she removed her tangerine shag coat and laid it across a chair. "Sally, shed that fur jacket. This room must be up to ninety. We'll have our tea. Then we'll take our bags upstairs and make ourselves lovely for din — supper."

"Is Miss Carter here for the week end?" Lois's eyebrows arched expressively.

Sally, who had opened her lips in protest when Kit had assumed she was staying, grinned.

"Sure, I'm here for the week end, so is Shep. When we heard that you and your mother had come, Kit said, 'Let's make it a real party.' And here we are."

"How did you hear?" Lois demanded.

"Underground. Marvelous system we have in the mountain states," Sally answered. "I could die eating these hors d'oeuvres. If eyes could talk, yours would say, 'Pity you don't,' wouldn't they, Lois? Shep, you haven't spoken since you came into the room."

"Just too hungry to talk," Shepherd Trask answered. "Now that I find Dick surrounded by cheerful company, I'm asking myself, 'Was this trip necessary?'"

"That's exactly what I'm thinking," Mrs. Langley declared. "Lois dragged me here because Richard would be alone. Now that he won't be I am returning to Mountain Lodge. Cal Smiley promised to be there. It is our gin-rummy night and I don't intend to miss it. You're coming with me, Lois."

"It's too late, Mother."

"It is *not. We are going.* We — "

"Will you excuse me for a few minutes, while you decide what to do?" Kit broke into the angry discussion. "I'll run across to Joe Carr's cottage for *Charlie.*"

"That vicious Airedale!" Lois shuddered. "I told the foreman not to let him loose while we are here."

"I'll see that he doesn't get in your way before you depart — if your mother insists upon leaving this afternoon. If you are going it would be wise to start, pronto. Wait here for me, Sally. I won't be a minute. Dick, look after Shep. Don't let him get the silly idea that he isn't welcome as the flowers in the spring, tra-la — "

"No one would suspect from the way you tossed off that pleasantry, Kathryn, you were flaming with rage," Kit assured herself as she started for Joe Carr's cottage beyond the bunkhouse.

The white tops of the mountains were purple against the afterglow. The days were shortening. Could she take it when winter really came? There she was, spang up against the Wailing Wall again. Lucky the men who were slogging through mud and snow, slashing through jungles to keep her safe, didn't weep against that same Wall.

In response to her rat-tat-tat, Joe Carr opened the door and greeted her with his split-face grin.

"Heck, here you are. Hey, young fella, go slow," he yelled at the Airedale who in a frenzy of welcome had flung himself on Kit. She dropped to her knees on the step and hugged him.

"Glad to see me back, *Charlie?* You needn't lick my face quite so hard. I know you love me." She rose. "Has he been bad while I was away, Joe? Miss Langley said he was vicious. Didn't you keep him here?"

"Sure, the dawg hasn't been inside the ranch house since you left. Bad? Cripes, no. He just didn't cotton to the ladies, that's all. He met 'em comin' from Dude's Rest. He knows quality whether it goes on two legs or four."

"Did you phone me to come home because of — of the unexpected guests, Joe?"

"You've said it. Them ladies arrived while the Boss an' me was out on the range roundin' up cattle for shippin'. They told Chang Loo they was expected an' the Chinee, knowin' nothin' better, said, 'Allee lightee, allee lightee,' and opened up the Dude's Rest for 'em, the way he used to for the Old Boss's friends. When your brother an' I rode up just before sunset an' see the smoke risin' out of the chimneys, he said, 'Who in thunder's in there?'"

"What did he do?"

"He stopped at the gate, slid out of the saddle, pitched the reins of his hoss to me, said, 'Hold everything till I come back, Joe' and stalked up to the door as if he knew the place was chockfull of Nips an' he was going to get 'em. Someone pulled open the door, a female voice squealed, 'Dick, *darling!* I've come.' I kept my back turned after that, I didn't know what to do."

"What did you do?"

"I'd got my orders. I waited. When your brother come back that big circle on his cheek was red as blood. I won't repeat what he said, it wasn't Japanese, just pure unadulterated American. They sure learn to express their feelin's in strong stuff in the service. He grabbed the reins, mounted and kicked the hoss with his heels before he bust out —

" 'All the fights aren't on the other side of the ocean or in the Pacific, Joe,' he says. 'I feel one workin' up right now at the Double H.' Cripes, it reminded me of Ma Snell's croak 'bout terrible trouble comin'."

"Did the Langleys have supper with Dick and the hands?"

"What was left here. Most of 'em was at the rodeo. I thought it over in the night while I listened fer the Boss to come home. I heard him start out on one of them wild rides. This mornin' his horse was back in the barn all lather. Didn't seem right fer him to be worried. Then when Swede Olsen asked fer his time I was plumb wore out with worry, I figured you'd better come home."

"Swede Olsen! Gone! I saw him at the rodeo yesterday afternoon."

"Sure, he and the other cowhands come back late last night an' believe it or not, Skip Cane had the nerve to come with 'em, his horse in the truck with ours. I guess none of 'em hadn't any stomach for whoopee after the spill. Terrible about Jack Singley. He'd oughter known he was too old fer bulldoggin'. He was a fine fella. Never heard him talk back to that wife of his an', heck, was she a nagger."

"Has Skip Cane gone?"

"He was off at daybreak. It's my guess he didn't want to face me. Tex reported he had a terrible black eye."

A quick dissolve as in a motion picture and Kit saw a fist lunge, heard a voice, "I'm not in uniform now, Cane." The cowboy never would forgive that blow. Thank goodness Rex was making his headquarters in town where he would be safe instead of at Rushing Creek Ranch where anything might happen.

"You're not worryin' 'cause Skip Cane bunked here, are you, Kit?"

"*No.* No. When did Olsen leave, Joe?"

"Jest before I phoned you. I figured his time an' when I saw him goin' along the road with his bedroll, dolled up in that classy outfit he wore to the rodeo, I had a hunch you'd better know how things was here."

"Did he say why he was leaving?"

"He got off a lot of stuff about me havin' it in fer him, said he couldn't do his work where he wasn't appreciated an' a lot more tripe like that. I figgered what set him off was I told him to carry firewood to the Dude's Rest fer the ladies."

"Did he do it?"

"Sure he did it. What d'ye think I'm foreman here fer if not to get things done? He was kinder strung-up an' seemed in a terrible hurry to go after that. He'd had considerable to drink at the rodeo, I figgered."

"Had he taken another job?"

"Yep. He'd contacted a stockman who needed an extra hand, said he knew I didn't like him, so snapped up the chance. Your brother hasn't said how he feels 'bout his goin' when we need every helper we can get. I suppose I could a kept him if I'd gone down on my knees, but, Swede Olsen was right. I never have liked or trusted him, besides I've heard he was seein' Skip Cane an' when that hellion come home with him last night, I got nerve screamies. It's gettin' darker, Miss Kit, you'd better trek to the house."

"The days are shortening fast, aren't they? I had to know just why you sent for me, Joe. I thought Dick might have developed symptoms about his health that worried you. I imagined a lot of other things, but I didn't think of guests. I'm sorry he went on the wild ride. I had hoped he had that impulse licked. I'm glad you phoned. Come on, *Charlie.*"

Joe had been wise to send for her, she thought as she walked slowly toward the ranch house. Her arrival had provided an excuse for Mrs. Langley to return to Mountain Lodge and Cal Smiley and their game of gin rummy. Was the spectacular diamond Lois was flashing the ring Dick had given her? Had she come to lure him into putting it on her engagement finger again? Would he do it before she left this afternoon? From Joe's account of his reaction to her arrival it seemed unlikely, but one never could tell what a man in love would do. He couldn't be so dumb as not to see what a schemer she was, or could he? He had said, "She can make a darn convincing bluff at loving."

"You can't carry him and his moods on your shoulders for the rest of his life, Kit."

Rex Danton's words echoed through her memory. He was right, Dick was a man grown, the complication was his to straighten out. If he was fooled again it was just too bad. She could do nothing to stop him.

Hard luck that Swede Olsen should leave and make him short one hand when he had the responsibility of his first shipment of cattle on his mind. Why had the cowhand left? She thought of her curious feeling of foreboding when his eyes had met hers at the rodeo. She had told him she wouldn't be there, would that account for his expression of surprise? "He was kinder strung-up an' seemed in a terrible hurry to go," Joe had said. In a terrible hurry to go. Why? The sound-track of memory went into action. She heard Shep declare: —

"That cowhand, Olsen, knows they are three strings of perfectly matched Oriental pearls. I know greed in a man's eyes when I see it."

Her heart stood still. Plunged on. Had Swede Olsen stolen her pearls? Silly, as if *Charlie* would allow him in her room.

"The dawg hasn't been inside the ranch house since you left."

Joe had said that. She pulled open the front door. Dashed across the hall. Ignored Dick's "Come here, Kit!" Tore up the stairs and into her room, the Airedale at her heels. Heart thumping, breath pumping, she looked around. Nothing had been disturbed. Relief took the stiffening from her knees. Her outsize imagination had seized the bit in its teeth.

"Why are you pawing and sniffing at the wardrobe, *Charlie?* Come away."

She caught the dog's collar. Her eyes widened in surprise. The wardrobe door was closed. Locked. Queer. She would have sworn she had left it open.

Had someone been searching for her pearls? Her fingers were none too steady as she turned the key and pulled open the door. Tense with excitement she lifted the gold sandal from the shelf. Set her teeth hard in her lip and thrust her fingers into the toe. Laughed in relief. The pearls were safe. She could feel them through the handkerchief in which they were tied. What a scare. She'd better put them somewhere else. Though they were safe the fact remained that the door she had left open *had* been locked. Someone *had* been snooping.

Seated on the side of the bed she drew the filmy handkerchief from the toe of the sandal, untwisted the knot, while the dog, squatting on his haunches, watched in absorbed attention. She stared at the three strings of pearls.

Pearls! They were not pearls. They were wax beads.

XX

TIME and the world stood still for Kit as she stared unbelievingly at the cheap necklace dangling from her fingers. The chime of the old steeple clock on the mantel shocked her into action. She checked a frantic urge to charge down the stairs broadcasting: —

"My pearls are gone. My pearls have been stolen!"

It would be dramatic but not according to the methods adopted by detectives in the mystery stories she had read. Hush-hush was the formula while one stalked the thief. Good as far as it went but while she was considering what to do, Olsen, if Olsen were the thief, was putting miles between himself and the Double H.

Thoughtful of him to have left the handkerchief. It was one of her finest. Was it? She turned it corner by corner. Hers were monogrammed "K.M." This had an embroidered fleur-de-lis. She sniffed. Perfume and strong. She had been too excited over the loss of the pearls to notice it before. She pressed the filmy linen against her nose. Her senses did a merry-go-round and steadied.

" 'Suivez Moi,' *Charlie*," she whispered. The Airedale cocked his head as if the better to hear. "As I'm alive — 'Suivez Moi!' The Langleys were drenched in it the first time they came to the Double H. Where do we go from here?" The dog whined in answer.

What was her next move? She crushed down the rising sense of panic and turned her mind back to her entrance into the library. Mrs. Langley, who had been moodily regarding the fire, had sprung to her feet as if in relief — did that mean a guilty conscience — had exclaimed, "Thank heaven you've come!" Hadn't she immediately told Lois that she intended to return to Mountain Lodge for her Saturday game of cards? The perfume was evidence that the handkerchief was either hers or her daughter's.

What did that prove? Nothing. That either of the two women had stolen her pearls was too shoddy a solution to be considered. Because Lois would have no compunction about snitching a woman's man didn't mean that she would snitch a woman's jewels. That last would be theft, punishable by prison, she could get away with the first without paying for it — perhaps. The Langleys were out as suspects.

Chang Loo? The suggestion brought her to her feet so suddenly that the Airedale, sagging into sleep, roused with a sharp bark.

"Everything's under control, *Charlie,* relax," she soothed and resumed her thought processes.

The Chinaman had served breakfast at the Dude's Rest this morning. Swede Olsen may have talked about the pearls within his hearing. The field had been clear for him to search for them. He was alone in this house till Dick came home in the late afternoon. He might have picked up the handkerchief — dropped, perhaps, while Lois and her mother were having supper with Dick and the hands last night — with the idea of throwing the suspicion of theft on the two women. But, an insurmountable "but," would Peter Danton have kept him in service for years and left him a pension if the man had shown signs of dishonesty? No. Cross off Chang Loo.

That brought Olsen in the lead again. He could have bought the wax beads in the city, but what chance would he have to secure a Langley handkerchief? He hadn't been at supper. He returned to the ranch late last night, had left at noon today. Memory flash. He had carried wood to the Dude's Rest this morning, Joe had said. That tied it. He was the man to follow.

Now what? If she consulted Shep he would say, "I told you so." She wouldn't give him the satisfaction. The next time he offered advice he would remind her of what happened when she hadn't listened to him about her pearls. Dick had enough on his mind. If only Rex Danton had brought her home. He would know what to do.

"Don't be reckless, gal, and throw away what you may need sometime." His laughing response to her snooty, "We really don't want your advice," echoed through her memory. He had been right. She needed that advice now.

"Kit! Kit!" Dick called outside her door. She tucked the wax beads and handkerchief under the folded green satin puff at the foot of the bed and flew to open it. Should she tell him?

"Why are you staying up here?" he demanded. "The Langleys have gone to the Dude's Rest for their bags and car. What's the matter? Your eyes are dazed. You look as if you'd been bopped. Boy, you're not going to be sick, are you? Didn't pick up the flu at the rodeo, did you?"

His horrified anxiety decided her. She would keep the news of the theft to herself for the present.

"Sick? Me? I reek with health, brainless. I was so mad that the Langleys had camped down here, I decided to remain in my room and count a hundred before I saw them again. Now, I'm smooth and smiling as a summer sea. Come on, let's speed the parting guests — and I mean speed."

Before she stepped into the sedan, Lois turned and laid her hand with the flashing diamond on Dick's arm.

"Darling," she said, tears in her voice, "I will stay now, if you say the word."

"Remember that fable, Lois, about the dog with a bone in his mouth who was crossing a log above a stream? He looked down and saw another dog with a bone staring up at him from the water. Remember that in snatching for that second bone he lost the first *forever?* You'd better get started if you want to reach Mountain Lodge before it is pitch dark."

Without a word in answer she stepped into the sedan and banged on the self-starter.

Sally, Shepherd Trask, Dick and his sister stood in the drive and watched the red tail light diminishing in the violet dusk. Kit sighed with relief.

"Thank heaven that complication is behind us. Oh, my goodness — "

"What's the matter, Kit?" Sally demanded. "You're staring after that car as if it were an enemy tank loaded with TNT approaching, instead of departing."

"Just a flash-back. Suddenly remembered something I — I had left undone at the hospital."

She couldn't explain that the flash-back had been related to the handkerchief with the embroidered fleur-de-lis, that it had reminded her of her intention to return it to the Langleys before they left. Their reaction when they saw it might prove a clue to the disappearance of the pearls.

"Forget the hospital." Sally's voice brought her to the realization that they were at the gate in the white fence. "That's behind you just as the late visitation is — " she chuckled — "we hope. I'm still dazed to discover that the sleek, soft, super-clinging-vine personality of Mother L. is an act, that underneath she's hard as nails. Notice how quickly daughter fell into line when she declared, 'We are going'? Lois is afraid of her Ma, who is 'Inez' to Cal, we discovered."

"You two girls don't understand Lois," Richard Marlowe championed impatiently. "You don't give her credit for her courage when she went overseas with the Red Cross. She had had it easy all her life, except that her mother holds the purse-strings and holds them tight. Lois has nothing of her own. Perhaps if either of you were in her boots you wouldn't do much better. Kit has had her own income for years, and I'll bet your father pays you a whopping salary for helping him, Infant. Come along to the corral, Shep. I'll show you a pinto as is a pinto."

Sally stared at the backs of the two men as they walked away.

"That was telling us, Kit. When Dick shot that Dog and His Shadow fable of the late Mr. Aesop's at Lois, I thought he'd discovered what a double-crosser she is, but his defense a minute ago sounded as if he were still in love with her."

"How do you know she's a double-crosser, Sally? Come on, let's wash the tea things. We can't expect Chang Loo to do that after serving breakfasts at the guest house."

"Do you think Dick is still that way about Lois?" Sally inquired as in the white kitchenette she and Kit, their suits protected by gay aprons, washed and wiped china and silver.

"How did you know he had been in love with Lois?" Kit asked as she polished a crystal cake plate till each facet glittered in the overhead light.

"Jeepers, hasn't she told Mother a dozen times that she and 'darling Richard' were engaged? That because of a tragic misunderstanding the engagement was broken? That she had come West to explain to him that she had never faltered —

that's her highbrow word, not mine — in her love for him? It's a lot of hooey, if you ask me. I'll bet a hat that Koh-i-noor she was flashing was the engagement ring he gave her."

"The cup you are drying is eggshell thin, Sally, don't vent your indignation on it. I don't know about the ring. The size and brilliancy of the diamond looked like Dick, he's lavishly generous." She vigorously polished the Thomas Daniel silver teapot. "I assume that Lois named Colonel Rex Danton as the cause of the misunderstanding? If she did, that's one time she was telling the truth."

"You've always been sour on Rex, haven't you, Kit? It sticks out all over you when you're with him. That being the case, perhaps you'll explain why you pretended you'd gone off the deep end about him the night at Mountain Lodge."

"Explain! I've been dying for the chance. When Lois began shooting her poison darts at me — you heard her — I had a brainstorm that was a brainstorm. I realized then how I disliked and distrusted her. I'm not like that usually, Sally. I've gone through life feeling friendly toward people I met. If one grated, I just side-stepped him or her. Lois roused in me a capacity for hatred I didn't know I possessed. The girl who determined to hit her and hit her hard — I was sure she was crazy about Rex—was a person I'd never known before."

"Pretty low-down of you to make him the goat."

"You're telling me. Think I don't hate myself for it?"

"That's what you say, but if Rex were to come through that door now you'd treat him as if he were the dirt under your feet."

I wouldn't, I wouldn't, Kit told herself passionately, I would hug him in my relief that I had a chance to tell him about the pearls, ask him what I should do. The pearls. In her excitement about them she had forgotten the importance of reporting to him that Ezra Dodge had called on Ma Snell. Aloud she said: —

"You've got me wrong, Sally. I would be a perfect little lady."

"That's because Shep Trask is here and you're on the crest of the wave. I'll bet he's come to ask you to marry him in a hurry. If you want to say 'Yes' don't stop on Dick's account. I'll take over for you. I could help run this ranch with one hand tied behind me."

"Sally Carter, I believe you mean it."

"Pipe down. Don't tell the cowhands in the bunkhouse about it. The minute I saw Dick something happened to me. Quick as that. He doesn't suspect it, though, he thinks I'm a kid. I'm twenty-two. Being a female, I've got to wait until he discovers that I'm old enough for him to love, I suppose."

"It will take time for him to get readjusted to life, Sally. His stiff arm and the scar are only the outward manifestations of what he has been through. The experience did things to him mentally and spiritually. He is frightfully nervous."

"Are you warning me against loving him? Too late. The use of his arm will come back. I'll bet if he were suddenly up against a life-or-death emergency he would use it. His eyes have lost that tortured look. The scar will fade. With the care of the ranch to keep him from dwelling on the past, he will conquer the nervousness. I'm not afraid, Kit."

"Then perhaps I might give him a little jolt — "

"One word from you and I'll twist your lovely neck. I wouldn't have told you now if I hadn't suspected that Shep Trask had come to ask you to marry him and you might refuse because of Dick."

"Wrong number. I shan't refuse because of Dick, Sally. There, everything is bright and shining. Come on, let's change for supper. We'll make it an occasion. I have a two-piece aqua crepe I've never worn that will make even my unobservant brother sit up and take notice."

"I'll complement it with a beige chiffon wool. It's simple but the green sequin belt will cause the male eyes at the table to bulge. Men are push-overs for glitter."

After coffee in the living room Sally inveigled Dick into taking her to the barn to see the ponies, he had already promised she might ride one before she left. Kit disciplined an urge to hurry after them. No use. If she avoided Shep now she would have to listen to him later. Better get it over. She snuggled into the wing chair. Aware that his eyes were fixed on her, she looked up at him. Dancing flames cast curious shadows on his grave face.

"You haven't asked me why I came, Kit," he reminded.

"Why did you come, Shep?"

"I'm reporting to the Coast Guard for service Tuesday."

Surprise brought her to her feet.

"Really, Shep. I'm — so happy for you. I know how it has hurt that you weren't with your friends. Who will carry on at the plant in your place?"

"That was easily arranged after I got Father's consent. He couldn't see it my way at first. Now, he admits I'm needed more in the service than where I am. He thinks the European-war-will-be-over-before-the-end-of-'44 optimism is a pain in the neck."

"I am glad for you, Shep," her eyes filled with tears, "but — " her throat tightened — "but sor-ry for myself. I shall miss you."

"Mean that?" He caught her hands and drew her close. "Marry me before I go, *please*, Kit?"

For one emotional instant his broken voice, his pleading

eyes, swept her along on the tide of his passionate longing. Why not? He was going into danger. She didn't love anyone else. As if he sensed her thoughts his grip on her hands tightened.

"You will? You will marry me, won't you, Kit?"

His jubilant voice, his touch, restored her sense of values. Marry him! She couldn't. She tried to free her hands.

"It wouldn't be fair to you, Shep. I don't love you that way. You mean a lot to me — "

"Enough to send me away with a kiss and prayer? I'll take the kiss now."

He caught her in his arms. Pressed his lips on her throat, her eyes and hard on her mouth with a force which terrified, repelled her.

"Sorry, for intruding at this ecstatic moment," a man's hoarse voice apologized.

XXI

REX DANTON watched Kit in the blue and white uniform walk along the cool, dimly lighted hospital corridor till it telescoped to a small square in which her figure shrank to midget proportions and vanished.

He shrugged his shoulders as if shaking a burden from his spirit. She'd be safe here till he came to take her home Sunday night. He realized by his sense of relief that Ma Snell's warning as to her safety had been pricking in his mind like nettles. With Sally's cowgirl outfit over his left arm, the white Stetson in one hand and the tops of the tall russet boots clutched in the other, he kicked open the green swinging door marked EXIT.

Why had "Ezra Dodge" gone to Mystery Gorge? Why had he taken a job at the Double H? According to Kit's report Ma Snell had confessed that her intention to marry him was a bluff. The questions which concern for Jane Singley had relegated to the back of his mind became front-page stuff as he walked to his roadster parked in a side street.

Ezra Dodge. He visualized the weathered face of the tall man in fringed chaps, black and white checked shirt and green plaid waistcoat hurrying across the arena, saw him stop as if shot. Had the sight of Rex Danton given him pause or had it been Cane's prone figure which had sent him dashing back the way he had come? Was he palling with Skip for a purpose?

Should he have told Kit the suspicions the man's presence here had set agog in his mind? He would give that question serious attention after he had traded Sally's outfit for the suit and week-end case and delivered them at the hospital as he had proposed doing.

That errand accomplished, he stood beside his roadster in front of the hospital and looked toward the east. A lopsided moon rested on the top of a mountain for all the world like part of a great red-gold button on the purple ski cap of a giant. Its brilliance dimmed near-by stars to diamond chips of light.

The last time he had seen a moon like that he had prayed for a cloud to cover it. A company of engineers had been wading through mud, ducking under water, to avoid the strafing of enemy planes as they worked feverishly to locate and cut the wires leading to dynamite charges with which the Krauts planned to blow up a bridge the Yanks needed. The cloud didn't appear. Each man stood out in sharp relief, but the job couldn't wait for the dark of the moon. They had accomplished their work without even a nick. The experience had left him with a devout belief in miracles.

Miracles. That smacked of Ma Snell and her Ouija. Ma Snell. How much truth and how much delirium had there been in her warnings? Dope wouldn't concoct a yarn like that out of nothing. Sam Ruthven's statement that his cattle had been highjacked had rung a bell. "Watch out — J — Jack," Ma Snell had whispered. He and Kit had thought she was referring to her brother-in-law, he was sure now that she had been trying to warn them that Dick's cattle might be stolen.

She had said she was dragging Kit and himself into danger. If there was truth in that, Kit was safe in the hospital for the present. Kit. The mere name set his pulses quick-stepping, flashed her lovely face before his eyes. She hadn't suspected that epoch-making night at Mountain Lodge when he said, "She hasn't seen love strike like lightning as I have," that he was speaking of his own experience the day he saw her for the first time in the line rider's camp. She had intimated that eventually she would marry Trask. Would she?

"Where's the fighting heart you bragged about, fella?" he asked himself and added on second thought, "You won't get her till you've convinced her that you disliked and distrusted Lois Langley at your second meeting and that's going to take some doing."

A near-by clock ponderously chimed eleven. If Ma Snell's warning that someone was out to get him were true, that person had missed the chance of a lifetime while he had stood here gazing at the moon, thinking of a job that was finished and one that lay ahead. A hand grabbed his left arm. Little chills pricked along his nerves as he turned in response to the clutch.

"And this is it," he told himself.

"Brother, can you spare a dime?" a thin voice whined.

Rex stared at the red-faced man with the bushy, square-cut beard and seedy navy-blue suit who was holding out a dirty hand.

"*Tim!*" he exclaimed incredulously. "Tim Blaney!"

"I didn't savvy youse was a tightwad or I wouldn't a asked youse." The man had raised his whine for the benefit of a couple passing. As they turned a corner, he whispered: —

"Got to see you. Need your help."

"Follow me to Uncle Pete's apartment. Watch out for the Double H hands."

"They've gone back to the ranch. See you in half an hour."

Rex waited till the scuff and shuffle of old shoes died in the distance before he slid behind the wheel of his roadster. Why was Tim Blaney here? "What's cooking?" he asked himself.

The pulse of the city was still quick-stepping from the excitement of the rodeo. It took more than half an hour to turn his car into the garage and reach the apartment which had been his uncle's and now was his.

As he entered the large, dimly lighted, ivory-walled living room the ghostly effect of the white linen covers which shrouded the furniture sent a chill along his nerves. Had he left on the electricity last evening when he had dropped in to look over the place?

"Welcome to the old home, Rex."

The dark eyes of the man standing on the threshold of the entrance to the dining room shone with laughter in a tanned face with prominent cheekbones. A World War button adorned the lapel of his well-cut brown tweed coat. He ran long, bony fingers through his short, crisp black hair and flicked the ash from the tip of a cigarette.

"Hold everything, Colonel. It's all done with mirrors."

Rex flung his gray topcoat over the back of a chair and crowned it with his hat.

"How did you get inside the entrance downstairs in the tramp make-up, Tim?"

"I shed that before I used the key I had from the Old Boss years ago."

Rex pulled the white linen covers from two deep chairs upholstered in dark green brocade. He sank into one and eased his aching leg over the arm.

"Sit down, Tim. I've been on my feet most of the day. My leg muscles can't take it yet without protest. Sorry not to offer liquid hospitality. I didn't open up this place till last night. It isn't provisioned."

"Okay with me. You're not the only guy who doesn't drink when he's on an important job, Rex."

"Then you are on an important job? You said you needed my help. It's in the bag, open up. What's on the little mind? Highjacking? Rooting out and following up cattle thieves was your job for Uncle Pete, or could it have to do with that piece of blue denim I deposited on your desk a few weeks ago?"

"It could. We'll come back to that. First and last we caught a bunch of cattle thieves, didn't we? In the early days they ran off the cows, now they snitch 'em by the truckload. Heard about Sam Ruthven's loss?"

"Yes. He told me the cattle just dropped out of the world."

"I know how and where they dropped. I'm keeping that information under my hat at present."

"Were you following the trail when you borrowed the Double H jalopy and took the road to Mystery Gorge — Ezra Dodge?"

"No keeping a born sleuth like you down, Rex." Tim Blaney lighted a cigarette before he admitted, "I've been scared stiff for fear I'd run into you at the Double H. My mind stopped functioning when I spotted you in civvies at the rodeo. Hadn't heard you were out of the Army. How did you get hep to the Mystery Gorge angle?"

"Joe Carr told me there was a patch on the right rear tire of the jalopy which had been borrowed by Ezra Dodge, ex-ranger-blacksmith — prospective husband of Ma Snell. When I reached the crossroads coming to town yesterday, I saw the impression of that patch in the mud. I didn't know you were contemplating matrimony until I saw you cross the rodeo arena and Miss Marlowe exclaimed: —

" 'The tall man with the weathered cowboy look hurrying this way is the happy bridegroom.' For whatever reason you were doing it, I don't like your fooling with Ma Snell's affections, Tim."

"Fooling the old lady! You're crazy. It just couldn't be done. She recognized me the first time I carried my stacked plates to the kitchen at the Double H. She plunked her hands on her hips, looked beyond me to make sure we were alone and whispered: —

" 'Ouija spelled terrible trouble. Is that what you've come for, Tim Blaney? Things were always messed up when you blew in.'

"I gave her the old hush-hush signal. 'It will add up to terrible trouble if you don't go along with me, Hetty' — she likes to be called Hetty. 'Going my way?' 'Sure I'm going your way,' she said, 'there's likely to be excitement and I'm fed up with this kitchen, an' cookin', cookin', cookin' three times a day. Christmas, how those cowhands eat. There's no food shortage on this ranch. Tell me what you want I should do.'

"We thought up the wedding story to divert the attention of one of the hands who showed symptoms of being curious about me. When she didn't meet me at the afternoon rodeo as planned I pretty near went haywire. She was to watch a man there for me. I thought someone had got wise to my business at the ranch and had kidnaped her to make her give what she knew. I was charging across the arena to ask Miss Marlowe about her when I saw you and beat it."

"She had the family and hands at the Double H fooled. I don't see how you got by Joe Carr with the Ezra Dodge yarn, Tim. I recognized you the moment I saw you at the rodeo and when you held me up for a dime in the street."

"There were times when I wondered myself if I were getting by. Joe's a keen old guy and he'd give his skin for the Double H if it were needed. He has transferred his loyalty from the Old Boss to young Marlowe. If he recognized me, he knew I was back for a purpose and I'll bet he didn't acknowledge it even to himself for fear it would get on the air."

"I'm sure now he knew you. Miss Marlowe told me that as the outfit was temporarily out of blacksmiths, Joe Carr had advised her brother to snap up Ezra Dodge."

"Perhaps he suspected I'm working for the Government." Rex whistled.

"The Government. Are we at last coming to the piece of blue denim with the red letter?"

"We are. I don't swallow all that mystery stuff of Ma Snell's but, cripes, if I don't believe you were led by an other-world force to the line rider's camp to find what was left of the fatigue discarded, if not burned by an enemy prisoner. If that isn't so, why was a scrap of it left, the scrap with one red letter and the strip of newspaper with its date line? Sounds cockeyed coming from me, doesn't it?"

"No man who has fought in this war, Tim, but gets to believe in that 'other-world force.' "

"That makes me feel less like a screwball. It is known that two escaped POWs are at large. The piece of blue denim suggested that one of them had been in the neighborhood of the Double H. The date of the scrap of the newspaper which had been used for kindling was a month before the day you found it. The person who burned it might have been miles away by that time. I was ordered by my boss to get a job at the Double H the Saturday after you came to my office."

"Quick work. Have you spotted your man?"

"I'm not sure enough yet to nail him."

"I've had a tip that Marlowe's cattle are in danger of being highjacked."

"I heard the buzz-buzz about highjacking while I was at the ranch. I may be wrong, but I suspect it's a cover-up."

"If they're not after cattle what do they want?"

"You're due for the surprise of your life, Rex. Our enemies are striving by every means in their power to discover the U.S. oil capacity, present and prospective."

"Are you intimating that an escaped prisoner has been assigned to *that* job?"

"One, or perhaps two. Either that or the saboteurs plan to blow up a few of your oil wells and perhaps put the whole field out of commission. Take your choice."

XXII

BLOW UP the oil wells!" Surprise brought Rex to his feet. "You mean there is an escaped enemy prisoner, doubling as a cowhand at the Double H, with one or both those dirty jobs up his sleeve?"

" 'You got your rope on the right pair of horns, mister' — Joe Carr speaking. What do you know about that Swede, Olsen?"

"Nothing. I've never seen him. When I dropped in at the bunkhouse he — *Wait* a minute! I remember now that when I entered a man sprang to his feet as if the sight of my uniform had snapped him to attention, then beat it out the back door. I had a fleeting suspicion that he was a discharged service man, not too honorably discharged perhaps. He had the stamp of a trained soldier. Consequent happenings crowded it from my mind and I haven't thought of it since. Is the man you're watching, Swede — ?"

Tim Blaney held up a warning hand.

"Better not mention names. The Swedish-American vernacular would camouflage another foreign accent. Any way of finding out from here if he returned to the ranch tonight with the rest of the hands?"

"Sure. I'll get in touch with Joe Carr. I ordered the apartment phone connected while I was still in hospital. He'll think I'm crazy but it won't be the first time." Seated on the end of the broad mahogany desk Rex dialed, and gave a number.

"This room is cold. The house superintendent must be conserving coal. Touch off the fire, Tim, while we are waiting for the call to go through. An open fire does things to my spirit and in the last twenty-four hours my spirit has had considerable shovin' round. What's that?" he spoke into the receiver. "Sure, he's there. Keep on ringing till you get him. This is Colonel Danton calling."

With the phone at his ear he grinned at Blaney.

"That ought to get service. For Pete's sake, open the draft in the chimney, Tim. The smoke will smother us. Use the poker — yes — *yes,* p-o-k-e-r. Use it, quick! Push up the window.

"Joe? Rex Danton speaking — No. I haven't a terrible cold — Sorry. Keep your shirt on, Joe. How could I know I was going to sneeze in your ear? A dumbbell just started the fire without opening the chimney draft and laid down a smoke screen that would start the Army eating its powder in envy — No. I didn't call you at midnight to tell you that. I gave you a buzz to ask if the Double H cowhands were home."

"Don't mention names," Blaney whispered. Rex nodded understanding.

"Did they all show up, Joe? . . . What sort of foreman do I think you are not to check on them? Don't be sore, fella. Sorry to rout you out this time of night, but I had to know. . . . You hadn't gone to bed? What's the idea? . . . Dick? . . . He has? . . . I'm glad, too. Don't worry about your baby, Joe. He'll snap out of it. This call is on the q.t., get it? . . . Okay. Okay. I know you're not a dumbbell. . . . What? . . . Yes. I caught up with Ma Snell before she had a chance to be married. . . . No. She won't be at present. You knew that when you started me after her, didn't you?

. . . He knows he didn't. . . . No, Kit isn't going home till Sunday. She's serving as Nurses' Aide in the hospital. I'll be seeing you. Good night."

"What's this about Joe and his baby?" Tim Blaney demanded. "Don't tell me that dyed-in-the-wool bach has been leading a double life?"

Rex crossed to the window, closed it and dropped into the green chair.

"No. Joe isn't the double-life breed. Dick Marlowe is off on one of his wild rides tonight. Joe was worried about him, he's gone all out for the young Boss. That's what I meant by his 'baby.' Said he was glad Kit was away and didn't know he had gone. I said 'Yes' to that. I suspect he was sitting up listening for his return."

"Wonder what set Marlowe off. Several nights I heard that black Satan of his tearing up the road while I was at the Double H. I had reason to keep awake there. Tough on his sister. It's a crime to bring an Eastern girl like her to a ranch in this country. She's been cooking for the cowhands while Ma Snell was away and, say, can she cook? You wouldn't know she wasn't sold on the job, though. Her voice never lost its lift."

"What's the matter with this country for an Eastern girl? Living in a mountain state doesn't necessarily mean cooking on a ranch, does it?"

"Sure, sure it doesn't, Colonel. I can see how and where life might be made smooth as cream for one of them." Laughter vanished from Blaney's eyes and voice. "We've been blown a long way off our course, Rex. Did you find out if Joe was on to me?"

"Sure, he knew. When I accused him of knowing that Ma Snell had no intention of marrying, he came back, 'Did that guy pretendin' to court her think he was fooling me?' I assured him that the aforementioned 'guy' knew he hadn't."

"Are *all* the hands back at the Double H?"

"Yes. Joe checked."

"That's a break. I was afraid the man I'm after might have got wise. He'll be where I want him this afternoon — I hope."

"Why wait till afternoon?"

"I must see Ma Snell before I go."

"Know where to find her?"

"She's in the hospital, isn't she? Why would you and Miss Marlowe go there if not to see her?"

"You've had us watched. Nize fella."

"Only one man on your trail. He had a way of finding out why you went there. He reported that Hetty to me, Ma Snell to you, saw Miss Marlowe before the operation. It might mean that, filled up with dope, she would talk, spill the beans. I can't take a chance. Not that she was wise to the real reason I was at the Double H, she just knew I was there on business. I've got to know what she said to 'Dearie.'"

"I can tell you." Rex repeated what Kit had told him. "What the dickens did she mean by 'J — Jack,' if, as you believe, the highjacking stuff is red herring?"

"Mm, she was mixed up, wasn't she? I'll see her and find out what she meant, take a few flowers, that will please her. She's a great old girl. I hope she'll get the fourth husband she's looking for, but it won't be me. Remember, I said I needed your help? Drive me out to the Double H this afternoon, will you? I'm still on the pay roll."

"Where's the jalopy you borrowed?"

"One of the cowhands snitched it, probably drove it back to the ranch."

"I'll take you out. Fortunately the ration board realizes

that I can't get back and forth to the oil fields without gas. As oil is my present job and you are working for the Government, that squares it. While I'm waiting for you I'll take a trip out there and put my head man wise to what may happen. To return to Mystery Gorge. I have a hunch Sam Ruthven's cows went that way."

"They did. The FBI lost an A 1 sleuth when you joined the service, Colonel. I discovered evidence of it there yesterday, but no preparations to shoot another bunch through a natural underground passage that comes out in the foothills."

"So that explains the mysterious disappearance of the 'dead tough' and his loot. Sounds plausible. In spite of the scare about the oil fields, I'm not so sure Ma Snell hadn't something on the ball when she babbled about 'Jack.' Didn't you notice when you were bunking at the Double H that Michigan Murphy and Texas Smith were feuding? Joe thinks that Tex suspects Mich is mixed up with a bunch of highjackers. Olsen and Mich don't hit it off, either. According to Joe, Mich rides the Swede. I'll bet a hat if cattle disappear Skip Cane will be in on the deal."

"That why you knocked him out at the rodeo, Rex?"

"No. That was entirely personal."

"You shouldn't have done it no matter what the aggravation. He's a bad egg. He'll try to get back at you and you are a vital link in the oil supply that's going to our fighting men. There is nothing more indispensable to defense and victory than petroleum and its products. The guys who sent me on this job drilled that into my mind. Having croaked my warning, I'll shove off. Ezra Dodge, that's me, mad as a mad coyote that he has to walk, will be hiking just outside the city toward the Double H at six o'clock or thereabouts. By-by."

The rising moon had been red gold. The disc that hung in

the sky was silver when Rex started for the oil fields. Mountains reared majestic peaks against a rose and opaline dawn. He had instructed the telephone company to get a message to his secretary that he had been called out of town.

For hours he interviewed heads of departments against a background of towering derricks with deafening sound effects of drilling and ditching machines and the suffocating smell of oil. He ordered guards doubled, warned the superintendent in charge to keep a keen lookout for trouble and to hold any man who applied for a job till he had been checked by the resident FBI. On no account was he to let anyone else know of the warning.

After the noon hour he called his city office. No answer. Saturday afternoon. It would be closed. Later he tried the hospital. Miss Marlowe had been called home suddenly, a nurse reported. *Suddenly.* The word ran like a refrain through his mind as he completed his inspection.

Suddenly. Did the summons connote trouble at the Double H? Had Dick Marlowe been smashed up in his wild ride? It would break Kit's heart. Why imagine the worst? Probably Trask had urged her to return to the ranch and devote her time to him during his short stay. Hang it, he must keep his thoughts and attention on this oil job.

"Nothing more indispensable to defense and victory than oil and its products," Tim Blaney had said. As if he, after years of fighting, needed to be reminded of that, needed to be prodded to keep Uncle Pete's wells flowing.

Stars were beginning to prick through when a man on the dark road outside the city hailed him with thumb up. He stopped. Fringed chaps. Black and white checked shirt. Green plaid waistcoat and a huge white Stetson. Tim Blaney, alias Ezra Dodge.

"Check. Hop in."

"You sure took your time, Colonel," Tim grumbled as he slid into the seat beside Rex. "I'm about frozen. The cowhand who snitched the jalopy got my mackinaw with it."

"Sorry. Put this round your shoulders." Rex drew a trench coat from under the seat. "Seemed as if Hades broke loose the minute I arrived at the field. Each head man had a question to ask or a grouch to register, from the chief of the geologic crew to the driver of a bulldozer. Just as I was ready to leave, a wildcat, two locations north of the Mammoth Spartan, came in with a rush. It was a big one and we all went mad. After that I made the best time I could getting here, not only for your sake but because I am anxious to know why Miss Marlowe was called back to the Double H suddenly."

"Perhaps her brother got bust up. He was on one of his wild rides when we talked with Joe Carr at midnight, remember."

"I thought of that. I hope we are both mistaken."

They were silent after that, each man occupied with his thoughts. The rumble of war-freight trains rolled across the stillness. Once Rex heard the screech of an owl and as they passed a small house a light flickered in the barn behind it from which drifted the strong smell of sheep and the pathetic bleat of a lamb. The field of stars shed a golden glow. When they reached the row of cottonwoods from which they could see the lights of the Double H, Tim Blaney threw off the trench coat.

"Leave me here, Rex. I'll cover the rest of the way in a few minutes. I'll tell the cowhands that I hitchhiked till I had to leave the highway and that I walked the fifteen miles from there."

"How about your bride? How explain coming back without her?"

"Tell the truth. Didn't have a chance to get married because she is in the hospital. Here I go." He stepped to the road. "Hope you won't find trouble at the ranch."

What would he find? Rex asked himself as he walked up the path to the house. Lights from the windows laid a pattern of yellow squares on the lawn. No answer to his knock. Why? He opened the front door. Quickly crossed the hall to the living-room threshold.

Kit in Trask's arms, Kit being furiously kissed.

"Hope you won't find trouble at the ranch house," Tim had said. Trouble. His heart turned to ice, his throat was tight but not too tight to let his voice through.

"Sorry for intruding at this ecstatic moment," he apologized hoarsely.

He turned on his heel and bolted across the hall and out the door. No girl would permit herself to be kissed like that by a man she didn't intend to marry, would she? That settled it. He'd find Joe Carr, tell him to watch Olsen till Ezra Dodge returned, then he would beat it for town — and stay there.

The foreman jerked open the door of the cottage in response to his furious knocking. He stared at the man facing him as if he couldn't believe his eyes.

"What in heck are you doing here, Rex, breakin' in my door, your eyes fairly burnin' in a muddy, white face? Who's dead?"

"Cut the comedy. No one's dead. I want to talk to you."

"Come in."

There was something in the absolute order and shining cleanliness of the room he entered that quieted Rex's racing pulses. The hearth was swept clean. A neat little fire burned without splutter of sparks. He sat on the corner of a large, flat, golden-oak desk, upon the top of which every article was placed with mathematical precision. The walls were covered with photographs of cattle, with the prize ribbon or medal each had won under the glass of the frame. In its heyday the Double H had been a leader in the ranching world.

"The Old Boss willed me that collection of pictures," Joe Carr explained as if he had read Rex's thoughts.

"He had the right idea. There is no one in the world to whom they would mean so much."

"Glad you feel that way about them. Let's quit stalling. What brought you here at this time of night lookin' as if you'd lost the battle?"

I have, one battle, Rex thought, before he answered.

"The hospital reported that Kit had been called home suddenly. Putting that with her brother's wild ride which you reported over the phone, I thought he had cracked up."

"Is that all. You certainly had me scared. I phoned Kit because the two Langley dames had arrived and camped down in the Dude's Rest an' — "

"The Langleys here?"

"That's what I said. I could see it was worryin' the young Boss. Them ladies come over fer supper, stayed playin' cards. 'Catchee young Boss pretty quick now,' Chang Loo whispered to me. 'Alle time they make big talk. Too bad. They no good. Him nice fella.' That gave me the willies. After they went to the Dude's Rest Marlowe started on that ride. When this mornin' Olsen asked for his time an' left — "

"Swede Olsen gone!" a voice demanded from the doorway. "Where? When?"

"So — you're back are you, Ezra Dodge?" Joe Carr drawled. "Where's that jalopy you borrowed?"

The man in the fringed chaps, black and white checked shirt and green plaid waistcoat came close.

"You know who I am, Joe."

"Sure, I know who you are. I knew you was playin' fer high stakes an' aimed to give you a break when I kep' my trap shut. I ain't afraid to tell ya that I didn't like ya foolin' Ma Snell 'bout marryin' her, though. You was dealin' her a mean hand."

"She was wise to it, Joe. I want Olsen. Never mind why. Where is he?"

"He said he had another job. Heck — "

"That wasn't the reason he left," Kit Marlowe declared breathlessly from the threshold, "he stole my pearls."

XXIII

WHAT do you mean, he stole your pearls?"

Kit shook off Rex Danton's hand on her arm. Why was he pretending interest? If she lived to be a hundred she wouldn't forget his face, his hard eyes, the icy voice in which he had said: —

"Sorry for intruding at this ecstatic moment."

Her mind went on flashing the past few minutes on the screen of memory. Her heart had stopped ticking, little shivers had quivered along her nerves. He was gone before she had a chance to speak, to ask him not to leave her. Something in the way Shep had seized her, kissed her, had been terrifying. She had twisted herself free, had called, "Don't go." Too late. Tears of anger had blinded her for an instant. Was Rex afraid she intended to claim him again, when she wanted only to tell him about her pearls? Someone should be told at once. She had waited too long.

"I must see Joe Carr," she had flung over her shoulder to Shep. He had called something she hadn't stopped to hear and —

"Miss Marlowe, if you won't answer Danton, answer me." A stern voice interrupted her thoughts. "When did Olsen take your pearls?"

Her contemptuous eyes swept the man speaking from head to foot.

"Just why should I tell that to one of my brother's cow-hands, Ezra Dodge? What's more, I have a strong suspicion you are mixed up in the plot to steal them, that your plan to marry Ma Snell was part of it."

"Cripes, come off your high horse, Kit, and tell us — "

"Don't speak to me as if I were a baby, Joe Carr."

"That's enough temperament, Kit. Ezra is here to get Olsen. Tell him at once what happened."

Rex's deep authoritative voice, his cold eyes, steadied her. She was acting like a silly child. Why care because he hadn't answered her frantic "Don't go"?

"Sorry I snapped at you, Joe."

"Miss Marlowe, you are wasting valuable time, Tim Blaney, FBI, *not* Ezra Dodge speaking. Go on. Let's have an account of your day."

FBI masquerading at the Double H as a blacksmith and a suitor to Ma Snell? Had he known that Olsen was a thief?

"Those pearls are hot stuff. He'll try to get rid of them quick and we'll get him and his fence. Talk!" Blaney snapped.

Beginning with Joe Carr's telephone call to the hospital, she told of what followed, of Ma Snell's change of attitude. When she came to her surprise at finding the Langleys in possession of the Dude's Rest and serving tea in the ranch library, the right words wouldn't come.

"Wait a minute," Rex ordered. "You're getting mixed up. Is it because you think it embarrasses me to hear of the Langleys' uninvited descent on the Double H? Don't mind me, I can take it. Go on."

If he could be flippant at a time like this she'd show him what she could do.

"Here the curtain drops for a few seconds to denote the passing of time," she said lightly before she told of her discovery of the loss of the pearls and her suspicion as to the thief.

"Have you told your brother or Trask that the pearls are missing?" Rex demanded.

"No. I had planned to reach you by phone this evening and ask you what I should do, but — "

"You were otherwise occupied."

"Don't be cantankerous, Rex, Kit's doin' right good," Joe Carr protested.

"What's the big idea running out on me, Kit?" This time it was Trask glowering from the threshold.

"I told you, Shep, I had to see Joe Carr and — " He caught her hand and twisted her to face him.

"Sure you didn't come to follow Danton? I saw and heard him at the door of the library. Look at me."

She was aware that Rex had thrust his hands hard into the pockets of his gray coat. He hadn't liked the tone in which Shep had mentioned his name. She had a sudden close-up of Skip Cane stretched on the ground.

"I'm looking, Shep," she declared hurriedly. "And what do I see? Two eyes, a nose. Isn't there a game like that?"

"Quit stalling."

Instead of calming the situation her attempt at the light touch had been a high explosive tossed into its midst. She had seen him hurt, annoyed, sulky, but never so fiercely angry.

"We'll put our cards on the table here and now." Shepherd Trask jerked at his collar as if its tightness were responsible for his choked voice. "This is the second time I have traveled hundreds of miles to ask you to marry me. It won't happen again. Let's have it. Yes or no?"

Why couldn't she love him? She had known him all her

life, knew his virtues and his faults as he knew hers. His blond good looks, his reputation as one of the coming politicians in his state, the social importance of his family, made him a hostess-pursued, noticeable and distinguished figure wherever he went. He would be generous — if always aware of his generosity — he would be kind, tender — No, no, not that last. She flinched as she felt again his savage kisses. Perhaps all men were like that when they loved a girl. Maybe, but she couldn't take it from him.

"You're taking your time answering my question, Kit," Shepherd Trask reminded bitterly.

"I have taken time because I would like to say 'Yes,' Shep. I'm sorry. I — I can't."

"I've heard that word 'sorry' before. I've heard you declare, also, that you were 'pretending' that night at Mountain Lodge when you implied you loved Colonel Danton. I'm beginning to doubt that word 'pretending.' Watch your step. Has he asked you to marry him? He won't. He's tied up with Lois Langley."

"What's your authority for that lie, Trask?" Rex Danton's voice was hoarse with fury.

"The best. Hers."

It was one of those photographic moments when emotions are at white heat and every detail is burned into the memory. She would never forget it. Joe Carr and Ezra Dodge disappearing into the hall. The light from the tidy fire turning the silver buttons on her aqua frock to rose color; the two men, Shep, haggard and demanding, Rex, slowly drawing his hands from his pockets, his slight smile evoking a sense of tension, only the flames in his eyes and the white line about his mouth attesting his anger, as he took a step forward.

Unaware that she had moved, Kit found herself backed against him, with all her strength holding him where he was. He caught her bare arms in his hands.

"Get out of my way. Quick."

"I won't stir until you two men stop fighting," she declared.

"Don't move on my account," Trask's voice lashed. "I can see that you've made your choice between a man who loves you and one who — "

"That's enough, Trask." Rex swung Kit aside and held her there, her wrists gripped in one hand. "Kit said she didn't want a fight here. *I* don't feel that way about it. Take back what you said about me or I'll give you the licking of your life."

"What's all the shootin' about?" demanded Dick Marlowe from the doorway. "What are you three doing in Joe Carr's cottage? We heard your voices as we came from the corral. Danton in civvies, how come?" He glanced from one face to the other before he spoke to wide-eyed Sally Carter beside him.

"How about those sandwiches you promised me, Infant?"

"They are as good as made, Captain. I'll dash to the house and prepare enough for all."

"Count me out, Sally," Shepherd Trask called as she disappeared into the hall. "I'm leaving for home at once."

"Leaving! Just like that," Dick Marlowe scoffed. "And how do you think you'll get off this ranch at this time of night, Shep?"

Kit rubbed her wrists after Rex released them. Shep was going. There would be no fight now.

"I can walk and hitchhike."

"Don't be a darn fool. I suppose you and Kit have had a row.

Don't tell me you have broken up another engagement, Colonel."

Kit hadn't known a bronzed face could go so colorless, or eyes burn as Rex Danton's burned as he answered her brother.

"I shan't tell you that, Marlowe, but after you speed the parting guest — apparently he insists upon leaving — there are a few items of interest in regard to your *business* I would like to pass on to you."

"My *business!* What's happened?"

"I said *after* your guest had departed," Rex reminded. A door slammed with a force which shook the house. "If you want to say good-by to the thwarted lover, you'd better hurry."

"What's that stupid fool, Shep, thinking of? He can't get away from here tonight," Dick Marlowe fumed before he dashed into the hall. A slam. The house shook again.

"That 'thwarted lover' was a cruel crack, Rex," Kit declared indignantly. "How would you like it said about you in that sarcastic voice after the girl you loved had turned you down?"

"The answer to that question would be out of order at this moment. Why did you take so long to consider if you would marry Trask?"

His cold eyes on hers set her a-shiver inside. It was an effort to hold herself tense so he would not suspect.

"It isn't really any of your business, Colonel Danton, but I don't mind telling you that I wasn't considering — not really. He has enlisted in the Coast Guard and I wondered if I ought — "

"We'd have a madder world than it is now if girls felt bound to marry a man because he enlisted. I enlisted, so what?"

"Ezra Dodge is back," Dick Marlowe announced from the threshold. "Just ran into him. Acted as if I had caught him stealing sheep. Do you know where he has been, Danton?"

"That belongs in the department of business I'm here to talk with you about, Captain. He — "

"That Trask fella has just driven off in your roadster, Rex," Joe Carr announced from the doorway. His voice shook with excitement. "I tried to stop him but, heck, if he didn't pull a .45 on me."

XXIV

WHAT "business" could have kept Dick and Rex Danton talking for hours and hours, Kit wondered the next morning as she arranged sprays of pine in a lustrous copper bowl on the library table. The murmur of their voices in this room under hers had made an accompaniment to her thoughts as the events of the day unreeled through her mind in technicolor accuracy.

She had hurt Shep intolerably. Why couldn't she love him? Why had Rex been so — Joe had a word for it, cantankerous, with her? Each time she thought of his cold eyes, she felt as if an icy wind blew over her. Good heavens, was she starting on that same old thought treadmill this morning?

Where was Shep? Last night Joe Carr had said he "pulled a .45" on him. Shep "pulling" a gun. It was too funny to believe. Where did he get it? Had he come to the ranch with the idea, gleaned from the movies, that a .45 was part of a ranch visitor's equipment?

"What's the joke, Kit?" her brother inquired as he entered. He drew a pipe from the pocket of his gray coat, lighted it, all with his right hand. "You were grinning like the Cheshire cat. Expected to find you low in your mind after Shep's theatrical getaway. What cooks?"

"I was thinking of that when you caught me grinning. Shep's exit, pulling a gun on harmless Joe Carr, was so out of character. Do you believe he had one?"

"I believe anything after the facts Danton handed me last night."

"About Lois?"

"*No*. Why should he and I talk about her? I'm through. 'You may fool all of the people some of the time' — you know the rest. If he wants to marry her it's all right with me. It was about Ezra Dodge. He is a G-man. While he was here he caught on to a lot of under-breath talk about a plot to steal my shipment of cattle. If it was straight goods — he doubted it — it was nipped in the bud. The suspected finger man, Michigan Murphy, asked for his pay, packed his bedroll and departed early last evening. Said he had a better job. Joe was sore, tried to keep him, but paid him and let him go. He wouldn't have gone if the plan was still on."

"Was that what brought Ezra Dodge here?"

"No. His boss had been tipped off that an escaped enemy prisoner was headed our way."

"He said last night he wanted Olsen. I have suspected that Swede wasn't what he pretended to be. I am sure he stole my pearls."

"Your pearls! No kidding. Why haven't you told me? Why do you think he took them?"

She told him.

"Shep warned me that Olsen knew they were the real thing. I came back smart-alecky: —

" 'I'll keep my pearls here, Shep. Who knows, they may start excitement and believe me, life on this ranch can stand a little pepping up.' "

"It's on the way to getting it," Richard Marlowe confirmed gruffly. "Every rancher within a hundred miles will be alerted to watch for Olsen. If he is as bright as he has proved to be to date by getting away with his Swedish disguise, he'll hide round this outfit figuring that the posse after him will think he would put miles between him and the Double H. This ranch will be in on the shooting party or I miss my guess."

"Has Ezra Dodge left? I still think of him by that name."

"Yes, he and Danton went in our jalopy, before the hands had their breakfast. Danton phoned later this morning that the hospital reported Ma Snell making a record-breaking recovery, that he had arranged with Chang Loo to stay with us till she was equal to the cooking job, if we wanted him."

"*If.* I'll say we want him. Did Rex speak of meeting Shep?"

"No. They picked up Danton's abandoned roadster just this side of the highway, with the owner's .45 Shep had brandished at Joe Carr. He must have thumbed a ride from there to the city. Crazy fool. I'm glad you decided not to marry him, Kit. He's an ego-deflater. That may be good medicine for some women, I would hate to see you sentenced to it for life."

What did Rex Danton think of a girl who had been kissed as Shep had kissed her and then refused to marry him?

"Grand morning," her brother's voice broke into her troubled reflections. He walked to the window. "Cold and clear. Usually there is snow before this, Joe tells me. Great country."

"You are happy here, Dick? You are not sorry you bought the Double H?" Kit asked eagerly.

"Sorry! You bet I am not. I'll never go back to a city for keeps. This country makes me feel contented, complete. It's so big, so clean, so fresh. Look at those mountains standing out as if their white tops had been painted against the sky."

"Ranching sold to the gent in the powder-blue pullover, gray slacks and coat," Kit intoned theatrically to hide her emotional response to his voice, to the glow of hope in his eyes. "Grandmother would be pleased to know you are wearing that outfit on Sunday instead of those faded blue Levis for which you have developed a passion."

"I like to observe Grandmother's little conventions when I can. Wish we were nearer a church for your sake, haven't forgotten that it means a lot to you, Kit. Remember the Grands used to remind us that the *real* people in a community always were church attendants? I saw that demonstrated among the officers in the Pacific. They had the right idea. Can't live up to it here. The Sabbath is no different from any other day to cows. There is considerable class to those black slacks and red blouse you're wearing."

"Not red, romance rose, my hearty. What became of Sally? When she left me after breakfast, resplendent in her cowgirl regalia, she was bound for the corral, said you'd promised she might ride a pinto."

"Right, but when she got there she sniffed at the pony, insisted upon riding my horse. I know she's good, but I'm worried. I've taken some wild rides on that black, I've made him a bad actor, and — listen!"

Kit's heart set up a loud tattoo in time with the pound of approaching hoofs.

"My God, that's Satan. He's running away with her."

Kit tore through the hall, down the path, to the road outside the white gate, at her brother's heels. The powerful horse with the girl pulling wildly on the reins was coming at a breakneck pace. Sally, incredible as it seemed, had lost her head as well as her hat.

Kit's heart stopped as Dick stepped into the direct path of the runaway. He would be killed. What did he think he could do with one arm?

She choked back the cry of warning. If she spoke he would know she was thinking of his disablement, doubting his ability to help. That would hurt more than anything the horse could do. The runaway was almost on him. Sally's face was colorless as she called: —

"Don't touch *him*, Dick. I'll jump. Catch *me!*"

Catch her? Dick? With one arm? She had forgotten. Kit's heart choked her with its pounding as Sally flung the reins over the horse's head and leaped from the saddle. If her foot should catch — if her skirt should — Dick caught her, held her tight in both arms.

"I thought for a minute I'd lost you, Infant," he said brokenly with his cheek against hers.

Lovely color swept to her auburn hair, glowing like red gold in the sun.

"You can't lose me ever, Dick, if you want to keep me," she said softly.

This was no place for a third party. Kit started for the house.

"Come back," Sally called. "I have something exciting to tell you." Her eyes, brimming with tears, swept from Dick's left arm about her shoulders to meet Kit's. She shook her head slightly. Was she cautioning her not to comment on the fact that the once useless arm was very much in use at the moment? Suspicion stirred in Kit's mind, crystallized to conviction. Rex had said that Sally was a trick rider, a whole lot better than some of the professionals who tour the rodeos. Had she staged the runaway to test Dick's arm? She had taken a frightful chance at death for herself, no wonder her face had been colorless.

"Won't it keep?" Her laugh was unsteady. "I'm definitely fifth wheel in this situation."

"It won't. Looks like danger to you with a large, large D. I — what's wrong, Dick?" Sally inquired anxiously.

He had withdrawn his left arm from her shoulders and was cautiously bending it at the elbow, flexing the wrist. His face was white, even the scar had paled. His eyes snapped nervously.

"You planned that runaway, Miss Carter," he accused furiously. "Risked your life, because you thought my stiff arm was an act I was staging to keep from returning to that hell in the Pacific, didn't you? Thought I was afraid to go back to see the jungle lighted by flares that showed the dead sprawled on the beaches, to the stench — "

"Where did you pick up *that* fool idea?" Sally's question crashed into his shaken voice. Her face was as colorless as his, her eyes were burning wells of horror. "Maybe I did plan the runaway, I've made that leap dozens of times, but not because I thought you were side-stepping the fight, I thought — "

"It doesn't interest me what you thought. You made a fool of me. You won't have a chance to do it again," he announced and stalked toward the barn.

Sally's eyes, which had followed him, came back to meet Kit's.

"Can you beat that? Of course I planned it. When we were together last evening I noticed movement in his left arm and I've heard that shock sometimes recharges the nerves. It did. So what? I get the brush-off. I'm going home."

"No, Sally, Dick will realize how unjust he has been and — "

"Then he can come to the Circle Q and tell me. I'm packing my bag — now."

In the guest room she changed to the navy costume in which she had arrived at the Double H.

"I'll leave the cowgirl outfit for you, Kit. I hope I never see it again. Jeepers, that reminds me, Dick's crazy accusation knocked it out of my head."

"You said something about danger to me, then the — the late unpleasantness — "

"Go ahead, wisecrack about Dick's fool idea. I can't. If you loved a person as I love — " she swallowed a sob.

"Sorry, Sally. Something tells me you'll see Dick tomorrow. In what danger am I?"

"Perhaps it isn't danger, but something queer happened when I was riding this morning — was it only this morning? I feel as if it were years ago, when I was very young."

"You haven't turned gray yet. Go on, *please*. Something queer happened when you were coming home from your ride," Kit prompted. "Take it from there."

"Just as I reached the cottonwoods on the ranch road, I realized I was being followed. I stopped my horse. The sound of hoofs behind me stopped. I did that twice with the same result. Mom's yarn about the escaped prisoner and desperadoes flashed into my mind and gave me an acute attack of heebie-jeebies. I pulled down my white Stetson hard, it had been on the back of my head, tightened my hold on the reins and prepared for a wild dash to this house. A hand grabbed my bridle, an oily voice said : —

" 'Don't be in such a hurry, Kit. You're coming with me!' "

"He said, '*Kit*'?"

"That's right. I swung in my saddle and stared at — *who* do you think?"

"For goodness' sake, Sally. Stop being mysterious. Who was it?"

"Skip Cane on that gray horse of his. You should have seen his face when he discovered I wasn't you. Mouth hanging open, gold tooth glittering. He snapped his jaws together, loosened them to swear and mumble: —

" 'Thought you was another party.' Then off he galloped for all the world like the bad hombre in a movie. It's your guess. Why did he assume I was you?"

"That is easy. I wore your cowgirl outfit at the rodeo Friday. I talked with him twice. A person would have to be color-blind not to notice that orange satin blouse, green skirt, fringed chaps and the outsize white Stetson. 'You're coming with me,' he said? What did he mean?"

"You didn't by any chance give him the come-on when you met him at the rodeo, did you?"

"I did *not*. I may have been a little too friendly, but I had a reason — "

"Perhaps he suspects that reason. Then again, Lois Langley may be mixed up in his plan, whatever it was. She was hanging to his arm at the rodeo like a bat to a rafter, begging him to explain the events to her. She has it in for Rex, a blind person could see that — and Rex knocked him out cold at the rodeo."

"How did you know that, Sally?"

"That bit of news shared the spotlight with Jack Singley's accident. It's a cockeyed world when a regular guy like Rex Danton gets mixed up with a girl like Lois. She's poison." Sally sniffed. "Dick was nuts about her too, still is, I guess, from the way he raved at me a while ago. Okay, I can take it." She picked up her suitcase.

"Mom was planning to invite you both to the Circle Q for the next week end. I suppose that's out now that I'm in the doghouse. Good-by."

Kit stood at the white gate till Sally's roadster was hidden by the row of cottonwoods. She thought of Skip Cane's

"You're coming with me," and she thought of Sally's belief that Lois was mixed up in whatever plan he had. She recalled her own suspicion that he might have heard of Ma Snell's warning about him at the hospital and had determined to stop the spread of it by kidnaping her. Kidnaping. Her imagination had run away with her. It was more likely that he knew of Olsen's whereabouts with her pearls and wanted to make a deal with her as to a reward. Tim Blaney had said: —

"Those pearls are hot stuff. He'll try to get rid of them quick and we'll get him and his fence."

Was Skip Cane the fence?

She was standing here motionless with the sun beating down on her head when she should be doing something, telling someone that Skip Cane had held up Sally on the road thinking she was Kit Marlowe. This wasn't the moment to confide in Dick. He had had a terrific shock. Give him time to realize the blessedness of it. Of course he was in love with Sally. His face, his voice, had proclaimed that when he had caught her in his arms.

If only she could reach Rex. She would swallow her pride and tell him about the attempted holdup. After all, Skip Cane was a menace to him as well as to herself. Hadn't he threatened at the line rider's camp, "Next time, Colonel, I'll catch you when you're not in uniform or with a lady"?

Joe Carr would know where to reach him. She glanced at the sun. Almost dinnertime. Being Sunday she might find the foreman at home. He cooked his own meals at his cottage.

She ran across the rusty grass. The front door was open. She lifted her hand to knock. He was at the telephone. She would wait. She sniffed. Delicious smell. He was having beef stew for dinner. No disguising the fact that he had been heavy-handed with the onions.

Seated on the top step she clasped her hands about one knee covered with the soft chiffon wool of her black slacks. How would she begin the story? She must be cool, a little amused, it wouldn't do to let him suspect that her pulses were quick-stepping —

"Yes . . . Sure, I've been here all the time. Blame it on the operator . . . What! Cripes! He has?" Joe's voice was heavy with disappointment. "And he's so needed here — I'll tell him. Good-by!"

Kit was standing on the top step, hand at her tightened throat, when he saw her and came to the door.

"Joe! Joe! What is it? What's happened?" she demanded. "Is it about Rex? Has he been — "

"Tim Blaney phoned that he had been called to Washington — "

"For how long, Joe?"

"Tim didn't know. Said to tell your brother. Cripes. What are them brass hats thinkin' of to pull him away from his job at the oil fields now?"

Joe had said Rex was needed at the oil fields. That wasn't the only place. She needed him terribly. Whom else could she tell about Skip Cane? No one. It looked as if it was up to her to play a lone hand.

"What you starin' at them mountains so hard fer, Kit? What'd ya come here for?"

Her laugh was shaky but it served.

"I — I came to tell you that Dick has regained the use of his arm, Joe. Isn't it wonderful?"

XXV

THE ROAD, bordered by gigantic pines on one side where the foothills loped down to meet it, was a checkerboard of sunlight and shadow. On the other, stretches of purple and gray-green sagebrush rolled eastward till it melted into the horizon. Acres of newly grown winter grain made a pattern of green against the black of freshly plowed soil. The occasional bellow of a steer came from the range beyond. A cock pheasant boomed out of the underbrush. For a split second its gorgeous plumage gleamed like varicolored enamel in the sunlight before it skurried back whence it had come.

The *Old Farmer's Almanac* had said of November, Kit remembered, "There is no month more alive, none more powerfully suggestive of the good things of living." It had the right idea.

She stopped her horse and looked up at the blue mountains with deep purple defiles between them. When she had first arrived they had chilled her by their remoteness and majesty. She had come to love them, to love the way their shadows fell on the foothills, to feel that in their great hearts they held the secrets of the universe. Almost as distinct as the nearer ranges, though miles beyond, peak above snow-capped peak, some isolated, some in groups, they stabbed into a sapphire sky.

Their steadiness and calm eased her aching anxiety, her troubled conviction that there was something mysterious behind Rex's summons to Washington. Had he been recalled to the Army? The feeling was spreading that V-E Day was not so imminent as had been expected.

"You look as if you might know. Why doesn't he return? Why did he go?" she asked softly.

The bay turned his head and regarded her with a white-rimmed, inquiring brown eye. Her pat on his satin smooth neck set her silver bangles jingling.

"I wasn't talking to you, Rusty, I was thinking aloud. You should be used to it by this time. I've spent hours in the saddle since the crisis, ten days ago, when the Langleys descended on the Double H, my pearls were stolen, Shep shook the dust of our ranch from his feet, Rex Danton departed with the G-man, Skip Cane held up Sally, mistaking her for me, she staged her spectacular leap and Dick's arm miraculously swung into action. A sprightly twenty-four-hour stretch, if you ask me. We'll hope it was the climax to the 'terrible trouble' Ma Snell prophesied and, speaking of Ma Snell, isn't it grand that she's home, bossing us all from an easy chair in the library? Let's go. *Charlie! Charlie!*"

In response to her call the Airedale rushed through the underbrush and capered ahead as the horse daintily stepped forward. The little wind that whispered eerily among the pines scented the air with their spicy breath. The naked branches of the cottonwoods and hackberrys creaked. The morning was so balmy that she peeled off her moss-green cardigan and tied the sleeves around the saddlebow. She had heard a shot soon after she started out an hour ago. No danger that she would be mistaken for game in her jonquil-yellow shirt and gray suède waistcoat with its shining silver buttons. A hunter hundreds of feet away could see it.

"In November, pheasant shooting," Rex had said that wet morning in the line rider's camp. Where was he now? Of course she was in love with him, desperately, it hadn't taken many sleepless nights to show her that, or that she had kept setting the memory of his affairs with Lois between them to fool herself with the belief that she distrusted him.

She had ridden away from the Double H in an attempt to escape from troubled thought of him. Curious how little the theft of her pearls occupied her mind. Here she was back on the worry circuit, on the Rushing Creek Ranch road, to which Joe Carr had almost tearfully asked her to stick.

"With them escaped enemy prisoners on the loose, you may be strikin' all four feet in a mess of trouble, if you ride anywhere else," he had warned.

The suggestion was blood-chilling. She wrenched her thoughts to the morning broadcast. The Eagle of the Pacific had begun to make good his promise, "I will return." That news ought to rouse Dick from the depression that had ridden him for the past ten days. MacArthur was his hero.

"Unprecedented fine weather in the mountain states for the first quarter of November, but watch out for a sudden change to snow," the announcer had warned. She thought of the advice of the commentator who had followed him : —

"Now that the shouting and the tumult dies, now that we know who will be the next President, we must once again be a united nation."

Had Shep Trask heard that? Was he bitter about the result of the election he had worked so hard to swing the other way, or was he too absorbed in the duties and training of his new life to have time or strength for apprehension or regret? Was he too busy or still too angry to answer her letter? She had sent it to his home address. They had been friends for so long she couldn't let him go into danger without assuring him again of her deep affection, of her interest in his life.

She stopped the bay with a jerk of the reins. Just ahead the sky was full of whirling, soaring birds. Their hideous chatter meant they had been disturbed while feasting on the decaying carcass of a cow or lamb. *Charlie* had a passion for investigating that sort of mess. Could she get him past it? She whistled. He tore out of the underbrush. Squatted on his haunches in the road he looked up at her expectantly.

"Your nose is brown with dirt, *mon brave*." She laughed. "You're a funny sight. Someday when you are snooping into a hole which is none of your business you'll get it tweaked off. What's that?"

She knew what it was, the click of a hoof against a rock in the road, the gentle creak of a saddle, the heavy breathing of a horse. Something undercover about the sounds gave her the creeps. Was she being followed? Memory broadcast Sally's account of Skip Cane's hand on black Satan's bridle; he had said, "You're coming with me, Kit."

The bay broke into a canter when she touched him with her heels. The Airedale tore ahead. She must go forward, she wouldn't go back, the sound had been behind her. She had been afraid of Skip Cane the first time she saw him at the line rider's camp, she had more reason to fear him since Rex had knocked him down at the rodeo.

What had *Charlie* run to earth this time? He was barking furiously. Rusty answered her touch on the reins with an increase of speed. They rounded a curve in the road and almost ran down the dog who was looking up into a tree at which he was clawing furiously. Her eyes followed his. A gray shape was stretched along a mammoth branch of a pine which bent under the weight. Great green eyes watched the frantic dog. A wet spot was spreading on the gray coat.

"There is a rumor that a mountain lion is prowling through

the forest," Mrs. Carter had said. Was this the creature coughing horribly? Had the shot she had heard wounded it? Would it drop on its tormentor? Fear paralyzed her for one horrible instant before she lashed the bay with her crop. The horse leaped forward.

"*Charlie! Charlie!* Come! Come!" she called frantically over her shoulder. Would the dog obey? It was the only chance to get him out of danger.

The Airedale looked at her in response to her frenzied call, clawed at the tree, gave an impatient "Whoof" of frustration. Her heart stopped. The lion's great gray paws were dangling. Was it preparing to drop?

"*Charlie! Charlie!*" she called again. With a final angry yelp at the gray shape the dog straightened like a whippet and raced after her. If only she could pick him up. She didn't dare stop. He might take it as a signal to turn back. As long as she kept on, he would follow.

"Faster! Faster!" she urged. The bay raced around a bend in the road. The stone house built into the sloping hillside in units on different levels was just ahead. Rushing Creek Ranch, the part of his uncle's property which Rex had kept. A filmy mist hung over the stream which gave the place its name, through it drifted the ceaseless sound of rapidly flowing water. No sign of life anywhere. A back road led to the other buildings. Log cabin. Storehouse. Bunkhouse. A barn with a corral. All appeared deserted.

Better stop here. If she turned back the hideous thing, crazy with pain, might drop on her, or on the horse, to say nothing of what it would do to *Charlie,* who would promptly renew hectoring the creature. If she waited at the house the lion might die, it had been bleeding. Then she could ride back.

At the gate of the stone wall she slid from the saddle, tied an end of the rein to the ring in the hitching post and smoothed the heaving satin neck of the bay.

"Sorry, boy, to lash at you, but it had to be done. You haven't had a workout like that since I arrived at the Double H, have you, Rusty? Look at *Charlie*. Flat on the ground, tongue hanging out, panting as if he couldn't get his breath. He deserves to be laid low for getting us into this mixup."

The iron gate creaked on its hinges as she opened it. Now that she was here why not take a look-see through the windows? The Airedale ran ahead of her up the path and sniffed at each step that mounted to the terrace level.

What was that? She turned from the long window through which she had been peering. Listened. Sounded like a shot. Another. Was someone putting the wounded lion out of its misery? Was it the rider who had been following her? Cheering thought. If it were Skip Cane she would be at his mercy here. If only she could get into the house and lock the door behind her.

She tried the window. Locked. She tiptoed along the flagged floor of the porch. Silly, as if the man on the road could hear her footsteps. She softly tried the knob of the front door. It turned. The door swung open. Her heart flew to her throat and raced its engine.

"How come? Is this a trick, *Charlie?*" she whispered. But the dog was not there to answer. Where was he? She called. Something brown was streaking back over the road along which they had come. *Charlie* had returned to the attack.

More trouble. Her stomach contracted to an icy ball as she visualized what was likely to happen. Only one thing to do. Ride after him, drag him away from his quarry and take a chance that in some way she could elude Skip Cane — if the person following her had been he.

She ran down the steps. At the exact moment her foot

touched the path the bay threw up his head, twitched the rein free and with a triumphant whinny raced after the fast-vanishing Airedale.

"You double-crossers! You *mean* double-crossers," Kit flared aloud. "This is what I get for exercising you together every day, whether I felt like riding or not. Buddies, aren't you. I hope the lion catches you and eats you up. I don't. I don't, really," she added remorsefully.

Now what? She could easily walk the four miles to the Double H. No dice. There were too many dangers on the road. A lion and a vengeful cowhand — perhaps. After *Charlie* and Rusty finished their sortie with the lion — if it didn't finish them first — they doubtless would return to the ranch. Someone there would suspect she had been deserted and start after her. She would wait, safely locked in the house.

Up the steps again, across the terrace, into the square hall. She tried to turn the key. It wouldn't turn. The lock was broken. It had been forced. Now what? It didn't necessarily mean that it had happened recently. The house might have been entered weeks ago. Whatever the explanation she would stay. She could hide somewhere if she heard Skip Cane coming.

She leaned back against the door. Opposite was an enormous fireplace, with ornate brass andirons. Above it, a large mirror reflected a hatless girl, in a jonquil-yellow blouse, silver-gray waistcoat, matching breeches, soft, polished, worn russet boots with high heels. Silver bangles on her right arm jingled as she brushed back a dark curl that had fallen forward over her forehead. "What sort of person are you inside?" Kit softly asked the looking-glass girl steadily gazing back at her. "Not the same one who came to the Double H weeks ago. Sometimes I think I don't know you very well."

A bench, upholstered in crimson brocade, flanked the fireplace on each side. At the left a staircase, railed with delicate iron tracery, carpeted with a rich Oriental runner, wound to the floor above. At her right five steps led up to the long room she had seen through the window. It looked as if it would provide more entertainment than the hall for a lengthy stay in case Rusty and *Charlie* did not return to the ranch. That thought helped. She still had two feet with which she had hiked miles, hadn't she?

A stair creaked. She stood rigid. Listening. Was the person who had broken the lock in the house? A tap at a window. Was it Skip Cane?

Her heart choked her with its beating. Silence. A curious pulsing silence. Tap. Scr-a-pe. Tap. Scr-a-pe. She thought of Joe Carr's warning to keep on the Running Creek Ranch road, he hadn't told her to come to the house. Was she about "to strike all four feet in a mess of trouble"?

Tap. Scr-a-pe. Tap. Scr-a-pe. She swallowed a laugh of relief. The creepy sound came from a vine brushing against a window. She ought to recognize it, she'd heard the same thing often enough in her room at the Double H. Wouldn't stairs in an old house creak? They would. Having explained that mystery to her satisfaction, why stand here with icy fingertips and racing heart? She, who had been so eager to get into the fight overseas, was putting on a scared-rabbit act because of a few weird sounds. If Lois Langley were to see her she would be justified in cracking, "It's so much safer cheering the boys on the home front."

"What beamed that headache into my mind at this minute?" Kit fumed under her breath. "Come on, 'fraid cat, let's investigate." She ran up the steps to the sunny room, lined with books.

She pulled off her gray pigskin gloves and laid them with

her riding crop on the large, flat desk, swung herself to a corner and with hands clasped around one knee studied the portrait above the fireplace in which logs were laid ready for lighting.

"You look as if you knew everything," she told the man who appeared to be appraising her with keen, dark eyes. Rex had features like his except for the mouth. Peter Danton's had an amused quirk at the corners. His nephew's was grim — the war had done that — except when he smiled, then the lips were boyishly tender. She sprang to her feet. Why think of Rex and start her heart aching? There was plenty of interest here to occupy her mind.

She walked from shelf to shelf looking at the beautifully bound volumes. The tall clock in a corner was a museum piece. The four-panel Coromandel screen that partially covered the opening into another room was exquisite. The background of a crimson brocade portiere that matched the hangings at the windows and the furniture coverings brought out its beautiful coloring.

The piano was open as if it had been used recently. The crimson *rebozo* of woven silk and linen and wool, thrown over one end, was a collector's item, so was a Mexican sombrero heavy with golden filigree hung against a dark panel. The gorgeous things should have been put away when the house was closed — the housekeeper in her speaking. Closed? Was it? If so, why had the door been unlocked? Footsteps overhead. She listened. Cautious steps in the hall. Hand tight over her heart as if to silence its loud beat, she stood motionless, unseeing eyes on the sombrero.

Someone had entered the room behind her. Tiny inchworms crawled up her spine loop by loop.

"Turn round."

XXVI

THE LOW ferocity of the command brought Kit's thumping heart to a jangling stop, but her motor nerves obeyed. Had Skip Cane caught up with her? She turned.

Her eyes widened till they burned like floodlights, even her bones congealed. The man glaring at her with hunted eyes set in dark rings in a dirty, unshaven face was Olsen.

"If Olsen is as bright as he has proved to be to date, by getting away with his Swedish disguise, he'll hide round this outfit figuring that the posse after him will think he put miles between him and the Double H," Dick had said.

He had been right, Olsen looked as if he had put in ten days doubling from foxhole to foxhole to escape his pursuers. A plaid mackinaw was fastened round his waist with a string. The legs of Kelly green pants flopped in wet, bedraggled strips over the tops of once red leather boots now scratched, torn and minus one three-inch heel. Light hair hung over his forehead like straw from a thatched roof. His drawn-back lips disclosed uncared-for teeth. A revolver dangled from dirty fingers, tipped with ragged nails. Kit's heart stopped.

"What's the idea of the holdup, Olsen?"

"Why are you here?" No trace of Swedish accent in the guttural voice. He spoke slowly, carefully, as if it were an effort to speak the English words correctly. The eyes that stabbed into hers were trapped, desperate, starved. The eyes of a man who had been hunted and knew it, who wouldn't stop at murder to keep his freedom. With an effort she tore free from his hypnotic glare and glanced around the room.

"I heard the house was full of interesting things. Dropped in to give it a look-see. Nice, isn't it?"

"*Ja.* Like the Colonel and you took a look-see at the stove in the line rider's camp?"

Surprise jolted heart and nerves and brain out of their semi-paralysis. The first pounded. The second hummed like telegraph wires on a highway. The third began to function.

"Wrong wave length," she denied as lightly as her tight throat permitted. "I didn't see — " A flashback of memory stopped her voice.

Rex had poked something out of the potbellied stove that rainy day at the line rider's camp. It all came back to her. He had stared at a piece of dark cloth with a strip of newspaper dangling from it. She had thought he appeared startled and she recalled that he had flung it down and kicked it behind the woodpile as if it were a matter of no consequence.

"You've remembered, *ja?*" The man's stealthy approach sent her back against the Coromandel screen. "I saw you go there in the rain. He came. Where is what he found and put in his pocket? I've got you, now I make him tell."

His gloating voice, his cruel eyes, terrified her. For a split second fright drained the strength from her body. She pressed her teeth into her lower lip until she tasted blood. "Idiot. You've never fainted in your life. Why begin now, when you need a fighting heart as never before?" The self-castigation steadied her, she even achieved contemptuously curled lips.

"Cut out the bluster, Olsen — perhaps your name isn't Olsen — the bad hombre act you're putting on is outdated. It doesn't get across even in the movies now."

Her light voice turned his weather-beaten face a purplish red. His fingers tightened on the revolver. It was madness to taunt him, but if she could keep him talking, help was bound to come. It might be the rider the click of whose horse's hoof she had heard behind her. Even Skip Cane would be better than no one.

"You're taking an awful chance, holding me up like this, Olsen." Was that really her amused voice coming from a throat that tightened like a vise each time his dirty fingers twitched on the gun in his hand?

"My horse and dog ran out on me fully an hour ago. When they show up at the Double H minus me, the outfit will dispatch a search party. You're an escaped enemy prisoner, aren't you? A German masquerading as a Swede. Now you're wanted as a common thief. You took my pearls, didn't you? Unless you're longing for the ease and comfort of a prison camp, you'd better go. Step aside. I am leaving at once."

"That is what you think." His chuckle was devilish. "You will come with me. I will trade you for my freedom. I have been hiding and dodging in the woods a long time now. I broke into this house for food. Upstairs I hear you come. Americans are soft. They will let me go to save you. We start for the mountain. If you scream, I will shoot." Was his stilted, labored English an act?

He brushed back the dangling lock of hair. Kit knew as she met his implacable eyes that nothing she could say would help. It was like a nightmare. A sunny outdoor world she could see through the window, death blocking her way to it. She, powerless to move. His fingers bit into her arm. With all her strength she shook off his hand.

"I am not going with you. Where did you get that crazy idea? Someone's coming. *Listen.* Footsteps on the porch."

The eyes of the man facing her went dead. Expressionless. They were opaque dots in skin gone gray.

"Get behind that screen. Speak and I shoot — "

He broke off to listen. Someone was pounding at the front door. Couldn't whoever it was see that the lock was broken? Suppose it were not Skip Cane? Suppose it were Joe Carr, suppose by some miracle it were Rex? Curious how the mere thought of him sent blood leaping through veins she had thought frozen. This man would kill him. No matter what happened to her she would warn the person at the door.

"Don't come in!" she called. "He has a — "

A brutal hand struck her mouth and cut off her voice.

"Hide, I tell you." He swung to face the door.

She slipped behind the screen, opened her mouth to scream for help. Fright paralyzed her throat. This, not the eventful twenty-four hours ten days ago, was the crisis of the "terrible trouble" Ma Snell had prophesied. She drew a handkerchief from the pocket of her breeches to dab at her bleeding lips, quickly thrust back her hand. The jingle of her silver bangles would betray her presence to the person at the door. Was it friend or foe?

A heavy tread across the flagged hall. Whoever it was had run up the steps to the living room.

"Shucks! See who's here!" It was Skip Cane's voice. "Put down that gun, Olsen. Don't act up as if I was breakin' an' ent'rin'. I got as much right here as you, ain't I? Where's the girl?"

Kit was sure that her heart had stopped forever this time, that her breath was permanently locked in her tight throat. Cane had been following her.

"What girl? Do I look as if I had time for women? Go, or I — "

"Each time you wave that gun, Olsen, you're walkin' straight into trouble. I got one too, see?" The warning was ugly with menace. "Have you gone plumb loco or do you think I have? Think I didn't savvy her hoss an' dog beatin' it fer the Double H? Think I don't see her swell ridin' crop an' gloves on that desk? I don't calc'late to swap talk with you any longer. Loosen up. Where's the girl?"

"Why do you want her? What is she to you?"

Olsen's voice had changed from bluster to appeasement. Did that mean that his resistance was weakening? Kit's muscles tensed. Suppose he gave her up to Skip Cane? Was there a choice between them? Something would happen to save her. It must. *Charlie* and Rusty would have reached home by this time unless the lion had killed them. Ma Snell was there. She would know that something was wrong and would send someone to look for her.

"What is she to me?" Skip Cane's voice was nearer the screen as he repeated Olsen's question. "She ain't nothin' to me but she is to Rex Danton, he's nuts about her an' I've got a score to settle with him. I kin hurt him harder through her than shootin' him. He's gone to Washin'ton. Ain't he goin' to be surprised when he comes back to find her missin'? Come across now an' come quick. Where is she?

"What d'ya mean, tippin' back ya head? Upstairs? Git goin'. We'll mosey 'cross the hall an' up them stairs with my gun at yer back — You coyote! You ornery coyote! That screen moved. Ya got her — "

Terror lent Kit strength. With all her might she sent the screen crashing against the two men. It hit Olsen's head. Skip Cane caught it, flung it aside, saw her standing against the crimson hanging and with a cocky smile stepped toward her.

"Shucks, there you are, Kit. Now we'll see — "

"Take one step, Cane, or you, Olsen, and I'll blow you wide apart," warned a hoarse voice behind Kit. "Drop those guns. Quick. Hands up."

Outside a bluejay squawked. Tap. Scr-a-pe, went the vine against the window. Tense silence inside broken by the thud of revolvers flung on the floor, the hard breathing of Olsen and Cane as, hands high above their heads, mouths working soundlessly, they glared at someone behind her. She looked over her shoulder. A face went into a dance routine and steadied. Rex Danton.

"I ain't got nothin' to fear from you or the law, Rex." The cowhand licked dry lips. "I got wind this fella was trailin' Kit an' follered to watch out fer her."

"I'm not deaf, Cane. I heard you say that when I came back I would find her missing. You know the penalty in this state for even an attempt at kidnaping. If you don't, the sheriff will remind you."

"Shucks, Danton, I was jest foolin', I didn't mean — "

"Shut up. Kit, the hump in Olsen's breast pocket may be your pearls. Investigate while I keep these men covered. If he moves so much as one finger he'll get it through the head."

Kit looked at the unkempt figure and winced.

"He's so dirty, Rex. I — I hate to touch him, but I will."

Teeth shut hard in her bleeding lip she stuck her fingers into the pocket. She sensed cruel eyes glaring at her, felt the man's muscles tensed to spring. She drew out a lump covered by a grimy handkerchief.

"Got them?" Rex demanded. "Hands higher, Olsen. That goes for you too, Cane. Are they yours?" he asked as three strings of lustrous pearls swung from her unsteady fingers.

She nodded.

"Sure, they're hers. Spot the 'K.M.' on the handkerchief, l

can see it from here," Cane confirmed eagerly. "I didn't have nothin' to do with that — "

"Save your breath, Skip. You'll have a chance to talk to the sheriff — and how. Put on the pearls, Kit, they will be safer. Pick up their guns. Use them if you have to. Joe Carr — "

He stopped speaking to listen. Kit strained her ears and heard the pound of hoofs. Rex turned his head. In that instant Skip Cane sprang for him. Seized his throat. Olsen started forward to help. Kit leveled a revolver in each hand.

"Let him go, cowboy, and I *mean* let him go. Stop, Olsen. I have you both covered. Good heavens, they're going off!"

Cane whirled at the sound of two shots and Rex poked a gun into his side. Olsen grabbed his foot and grimaced with pain.

"Stay where you are, Olsen. You'll get it coming and going, if you don't," Rex reminded breathlessly. He moved his head as if to test the muscles of his throat. The chalky-faced man with the thatch of straw-color hair clicked back the foot he had put forward.

Tim Blaney, doubling as Ezra Dodge, followed by Marlowe and Joe Carr, catapulted into the room.

"Kit! Kit!" Richard Marlowe flung his arm around his sister's shoulders. "Are you whole? Unhurt? Dodge appeared from nowhere and yelled that your horse and dog came back without you. Joe and I grabbed our horses and started on the gallop. We — " His voice stuck in his throat.

"I'm not hurt, Dick." With a sobbing sigh of relief he thrust his unsteady hands into the pockets of his faded Levis.

"What gives, Rex?" Tim Blaney inquired. "I was gassing the jalopy when the horse and dog appeared. I knew something was wrong. Joe yelled, 'Rushing Creek,' and I burned up the road till that patched tire burst and slowed me. Cane's a nice dirty yellow. What's he been doing?"

"I heard him threaten to kidnap Miss Marlowe. Olsen had her pearls."

"Kidnap. That's going strong, Skip. Escaping from the prison camp was enough for you, Olsen. You shouldn't have gummed up the works stealing pearls."

"What business is it of yours what I do, Dodge? You're nothin' but a — " Cane's voice died in a rattle as the man at whom he was glaring casually lifted the flap of his breast pocket and revealed a shining badge.

"Get these men out of here, will you, Tim? Miss Marlowe has taken about all she can stand."

"Sure, Rex. Marlowe, take Skip with you in the jalopy. Joe, ride beside them. Take one of the guns Miss Kit is holding, if Skip gets fresh, shoot. Give me the other. I'll ride the black. We'll take Olsen back in good old Wild West style on Skip Cane's gray. Heck, we might even stop for a little roping party." Blaney's pleasantry turned Olsen's already colorless face to chalk. "That's an idea."

"Shucks, you ain't goin' to treat me, a citizen, like this war criminal, are you?" Skip Cane demanded.

"Ain't he simple to think he'd go free caught red-handed kidnaping. Pick up yer big feet, Olsen. Get goin', ya — " Joe Carr blasted him with a few well-selected epithets.

Dick Marlowe stopped on the threshold.

"How will you get home, Kit?"

"Don't worry about her, Captain. You've got your hands full to get these men into the custody of the sheriff. I'll make sure she gets there safely," Rex Danton promised.

He followed Kit to the window. They watched the cavalcade start. Skip Cane in the jalopy with Dick Marlowe, Joe

Carr on his calico mare riding close beside the cowhand. Olsen on the gray followed. His hands were tied behind his back, a rope ran around his waist and down on each side through a cinch ring. He sat humped forward, chin on his breast, the yellow hair on his forehead moving in the light breeze. Tim Blaney, as Ezra Dodge in fringed chaps, black and white checked shirt, green plaid coat and huge white Stetson, on black Satan rode beside him.

"I can't believe I'm not looking at a Western on the screen. Is that trussed-up effect 'old Wild West style'?" Kit asked.

"Not so old. It is still effective. You're shivering. Come away from the window. We'll have a fire."

He touched a match to the kindling under the logs. When flames mounted up the chimney he drew forward a chair.

"Now that the excitement is over my knees have let me down," Kit admitted as she dropped into the crimson chair. "I was scared stiff when I picked up those revolvers."

"You handled the guns like an expert and at just the right minute. Cane had me by the throat. Good Lord, what happened to your lips? They are puffed and bleeding. I was so intent on keeping those two thugs in line I haven't noticed them before."

"A member of the Master Race struck me when I shouted a warning to the person I heard in the hall. The blow must have been what is technically known as a right to the jaw — and what a right."

"Damn the brute. Come here." He caught her hand and drew her to her feet beside him, tilted up her chin and gently dabbed her swollen lips with a fine white handkerchief. "Steadier now?"

"Steady as that highest mountain. How did you happen to arrive at the exact moment you were needed?"

"Got in from Washington yesterday afternoon and drove out here for a coat I had left. Decided it was too late to return to town so parked my car in the barn and slept here. This morning while I was packing some clothes, from the window I saw a figure dodging among the shrubs.

"What gives, I wondered, slipped into my pocket the gun that Trask had thoughtfully left in the roadster, and ran down to the hall. Heard the front door open and slipped behind the portiere back of the screen. Footsteps on the stairs. Then someone came into the library."

"Enter the pur — sued heroine."

"Nice girl. You're getting back to normal fast, aren't you? Before I could find out who it was, I heard a voice growl, 'Turn round.' You know the rest."

"What an incredible coincidence that you should have been there when so terribly needed."

"Was it coincidence or part of a preordained design?" He cleared his voice. "When Cane grabbed my throat I lived a lifetime of terror as I thought of what might happen to you if he got me." He brushed his hand across his eyes as if to clear them. "Let's forget the nightmare. I did a bit of shopping in Washington. Want to see what I bought?"

He drew a white velvet ring case from his pocket and snapped it open. A diamond shot out sparks of color where the firelight caught it.

"I'm old-fashioned. I like the idea of a solitaire for an engagement ring. How do you feel about it, Kit?"

Because she feared he would hear the hard beating of her heart she asked gaily: —

"Am I being psyched for my response to jewels? I'm for them singly or collectively. Do you call that a solitaire? Looks more like a headlight — "

"Forgotten that you begged me to meet you here, that you said you had something to give me, Rex, *darling?*" a spoiled-child voice inquired. Lois Langley, complete in light blue tweeds and a wistful smile, stood on the threshold.

XXVII

KIT, come back!"

She ignored Rex Danton's sharp command, caught the triumphant gleam in the eyes of the girl standing on the threshold of the library as she brushed past her, charged down the steps to the hall and out the front door.

She didn't stop running till she had turned the bend in the road which hid her from sight of the stone house. Then the excruciating pain in her left side stopped the breath which tore up from her lungs. She slowed to a walk, always with her ear alert to a sound behind her. Silly. As if Rex would follow. He had asked her advice about a ring. For one rapturous moment she had thought it was for her. Then Lois's voice had smashed her happiness to fragments. He had "begged" her to meet him there, he had said he had something for her. The ring of course.

Lucky she had heard it. She walked on drawing harsh, quick breaths, pressing her hand hard against her side to relieve the pain. Loving him as she did she wouldn't have believed it. Had, not did, was the right word. Love went out like a candle in a cold wind, when she saw the girl on the threshold. How did she get there?

Ooch! That stone in the road had given her foot a vicious turn. Riding-boot heels were not designed for hiking. She was now out of sight of Rushing Creek Ranch. Her limp couldn't be seen from there. That was a dumb thought, as if Lois and her "darling" — No. No, she wouldn't give the beautiful word that had meant so much to her as a child and young girl that hateful twist, even in her mind. It had plunged her into trouble once.

Blood surged through her in a scorching tide. Who was Kit Marlowe to condemn Lois Langley for pursuing her man? Hadn't she appropriated Rex Danton at the third meeting? That memory ought to slap her down when she became critical of the holdup tactics of other girls.

She hobbled on. The sun was hot for walking even in November. It was slanting a trifle. Must be about one o'clock. She glanced at her wrist watch. Right. Dodge had appeared at the ranch and yelled to Dick and Joe that her horse and dog had come back without her.

She shivered as she lived over the moment when Skip Cane had stepped toward her with that cocky smile.

"You have to go forward in life, you can't go back." Rex's reminder broke into the terrifying memory. He was right, she must stop thinking back.

She forced her attention to her surroundings. It was about here — she had forgotten the lion until this minute. There it was. That long, gray, bloody shape by the side of the road. The sick sensation in her stomach frightened her, sent her skipping, hobbling on till the shortness of her breath made progress impossible. She flung herself flat in the brown leaves under a tall cottonwood. She would rest for ten minutes. Perhaps the paddles churning like mad in her stomach would settle down.

What was that sound? A car? She snuggled deeper into the leaves. If it were Rex she wouldn't take a chance at hi seeing her. Heroine-with-sprained-ankle situation was outdated. He might think she was faking to win his sympathy. Besides, her ankle wasn't sprained. Now that it was rested it was better, a whole lot better. The car had stopped.

"Come here, Kit."

She had heard that same "Drop those guns" voice a short time ago. It sent curlicues of icy tingles along her veins.

"Coming? No?"

It seemed but a minute before Rex had lifted her in his arms. He looked down at her face so near his.

"You're white as a sheet. What did it? That thing by the side of the road? It is dead, honey. It can't harm you now." She steeled herself against the tenderness of his voice. His line, just his line, she reminded herself.

"No answer? All right. Gals in yellow blouses shouldn't hide in brown leaves if they don't want to be found," he remarked as he deposited her in the seat of his open roadster.

"Just by way of a reminder. When I say 'come' I mean come," he declared and threw in the starter.

"You and General Ike. You don't have to tell me that. The following is a transcription: —

" 'Forgotten that you begged me to meet you here, Rex' " —the word "darling" wouldn't come.

"Why didn't you finish it? Look at me."

She shook her head and kept her eyes on the blue glint of a lake high above the timber line of a snow-capped mountain.

"Ashamed to, aren't you? You ought to be, riding round this country alone, breaking into a closed house, frightening the people who love you, stiff."

Surprise that he had abandoned the Lois Langley angle sent her indignant eyes to his.

"The house wasn't closed. The lock of the front door had been forced. An accident sent me there."

"Your eyes are deep blue, aren't they? I've never been quite sure before. What do you mean, accident?"

She told him, even went back to Skip Cane's holdup of Sally Carter near the cottonwoods that Sunday morning.

" 'You're coming with me, Kit.' " Rex repeated. "You were too friendly with that bad egg at the rodeo."

"I wasn't friendly, I was trying to find out if he fitted into Ma Snell's warning. Your friend Lois hung to him like a bat to a rafter, Sally said."

"Leave Lois out of this. I've had all I can take of that without — " His grim lips cut off the sentence.

They drove on. The harder Kit tried to think of something nonchalant to toss into the strained silence, the more stubbornly ideas refused to germinate. They were in sight of the Double H when Rex said: —

"Skip Cane is a heavy drinker when he is out of a job — he's an efficient worker when he has one — but a troublemaker, as I told you once before. I overheard two cowhands say he was on the wagon, they wondered what he had up his sleeve. I reported their speculations to Tim. He had a hunch that Skip was wise as to the whereabouts of the escaped prisoners. After overhearing his talk with Olsen today, I am sure he didn't know that the Swede was one of them. Has Ma Snell returned from the hospital?"

"Yes. You skip from subject to subject with the agility of Eliza on the ice cakes. She's back and on the crest of the wave. She says that for the first time in her life she is being waited on."

"She rates it. Try to find out what she meant by 'danger' to you and me. That's one of the few strings left untied. Your brother told you that the plot to steal his cattle was merely a flash in the pan, didn't he?"

"He did. It would have been a terrific blow if he had lost them. The cows brought the highest market price, but, sometimes I wonder if he wasn't a little disappointed, if 'shooting it out' for his cattle wouldn't have made his dreams come true of the thrills life on a ranch provided."

"Don't run away with the idea that what you saw today is typical of life in the ranching country. In all the time I have spent here I never met up with anything like it. It was just one more backfire from these tragic wars. The United States needed men and took cowhands when they qualified. Your brother had to hire what came his way to keep meat going to the fighters. I hope this experience won't discourage him."

"It won't. He told me that he loved the country, the life. Did you notice he used his left arm?" she asked eagerly.

"Yes. The mere telling of it has brought back your radiance. Here we are." He stopped the car at the white gate.

"Will you — come in?"

"Sorry to refuse your *cordial* invitation. I'm expected back at my ranch. Been nice meeting you. Good-by."

She resisted the temptation to watch his roadster out of sight. He was expected back at his ranch. It wouldn't take a master-mind to figure out by whom.

Serena Carter's observation about the Double H library recurred to her as she entered the room.

"Always I have a feeling of warmth and comfort when I step into it."

She felt as if protecting arms had closed about her, easing the smart and ache of her heart.

"Was that Rex driving off as if he was goin' to a forest fire?" Ma Snell inquired from the depths of the wing chair by a fire which had died down to glowing crimson embers. Her upswept hair-do glittered like gold. Firelight tinged to pink the gardenia tucked in the wave. Her make-up suggested peaches and cream. A ball of navy wool rolled from the lap of her green and white gingham dress as she looked up from her knitting. "What's he in such a hurry about?"

"He had business at his ranch."

"Perhaps Cal Smiley'll reach him there. He's had this phone tied up tryin' to get in touch with him for the last half hour."

"Did he say what he wanted?"

"No. He was terrible mysterious when I asked him could I take a message. Where you been to make you look so — so greenish, dearie?"

"Greenish!" I must have been an enticing sight for a man to look at, Kit thought. "It isn't where I've been, but what I saw that turned me green, Ma Snell."

She told of the encounter with the wounded lion, of her race to the stone house, of the desertion of her horse and dog.

"Christmas, so that's why that Airedale came sneakin' in lookin' as if he'd been caught stealin' sheep an' smellin' like all get out. I called Chang Loo to chase him out to the barn. Better not have him in the house till one of the cowhands has given him a bath."

"I won't. Discipline won't hurt him." Kit perched on the arm of a chair. "Ma Snell, what did you mean that night in the hospital when you warned me there was 'terrible trouble' ahead, that Rex and I were in danger, that Olsen was to be watched? 'Look out for Jack,' you whispered."

"I told you later I was all mixed up. Terrible that Jack Singley just threw away his life bulldoggin'. It was all Jane's fault. She egged him on."

"It was tragic, Ma Snell, but let's get back to your warning. Rex asked me to find out what you meant."

"If he wants to know, that's different. You see, the fella who sold me the Ouija board said he could tell by lookin' at me that I was cy — cy — "

"Psychic?"

"That's just the word, dearie, psy-chic. He said I could tell the future, if I'd put my mind to it. Sounded kinder int'restin'. Christmas, I sometimes get so fed up with cookin' seemed 's if I'd scream, but cookin' is all I know how to do, an' money's a useful thing to have. I couldn't desert the Old Boss or the Double H when Rex was fightin', my war job was right here, then when you an' your brother come I was sold on you an' — "

"You began consulting the Ouija board about us?" Kit prodded.

"That's just it, dearie. I can't explain how I come to suspect Olsen an' Mich was here fer mischief — guess 'twas that psy-chic stuff gettin' in its work — then along come Tim Blaney, pretendin' to be Ezra Dodge, a blacksmith, an' I knew trouble was right round the corner. Perhaps I wasn't surprised when he said we'd pretend to be married. I thought he'd gone plumb crazy."

"You knew all the time that it was pretense, Ma Snell?"

"Me not know the real thing?" She preened. "I've had three husbands if I am sixty-five. I reckon I know when a man's courtin' regular. The night before I lit out for the hospital, Olsen an' Mich helped with the dishes. I went to the pantry, but I didn't close the door. I heard Mich say: —

" 'All set to run off the cattle — get Danton — I'll — ' He must have whispered something because Olsen said: 'Danton and the girl may stop — ' Then I went back an' they began to hand out the old oil an' something told me they'd meant me to overhear 'em, that they was up to some other deviltry. I tried to get hold of Tim Blaney somewhere. He'd gone. I went along to the city. We'd agreed I'd meet him at the rodeo. He didn't know I'd made a date at the hospital. No man's goin' to hear me talk about aches and pains long's I'm conscious."

"Didn't you intend to let Ezra know you wouldn't meet him?"

"Sure, but when I got to Jane's she talked so much I forgot. All the time I was going to the hospital, I kept thinking, 'I must tell someone what I suspect, I'll send for dearie.' Then you came an' I was so mixed up I couldn't tell you straight. Perhaps I haven't made it very clear."

You haven't, Kit agreed to herself, but it will serve.

"That's all there was to it. Joe Carr says when he came in a few minutes ago that Olsen — I knew he was a tough hombre — an' Skip Cane were on their way to the sheriff. Tune in on the radio, dearie, let's see if the news about 'em has got out."

Kit twisted the dial, turned off a musical, "Something to Remember Me By," tuned in an excited voice.

"A man who applied at the Danton oil fields for a job turns out to be an escaped enemy prisoner who has been working for months as a cowhand at the Double H under the name of Michigan Murphy. He is an American citizen who had joined the German Army, was captured and sent to this country as a prisoner. He boasted that he and Swede Olsen, working at the same ranch, had been assigned to procure information as to the supply of oil and blow up a well or two. They were to get their time at the ranch on the same day and work their way to the fields. The fake Swede stopped to snitch pearls and was caught. What Michigan Murphy said about his co-worker I wouldn't be permitted to repeat over the air."

"Mich Murphy! I'll be hornswoggled," Joe Carr's hoarse voice came from the doorway, "if I didn't give that coyote his time an' turn him loose myself."

XXVIII

IN THE roadster, beside her brother at the wheel, Kit
looked ahead at the great, low-spreading house at the base of
the foothills.

"We are really here, Dick. I've held my breath since Mrs.
Carter's invitation came to spend the week end, for fear something would happen at the ranch that would keep you from
coming." Or your feud with Sally might, she added to herself.
"The house is old Mexico at its most perfect, isn't it? Except that it has large windows instead of slits in the thick
adobe walls."

"Sally said her father wouldn't stand for those. An archi-
tect spent weeks on the hacienda which was Mrs. Carter's
home for years and made plans of the old house."

"I love it, it is so solid. Like those white-capped mountains
behind it, it gives a sense of permanence, as if wars might
rage, nations rise and fall, hearts might break the world over,
without rattling so much as a shutter."

"Nothing short of an earthquake would shake that. Wait
till you see the inside. The dining room is what the advertising big shots would call 'in the suave luxury tradition,' definitely black tie for daily living. You're looking pretty snappy.
Whence the white fur coat?"

"Grandmother sent it for me to wear when I 'ran out to a
neighbor's in the evening.' Don't you love that? I decided I'd

better get some use of it so twisted a white scarf for a turban and fastened it with the smashing gold pin. Like the result?"

"Sure. It makes your hair and eyes look darker, brings out the color under your tan. Gosh, what a perfect day for the middle of November."

"All blue and gold and bronze and dark green. Joe Carr says there's snow in them thar hills."

"Glad to hear the laugh back in your voice, Kit. There hasn't been much lift to it since that run-in with the thugs at Danton's ranch."

"You haven't been dancing in the street yourself, Dick."

"I know, moody as the devil. When Sally made that spectacular leap it did more than straighten the kinks out of my arm, it shocked me to a realization of my selfishness when I brought you out here to cook on a ranch."

"Forget it. That cooking bout will be one of the enduring satisfactions of my life. It's a grand feeling to know you had the stuff in you to make good in a difficult situation. Once I wouldn't have thought I had the physical strength or the spiritual fortitude to put it through. Strange how a crisis brings out unsuspected facets of human nature. Once in a while a person ought to re-evaluate herself."

"You have made good in every way. No other girl would have put up with my depression. It's a poor excuse, but I've had a lot on my mind, been up against a tough problem."

She wanted to ask if his love for Sally Carter was part of the tough problem, if he had seen her since the Sunday she had faked the runaway, decided against it. Twice during the last week she had heard him charge down the stairs at midnight, had thought he was starting on one of his wild rides; then while her head was still lifted from the pillow listening, she had heard him come back.

"Have others besides the two prisoners we hired for the Double H succeeded in getting the information they were after at the Danton oil fields?" she asked. "I have practically sat in the lap of the news commentators, but I haven't heard a mention of it."

"You won't. It's hush-hush. Olsen gummed up the works for fair. Instead of heading straight for his assignment when he got his time and pay at the Double H, he stopped to snitch your pearls and became a hunted man. By the time Mich Murphy appeared there to ask for a job that would give him a chance to snoop, they were waiting for him. Even though the plot didn't succeed, anxiety about it has powdered Rex Danton's hair at the temples with another layer of white."

"How do you know?"

"He dropped in at the ranch a couple of days ago to see Joe Carr and I ran into him."

"Why didn't he come to the house?" That was a dumb question. Because he didn't care to see her, was the answer.

"I didn't inquire and he didn't say." Color flushed Richard Marlowe's thin face. "I'm ready to admit I had the wrong slant on Danton, Kit. I'm convinced that Lois lied when she declared he tried to make her love him. From what I have seen of him he isn't that kind. There are times when I have a hunch he is slated for Sally Carter."

"For Sally! You're crazy."

"What's wrong with the idea? They grew up together. She thinks he is perfect."

"That's a brand-new thought to me."

"Keep your eyes open and you'll see what I mean. Here we are. Get hep to the two grizzled Mexicans in dark red native costumes holding back the carved iron gates. They are naturalized American citizens but you'd never know it to look at them or hear them speak. Sally says her father loathes the formality but adores her mother so puts up with it because she loves it. Hollywood, here we come," he declaimed and drove the car between the bowing men.

A tall major-domo in black with silver embroidery swung open the heavy-timbered, brass-studded door of the house.

"*Buenos días, Señorita, Señor. La Señora —* "

"Welcome to our city," Sally Carter interrupted. In her yellow frock and auburn hair she gleamed like a golden girl against the rich background of the square hall. She tucked her hand under Kit's arm. "Come on, I'll show you your room. You'll find tea, sherry and *dear* friends in the living room, Captain." She flung the words over her shoulder in a voice from which all the previous warmth had been drained.

"Your servant, *Señorita.*" Richard Marlowe bowed low in imitation of the major-domo.

It was evident that Dick had not seen Sally since that eventful Sunday, Kit decided, before she crossed a floor burnished to rich bronze, mounted a broad, dark stairway, to a railed gallery.

"This is yours," Sally said and threw open a door. The room was warm and pink with late afternoon sunlight that set agleam the polished brasses on the heavy Spanish pieces.

"The furniture is gloomy but so definitely Mexican I thought you would like the atmosphere. Shed that super white coat and turban and come to the living room. The lime-green jacket and black skirt outfit you're wearing is something out of this world."

Sally was chattering, Kit realized, as she renewed lipstick and powder. Why? In the mirror she met the eyes of the girl lingering on the threshold.

"Lieutenant Bob Kent and Cal Smiley are here. So — so

are the Langleys," she announced. Then defensively, "I *made* Mom invite them."

Kit whirled to face her.

"What gave you — " she realized she was speaking in capitals and disciplined her voice — "that hideous idea for a piece of stage direction? Don't you know that it will ruin Dick's week end?"

"That's what *you* think." Sally closed the door forcibly behind her.

From the threshold of the enormous living room Kit had a fleeting impression of magnificent wall tapestries, massive carved chairs glowing with the crimson and gold of Spanish leather; the scent and color of yellow roses in two tall silver vases; of a great window framing a picture of snow-topped mountains; of voices, laughter and the tinkle of silver on china. Mrs. Carter, in a silvery gray frock, came forward with outstretched hands.

"My dear, it is a joy to welcome you. *Esta es su casa,* as we say in Mexico. 'This is your house.' "

"I wish it were, Señora, that title seems to fit better here than commonplace 'Mrs.' I've never seen anything so heart-satisfyingly gorgeous. It is perfect."

"Now, you've made my wife your friend for life," Seth Carter assured beside her. "Welcome, Miss Kit. You know everyone here."

She did and fervently wished she didn't as she nodded to Mrs. Langley presiding at the tea table. The huge diamond sunburst at the shoulder of her black frock outdid in sparkle the flicker of firelight on silver and crystal. Cal Smiley stood beside her holding a glass of sherry in one hand, a *canapé* in the other as he talked. Blond Bob Kent in the uniform of a lieutenant of infantry was standing in the firelight by the mantel. Lois in turquoise wool with a belt of silver filigree, head uptilted against the tall back of a Spanish chair, smiled at Dick as, arms folded on the top, he talked to her.

"Has he gone stark crazy, doesn't he know she's playing him off against Rex?" Kit asked herself and stole a glance at Sally standing near the great window. Her hand showed white against Rex Danton's dark blue sleeve. He was bending his head, smiling as he listened.

Dick was right. His hair was whiter. The realization contracted her heart. Had he been right also when he had said that he and Sally were slated for each other? Suddenly she was violently, unbearably homesick. Mr. and Mrs. Carter had left the room. There seemed to be no place for her. She was unmistakably fifth wheel.

"Kit Marlowe, you look lonely as an atoll in the Pacific. When did you steal in?"

"All of two minutes ago," Rex answered Sally's question. "Tea or sherry, Kit?"

He had seen her enter the room and hadn't been interested enough to look up and speak. Memory burst into the picture like a clown's head through a paper hoop. She saw Lois on the threshold of the living room at Running Creek, heard her voice, "Forgotten that you begged me to meet you here, Rex, darling?"

"I'm awaiting your order, madam. Will it be tea or sherry?" His amused voice broke into her troubled reflections.

"Neither, thanks. I will ask the Lieutenant to get tea for me later." With a smile and nod she turned away. Bob Kent was staring at the two absorbed couples as if suddenly aware that he had been cast for a bit part in this week end. Apparently she had been also. Why not go all out to build him up to the juvenile lead, give him the time of his life? She joined him in front of the fire which gave out the spicy scent of burning pine.

"You may have all the sherry, Lieutenant, if you will take pity on this starving female and get her a cup of tea," she declared.

His bored face brightened as if a lamp had been lighted behind it.

"Tea coming up. Park your lovely self in one of those two chairs tête-à-tête in the corner and I will be with you before you can say, *Esta es su casa*. How's my Spanish?"

"Perfect. Hurry. I'm crazy to hear more of it." She settled into the soft depths of the chair. The week end has possibilities, she decided.

It had had more than possibilities, she told herself the next evening as in a pink and violet frock, shimmering with silver, pearls about her throat and a diamond comb in her dark hair, she pulled aside the long hanging to look at the outside world. It had snowed in the night. Trees which had been stark and bare yesterday, this morning had been coated with snow. Telephone wires looked like white ribbons stretched across the darkening sky. The patio was carpeted in white, dotted with queer-shaped humps which must be the shrubs.

She thought of the hours they had spent, skiing, bobsledding, lunching round a campfire, Dick and Lois, Sally and Rex, Bob Kent and herself. All day the pattern had remained unbroken. Did Rex love Sally? Had Lois recaptured Dick? Didn't he know he was fooling with dynamite to pay her such marked attention? Once or twice she had caught Lois's eyes on her in mocking derision.

Why stand here thinking? Why not do something about it if she had to drag him back to the Double H by pretending she was ill? That was an idea. Better not waste time. They would leave directly after dinner. She would suggest it to him at once. She opened her door. Rex Danton in dinner clothes leaned against the gallery rail directly in front of her.

"Well, see who's h-here." Anger at her startled catch of breath vanished in concern. "What is it? Has anything happened to — "

"Nothing has happened to your brother. I have something to say to you." He caught her wrist and drew her toward him. "What are you doing to that boy?"

"Boy?" Kit's brows knit in a puzzled frown.

"You can't get away with that wide-eyed innocence. You know what I mean. You know you've been encouraging Kent to fall in love with you."

What would he say if he knew that most of their time together had been devoted to listening to the Lieutenant's homesick reflections on the girl he had left behind him? One of her duties at the USO had been to listen to the heart outpourings of lonely men. She had become adept. She shrugged.

"Why shouldn't I encourage him? Perhaps I want him to love me. Perhaps I have found my dream man at last."

"If that is the case, I am on my knees in apology for butting in. There go the dinner chimes. Come on."

They were the last to enter the library. Sally caught her arm.

"Cal Smiley has taken stage center," she whispered. "Look at him backed up against the mantel. I bet — "

"News flash." Smiley's eyes glanced from one startled face to another. "Inez and I are happy to announce our engagement."

"Pity her che-ild left all alone, Dick." Lois's pleading eyes sent a wave of red to Richard Marlowe's face which quite obliterated the scar.

You had it coming to you, young fella, for the way you've acted up these last twenty-four hours, Kit thought.

"Felicitations, Cal" — Rex Danton's cordial voice covered Dick's embarrassment, had he noticed it? — "and best wishes to you, Mrs. Langley. I can see that I owe you an orchid."

"Then you notice the absence of fountain pens?" Kit, standing near, heard Mrs. Langley's whisper as she returned his grin with a smirk of self-satisfaction.

"I didn't believe anyone could separate him from them. You're a diplomat. I prophesy you'll be this state's next first lady."

"Oh, Rex, how cute of you." She raised her voice. "Now if you'll only sell us Rushing Creek Ranch, my happiness will be complete and — "

"Don't look so flabbergasted, Rex," Cal Smiley interrupted. "She's seen the house and wouldn't say 'yes' to me till I promised I would try to buy it. I had the keys. You were in Washington, couldn't sound you out. Lois, her mother and I had driven out to give it the once-over that day the escaped prisoner was picked up there. We passed the cavalcade. Lois declared you must be in the house and dashed up to the front door while Inez and I were investigating the swimming pool. When we reached the library you had gone. I phoned the Double H thinking I might catch you there. No soap."

Kit's eyes flashed to Rex Danton. His, faintly amused, faintly cynical, met them. Memory broadcast his voice.

"There is no foundation of trust to build on and trust will solve many a situation which appears hopeless."

She hadn't trusted him. Each time she had seen him with Lois the thought that once — perhaps now — he loved her had prickled like nettles. Dick had said he was sure Lois had lied.

"Sorry, Cal." Rex's voice brought her attention back to the great room, to the romantic comedy being staged there — if one could think of red-faced Cal Smiley as the romantic lead. "If the lady of your heart won't marry you unless you bring love in one hand and my ranch in the other, you're out of luck. It is not for sale. I'm keeping that for my children and my children's children."

"Cal's announcement calls for champagne at dinner," Seth Carter said jocularly. "We must make this an occasion."

It was an occasion, Kit thought, as later she sat in the beautiful dining room at the left of the host. There was but one picture on the dark paneled walls, a Mexican Madonna. A crystal and gilt mirror with green baguettes reflected the sheen of silver on her pink and violet frock, her pearls; her eyes, which seemed so outsize that she turned away from them, gave back Sally in limelight green and Lois in pale blue. The dark, elaborately carved chairs had white leather backs. The long table was covered with a yellow lace and organdie cloth. There was a service of crystal heavily overlaid with gold, and gold-banded service plates. Deep orange chrysanthemums and four tall matching candles glowed in the center.

She had a sudden close-up of the long, black and white linoleum-covered table at the Double H. Rex had been right when he had said it was absurd for them to live like that. When she returned to the ranch they would use the small dining room if it meant a pitched battle with Dick.

Coffee was being served when she remembered her plan to start for home immediately after dinner. Cal Smiley's explanation of his presence at Rushing Creek had wiped it from her mind. Too late to suggest it now.

"Snap out of your trance, Kit," Sally ordered. "Get a wrap. Pull on overshoes. You'll find them in the coat closet.

We're all going to the patio to see the moon rise over the mountain. The paths have been shoveled. Rex, wait for me, *please*," she flung over her shoulder before she disappeared in the cavernous hall.

In her room Kit threw the ermine coat over her arm. Why go to the patio? Why be a spare tire? Why listen to more of Bob Kent's ravings about his girl? Why be a short sport and not go, she challenged herself and closed the door behind her.

Halfway down the broad stairs she stopped. With outstretched arms, Dick was barricading the lowest step on which Sally Carter stood.

"No passing, Infant. The others have gone out. This is where I come in. You've dodged me since the moment I arrived, now you'll listen."

"Better run after Lois. She'll eat up what you have to say."

"We'll leave Lois out of this. Both she and I have been playing a game. She knows it. Play fair, Sally. I'm sorry I lashed at you that Sunday, but, the world I had made up my mind I would have to live in the rest of my life was ditched when I found I could use my arm and — "

"So you ditched me."

"That was because a moment before, when you risked death for me, I had discovered I loved you terribly, Infant."

"If that is the effect love has on you, I'm not having any. thanks."

"Yes you are. You're going to decide this minute whether I'm your doormat or your dream man." He caught her close. "Love me?"

Kit roused to a horrified realization that she was avidly listening in on a situation that concerned only the two persons below. She sank down on the stair, stuck fingers in her ears and closed her eyes tight.

It seemed hours that she sat there rigid. How would she know when they had gone if she could neither hear nor see? Was that faint clang the front door closing?

She opened one eye. Caught her breath. Rex Danton stood at the foot of the stairs looking up at her.

"I've been waiting for you. What has happened? You are hunched up like a sparrow with its head under its wing. Are you *hurt?*"

"No. *No.*" She caught up the ermine coat and ran down the stairs. "I found myself playing gooseberry to Dick and Sally and I tried not to see and hear."

"They've made it up, have they? I love Sally, but I object to being a listening post for her to practise on. Where's your Lieutenant?"

"Out in the cold, cold world waiting impatiently for me, I suppose. One should never keep a man in love waiting."

"You're jeering at me. You'll have a thousand chances to see the moon rise above the mountain. I have something to say to you. Come with me." He slipped his hand under her arm.

Unsuccessfully prodding her mind for an indifferent reply she entered the softly glowing living room. As she passed the great window she could see the purple shadows of trees on snow, hear laughter and voices. The moon was just coming up, topping a mountain with a luminous silver rim. The tips of tall snow-covered trees caught the light and sparkled like diamond dust.

"You heard Cal break the story of why Lois was in my house the day we rounded up the escaped prisoners, didn't you?" Rex was terrifyingly tall and grim as he took her coat, dropped it on a chair and faced her in the firelight.

"Yes."

"Believe him?"

"Yes."

"How come, when you wouldn't believe me when I told you that never had I even thought of loving Lois? No answer? We'll let it go — for the present. From your report of what you saw in the hall, looks as if you were about to lose your job as companion for your brother, doesn't it?"

"It does. Something tells me I should be about the business of looking for another." The voice she had attempted to make gay didn't make the grade.

"There is one waiting for you." As she retreated a step he caught her hands in his. "As my wife. Think of the hours you could spend at the hospital helping if you lived in the city."

It was like stepping from a fog into a gloriously shining world, a world in which nothing mattered but the fact that he wanted her.

"Don't tell me you are descending to bribery, Colonel Danton," she accused unsteadily. He caught her in his arms and pressed his cheek against her hair.

"I've been wanting to do this since the day in the line rider's camp. Kit, will you live with me here, give up your beloved East?"

She leaned away as far as his arms permitted.

"You haven't said you love me. Are you sure you are not saying this because of my crazy declaration that night at Mountain Lodge?"

He pressed his mouth hard on hers. Held it there till she turned her head and hid her face against his shoulder.

"What do you think about love, now?" He cleared his husky voice. "I'm playing for keeps, Kit."

"So am I, Rex — for always."

"That promise needs to be sealed. Hold out your left hand."

From his waistcoat pocket he drew the ring he had shown her at the ranch and slipped it on her finger.

"Still like it?"

"Love it."

"Kit, you are the most heart-warming — " He kissed her throat, her eyes, her mouth, not fiercely as Shep had kissed her, she remembered, even as she responded to the pressure of his lips on hers, but with infinite tenderness. He released her suddenly.

"Come on," he said gruffly. "Let's go out and see the moon." He picked up the ermine coat.

As she slipped into it, his arms closed tight about her again. Cheek against her hair he said : —

"You are very lovely tonight, my darling."

She tipped her head back against his shoulder and looked up at him.

"Rex! Rex! You remembered?"

"Sure, I remembered. But I was saying that on my own, too. Don't you know I think you are beautiful? Don't you know I have loved you from the moment I saw you in the line rider's camp?" He steadied his shaken voice. His eyes, warm with laughter, met hers. "My crystal ball tells me the lady will need a lot of showing — later. Come on, honey, or — or we'll miss that moon."